AGAIN MY LOVE

DIANA KNIGHTLEY

For my readers, this one is especially for you...

ONE - HAYLEY

My eyes were not working right. Everything was super dark and close and pressing and totally overwhelming me. I concentrated on the horse's mane and tried not to think about the big man-thighs in close proximity, pressing against my own. Those thighs were wrapped in a kilt, smelling like it hadn't been washed in a really long time, if ever, like a wet dog. Or a sheep. And of course there was nothing under his skirt. This I knew, having seen Braveheart, my dad's favorite movie. I was grateful to be wearing military clothes, layers of cargo pockets between me and this scoundrel.

Because without a doubt he was a scoundrel.

He literally looked like a pirate. Or a Viking. Like a guy that might seem sexy on paper but in close proximity, on the back of a horse together, was mostly terrifying. Because this guy was definitely all sword, no manners.

Just my luck.

Our route wound through an ancient wood, then emerged onto a well-travelled path with fewer trees. The thick-clouded sky looked oppressive and heavy, a neutral gray against the deep green of the pine behind us and the lighter green of the grass ahead of us.

Fraoch shifted, looking over his shoulder. Our horse slowed.

He turned the horse around and headed us in the opposite direction, back towards the forest, our pace barely a walk.

"Why did you do that?"

"This is the road tae the castle."

"Yes, and... where were we going?"

"Tae the village, where I live."

"So again, why did we turn around?"

He grunted. "I canna decide where tae take ye. Tis a great deal of trouble either way."

"Oh."

We rode in quiet. I was trying to get liquid from my saliva. "I'm really thirsty."

He reached into a leather bag and fished out a bottle of thick glass wrapped in leather strips. With his teeth he gripped the cork, pulled it free, and passed the bottle.

I sniffed the opening. It smelled like whisky and beard. "Shit, I really want water, but I guess it's five o'clock somewhere."

He chuckled. "I canna understand half of what ye are sayin'."

I drank, grimaced, then returned the bottle.

He swigged from the bottle, twisted the cork into the top, and dropped it into the bag. "Where are ye from?"

"Florida. A place called Amelia Island."

"Tis in the colonies?"

"Yeah, I guess, now it's called the United States."

"I have been tae St Augustine. I was garrisoned at Darien."

"Cool. St Augustine is south of Amelia Island, Darien is north." We rode in silence for a bit. Our horse shifted beneath us, back and forth, a steady cadence that calmed my nerves.

Finally I asked, "When?"

"Durin' the War of Jenkins Ear in the year of our Lord 1740."

"That's before the United States was even a thing." I added, "Weird."

Then I added, "What do you mean by trouble?"

"Madame Lizbeth lives at the castle, have ye met her?"

"No..."

"She is Magnus's sister, she would take ye in until he comes for ye, but tae get ye there we have tae enter the castle, past the soldiers, and twill be difficult tae explain yer arrival. I have only spoken tae the Earl once. He was nae an easy man tae converse with. I would prefer tae send a message tae Lizbeth and have her come gather ye, provide ye with a proper dress."

"That sounds good. I don't mind the idea of a castle."

He grunted again, close to my ear, and slowed the horse.

"I daena believe I can take ye home, tis Madame Greer's house, she has been..."

"What?"

He chuckled. "Naethin'. I have been off huntin'."

"Hunting. So where do you live?"

"I have a camp house farther east along the River Tay."

"Do you have food? I'm very hungry. Then we can watch for the storms. I may not even need a dress, you know, I only have a few hours to wait."

"Aye, I have food." He turned the horse a third direction, yelled, "Hie!" and set the horse galloping into the woods.

We came to a clearing and at the edge stood a small, thatched-roof cottage. The walls were dirt, the window was a hole with no glass, and there wasn't a door. It was basically a hovel. Or a pigsty. It looked barely large enough for one person.

My townhouse's master bedroom had a larger closet. This

was like what someone might use to store their rakes before the contractor arrived to build a proper tool shed.

Fraoch guided our horse to a tree, swung to the ground, then headed into the house. I did not want to be outside, alone, so I dropped to the ground, trying to seem professional, and followed him.

Inside, the room was dark, dank, and musty, and with Fraoch beside me, pretty body-odorous too. A dead rabbit hung from the wall.

"Ew."

He followed my eyes to the murdered bunny. "Tis dinner."

"Ugh. I mean, thanks. I mean..." I swatted at something tickling my cheek, to see a spider hanging from a thread near my shoulder. "I think I need to pee." I really just wanted out of that stiflingly small, spider-dwelling, smelly place. I pushed my way past Fraoch, trying not to breathe until I was back in the fresh air. I needed the fresh.

He grunted and followed me out.

I said, "So there's not an outhouse or anything? Like no indoor plumbing?"

He grunted again. "There is a bush beyond the alder."

"Great." I trudged into the woods the basic direction he pointed and crouched behind a tree, pushing my pants down around my calves and holding the waistband away from my urine stream. I called, "I guess toilet paper would be too much to ask?"

Another grunt from Fraoch and this time it sounded close, way close. I was super embarrassed about how loud I was peeing. Great again, this was all fucking great. I pulled up my pants and followed him back to the cottage.

. . .

I finally took off my bulletproof vest. It was cold without it, but it had been heavy. I leaned it against the front wall of the house, then crossed my arms and shivered.

His brow drew down at the sight of me.

I followed his eyes as they appraised me — my khaki vest covered in cargo pockets over a white T-shirt. My pants covered in more pockets. Why I was wearing so many pockets, I could not explain — they were completely empty, not a sandwich, a blanket, a roll of toilet paper, nothing useful. My shoes were Adidas trainers that did not pass for eighteenth century *anything*.

He crouched to build a fire. I sat across from him, but, just my luck, the wind blew smoke in my face and, like a dork, I tried to wave it away. My eyes teared up. I coughed—

"Ye are sittin' in the smoke."

"I know," to make it sound reasonable I added, "the wind switched."

I crawled around to sit beside him. He was wearing an obvious smirk on his face.

"So you live here, in this... where's your bed?"

His eyes twinkled mischievously. "'Tis brazen tae ask it, dost ye want me tae show ye?" He patted the dirt.

I rolled my eyes. "God no. I just wanted to make sure I was correct. There's no place to sleep, no bathroom, nothing. I've been in nicer tents before."

His brow drew together. Then he asked, "Are ye hungry?"

"Famished. Thirsty too."

He tossed me the bottle of whisky. I caught it with both hands, pulled the cork with my teeth, and swigged. "No water?"

"Nae, I will get some in a moment." He clutched the skin

across the back of the rabbit, made a small cut with a dirk, ripped the rear half of the skin off, then ripped the front half off.

I looked away with a shudder.

He asked, "When dost ye think they will come for ye?"

"Any minute now. We just need to watch for the storms."

"You are lucky tis warm and dry."

I had been thinking of the day as cool and wondering if it would rain. "What month is it?"

"We are soon tae be arrivin' at grian-stad samhraidh." He carved down the middle of the rabbit and butterflied it open.

I tucked my eyes to my knees and tried not to throw up. "What is krea-stat saureg, or whatever you just said?"

There was now a stick jammed through the poor murdered rabbit and Fraoch was rotisserie-ing it over the fire to cook on all sides, though, at this point, one side was black and crispy while the other dripped raw and bloody. "If ye are hungry, Madame Hayley, ye can eat from the done parts, daena eat the raw side."

I gagged.

He looked up at the sky and appraised the trees. "Tis the beginnin' of the braw days."

I pressed my face into my knees. "So this is summer? This is warm? Okay, at least it won't snow." But it was cold and I was from Florida so I thought to ask, "Will it snow?"

"Probably nae."

It didn't seem like he was joking.

Done, he slid the rabbit onto a piece of wood, tore off a hunk of meat, and stuffed it in his mouth. He gestured for me to join in.

I peeled off a bit, put it in my own mouth, chewed, and gagged it down. It was a little like chicken but also, not at all. Maybe like the dark meat of turkey but dry. It needed some salt.

I had been very hungry though, so this was completely necessary.

We ate quietly, barely talking. He grunted a lot.

I couldn't tell if his grunts were exasperation or if he thought I was funny, or confusing, possibly repulsive — I had worked through my deodorant and hadn't slept well in days. My mood was craptastic.

"Will yer husband be worried on ye?"

"Oh, um..." Without a doubt it would be best to say yes — I was at his mercy, no phone, no 911, no neighbors, no ride home. I needed protection, he needed to be too nervous to try anything.

"Definitely. My husband — I'm sure he'll come with Kaitlyn and Quentin, possibly Mags... any minute now." I added, "He's big, just so you know, like an MMA fighter."

His brow furrowed. "What is an ememay fighter?"

"Fighting, like with full-contact and... um... I'm not exactly sure how to describe it."

"Nae with swords or guns?"

"No, but he has a gun. He can shoot."

"Aye, and why did he allow ye tae embark on such a dangerous journey? He should take better care of ye."

"Yeah, true..." I changed the subject, "So which direction are we watching for the storm?"

He grunted and pointed.

I turned that way and watched the sky.

TWO - HAYLEY

The sun was starting to go down. The woods around the clearing were cast in deep shadows and the temperature dropped. I was not worried though. Katie and Mags usually gave it a day before they'd retrieve someone, not wanting to overlap or something. I just needed to hold tight.

Fraoch, after instructing me to stay very quiet and to yell if there was any trouble, "I will hear ye," he said, disappeared into the dark woods.

He returned about forty-five minutes later carrying a ceramic jug of fresh water and a bundle of wood for the fire.

I said, "No storms, but tomorrow there is sure to be a rescue committee."

"Aye."

I shivered as a wind rustled the limbs of the pine above us.

"Dost ye need a wrap?"

I huddled round my knees nodding. "I really do."

From the bag on the side of the horse he retrieved a thick

wool blanket, folded it over his arm, and whacked it repeatedly with his palm causing dust to billow from it. After a few more whacks he passed it to me to wrap up in.

I ignored the smell and tried to think about how kind it was of him to dust it for me. "This is really summer?"

He grinned a big grin accentuating his missing tooth. "Och aye, tis balmy." He added more wood to the fire, building up the flame, hot coals warming for at-most six inches around.

I lay down on my side wrapping the blanket tighter. "So how do you know Mags?"

"I met him just after a battle. He had escaped a prison, I had deser..." He stopped and continued differently. "Twas time tae come home tae Scotland for both of us. We gained passage on a ship from Savannah and then across tae London. Twas a verra long journey."

"Where I come from that would take about six hours."

"Och, really? Would ye use the vessels?"

"No, we fly," I leaned up on an elbow. "In something called an airplane. I don't really understand how they work, but a hundred people, sometimes more, get into seats and the plane flies them across the ocean."

Fraoch concentrated on my face as I spoke. "Madame Hayley, are ye tellin' me a story?"

"Nope. It's true."

"Tis nae witchcraft?" He stared at the smoke rising in a spiral from the fire shaking his head. "Kaitlyn told me twas nae black magic, but it seems..."

"It's not, Fraoch. It's science and engineering, and..."

"And invention, like Og Maggy said?"

"Yep." I giggled. "That's what you call him?"

"Aye, young Maggy. It suits him, he is much like a verra young boy who thinks he is a man, I hae tae remind him he is a wee-un." He laughed.

I rather liked his laugh, low and deep.

The night had grown very dark, the fire our only light, the sounds around us close and spooky. I pulled the blanket up around my ears.

"In the crossin' from the colonies, I was verra close tae death. Og Maggy and Madame Kaitlyn saved m'life. Tis why I live here now, in a different time and place, tae help him keep his family safe. I watch for storms."

"That's nice of you. They deserve it. They have a lot of assholes after them and need all the help they can get."

He nodded and watched the fire for a few minutes. "They will come for ye on the morrow, Madame Hayley."

"Yes, definitely. Is this where I'm supposed to sleep tonight?"

"Aye, for the warmth. I will stay awake tae watch for the beasts."

My eyes went wide. "What beasts?"

"Tis nae matter in it, I am watchin' for them."

The night was weird. Fraoch barely slept, or at least I barely slept, and whenever I opened my eyes to wonder where I was, he would be in a different position. Once, he was crouched at the fire. Later, standing at the edge of our clearing. And then freakily, crouched near my feet, facing away. When I startled awake, he whispered, "Wheesht."

After a few moments he settled back down, whispering, "Nae worries, ye can sleep."

"What was it?"

"I daena ken."

Oh.

When I woke in the morning, he was already up.

I stretched, sore from sleeping on the hard, cold, medieval

dirt. "I'm thirsty." At home I would have had a glass of water on my nightstand. I would have a water bottle with me constantly.

"Well, get ye up."

I squinted my eyes. "Get ye up? Get ye up, *really*? Let's try this again. Fraoch, would you be kind enough to bring me some water? Then you say..." I rolled my hand.

"Madame Hayley, I will accompany ye tae the stream."

"Perfect."

I stood, keeping the blanket wrapped around my shoulders. "Were you cold last night?"

"Nae, twas warm enough."

He led me down a well-traveled path, through the woods, to a small stream where he picked a path to a large flat rock and crouched. He washed his hands, then drank from his palm. I dropped the blanket to the path and kneeled beside him, washing my hands in the ice cold water, drinking from my palm, then with panting breaths I built up the courage to splash water on my face. "Cold cold cold cold, oh my god, cold!"

I asked, "Do I have mascara all under my eyes?"

He said, "What is it? Tis all around dark."

"It's my makeup. It's supposed to be making my lashes long, not smearing all under my eyes. Just perfect." I splashed more water. "Waterproof until this moment." I rubbed with my fingers. "Now?"

He put a big, rough, worn thumb to my skin but drew away quickly, instead gesturing at the corner of his own left eye. "Tis here."

I used my sleeve, smearing black on it, but then again I had been wearing this shirt for days. It was already a dirty, filthy, mess.

I also noted that Fraoch didn't wash, and frankly his stench was... "While we're here, talking about cleanliness, Fraoch, cleaning ourselves — you should take some water and splash it all around your parts."

I gestured for his underarms, because it was all a lot ripe. "Maybe up under your kilt too." I gestured as if I were pulling my kilt up and splashing water on my undercarriage. "It's been hot and sweaty and you could use a wash down, because of smell. Please, don't be offended. I'm not telling you to be mean, just telling you as a friend."

"Och." His brow drew down.

"I'll go pee behind the bushes and I won't look while you do it. But seriously, when I come back, be kind of cleaned up."

Without waiting for an answer, I went behind a tree, crouched down, and peed and pooped, using a large leaf to wipe. When I peeked around the tree, Fraoch was applying himself to the chore of washing his armpits with fresh water, splashing some on his hair too, smoothing it back, and scrubbing water up and down on his face. Then he took off his boots, walked knee deep into the water, and splashed water up under his kilt. He waded back to shore and patted his legs dry.

I returned, noting that his shirt was very wet and his kilt dripping. "Thank you very much, Fraoch."

"Ye are welcome, Madame Hayley."

I put my hands on my hips and surveyed the situation, babbling brook, bright morning, breeze on the high branches of the trees, no coffee — bleak. "I guess coffee would be too much to ask for?"

"I had it when I was in London, twas verra good. Ye like it?"

"So good, so necessary, it helps you wake up. But there's none here, right? There isn't a Starbucks?" I sighed.

"What is a starbuck, Madame Hayley?"

"It's a restaurant, kind of like a pub, you know?"

"Aye, I ken a pub."

"Except they serve coffee and sweet drinks and things that are whipped and sugared and so delicious."

"Aye, it sounds verra good. I canna offer ye somethin' such as that."

"They'll be here soon I suppose, I can wait. But, while we wait, what's for breakfast?"

"I was goin' tae return tae Madame Greer's this morn. I daena have much left tae eat." He pulled a piece of hard bread from a dusty bag and looked at it so hungrily I knew the kind thing would be to let him have it.

I said, "No thanks, watching my gluten."

He ripped off a hunk, stuffed it in his mouth, and chewed ravenously. He spoke with his mouth full. "What is gluten?"

"It's something in bread — nothing, I was joking."

"I am supposed tae be eatin' dark greens, oranges, if I can find them, rose hips, thyme and parsley, and berries. Madame Kaitlyn made me promise, but I haena had any in a long while. I had the scurvy."

"Oh, right, that's why you're missing a tooth?"

"Aye."

He added, "We will watch the skies for the storm but if they daena come soon, I will go tae get ye some food."

"Okay, it's a deal." He passed me a bit of bread. It wasn't enough but I was half his size, it would have to do.

*B*ack at the hut, I sat in the dirt watching the sky, but soon grew bored. "Where's your wife?"

"She passed when tryin' tae bring forth a bairn." He was strapping the bag of vessels to the horse.

"Oh, I'm sorry about that."

"Tis nae matter in it, has been verra many years. I hae gone tae the colonies and returned since." He tightened the strap. "I daena think on it much."

"Who's Madame Greer?"

"She is a friend of Madame Kaitlyn's and one of Og Maggy's aunts by marriage."

"You live with her?"

"Aye, sometimes. Many days she finds me difficult tae have about. She tells me and anyone else who will listen tae her on it, that I am always loomin' around corners givin' her a fright. The other day she said, loud enough for the whole village tae hear, that I was 'givin' her a headache always in her kitchen wantin' somethin' tae eat.' I told her I was hungry and couldna help bein' hungry, so she told me tae go on and do somethin' else. She makes me leave quite regularly."

I laughed. "She just kicks you out?"

His eyes twinkled with humor. "Aye, sometimes with a broom in hand, so I come here tae have some peace."

"So this is your man cave." I looked around the clearing: the hut, the dirt, the smoke, the temperature, the wild beasts just beyond in the woods. "This is a terrible man-cave. I mean, thank you for your hospitality, but you don't even have a television or a pool table or anything cool. It's literally just a fire-pit and a horse."

He chuckled. "I hae nae idea what yer words mean."

I waved him away. "That's okay, I rarely have a point, anyway. Michael used to say all the time 'I just nod and smile when you're talking.'"

"Tis your husband?"

"Oh, um, yeah, I guess he is. Yeah, he says that all the time."

We sat quietly for a moment then I said, "Okay, now I'm starving."

He lumbered to his feet. "Dost ye ken tae use a weapon?"

"Like what, a sword or a gun?"

"Ye ken tae use a rifle?"

"I do a rifle, but not a sword. Though if I had a blade I could probably do some damage. Why, what are we fighting?"

"We arna fightin' anyone. Tis in case of highwaymen."

"Oh, like thieves?"

"Aye." He ran his hand through his hair. "I am nae sure how best tae keep ye safe, Madame Hayley. I daena want tae attract attention tae ye until I have ye dressed properly. I am sure Og Maggy would be able tae handle ye better."

"Mags doesn't have to handle me, I can take care of myself." I thought for a moment. "I do wish he would get here though. And I'm totally aware that that's an inconsistency on my part."

"I will leave ye here with a weapon if ye ken tae use it. Ye can hide in the hut."

He passed me a gun that was so old fashioned that, for a moment, I thought he was joking. "This?"

"Aye, twill be enough tae aim it at them, ye winna have tae fire. Daena worry, I winna be gone for long. I will return with a meal."

"What happens if there's a storm?"

He cinched the drawstring on a bag. "If there is a storm daena go tae it, stay here and wait for me. I will go tae it and if it has Og Maggy—"

"It will, not if, definitely Mags, or the black man, Quentin, or Kaitlyn. One of them, definitely."

"I will bring them here, so daena leave. Ye might be lost or hurt and I daena have a way tae protect ye."

"Okay, got it. What about the bag of vessels?"

"They are valuable, I will carry them with me."

"Okay fine, that makes sense." He swung up onto the back of the horse.

"Will you protect the vessels though? Like *really* protect them?"

"Aye, get ye in the—"

My chin trembled. I looked down at the gun to try to cover that I was about to cry. I couldn't believe I was stuck in the eighteenth century and this big burly man on the back of the horse was my only hope for survival. He was leaving me all alone.

"I mean, Madame Hayley, if ye would please go intae the hut, I will go tae the village for some provisions."

It hadn't been what was upsetting me, but I decided to take a deep breath and pretend like it was better. "You're really getting the hang of that being polite thing."

I stood in the doorframe of his closet-sized hut, with all the spiders, just inside of the shadows, and watched as his horse galloped away.

~

That was a freaking terrifying couple of hours. Because it was indeed a couple of hours and every sound spooked the shit out of me and there were all kinds of crazy sounds and also, no sounds at all — no ocean, no sirens, no electricity, just the reverberating, echoing silence, the sound of my breath and heartbeat in my ears.

I clutched the flintlock gun to my chest, remembering its name somewhere down in my psyche, from history class or some kind of reenactment I had watched, not for instructions, but for entertainment. Now I was holding a flintlock rifle and wished I had instructions. Like how safe was this to clutch to my chest?

I watched through the door. Sometimes I clung to the inside, not watching at all because it was terrifying, so terrifying to stare out at the desolate woods. And these were desolate woods at some point in past history, there were no police, no malls beyond that tree line, no highway out of here. I couldn't look at it. But also not looking at the woods was horrific, because shit. could. sneak. up.

It was not lost on me that this would be an epic plot-line for a horror movie.

And also not lost on me that a homeless, missing-a-tooth, barely bathing man in the eighteenth century had hidden me in his hut in the woods and was keeping me there, and not one person in the history of the world knew I was here.

Except Kaitlyn and what if she died in the arena?

She could have died.

Died.

And if she died, I would probably die.

FOUR - HAYLEY

raoch returned. We sat beside the fire pit and he spread out the meal. There were loaves of bread, some berry preserves, some cheese, a jar of milk.

As I ate most of my fear dissipated. "Thank you, this was so necessary, I was starting to get kind of freaky."

"Freaky?"

"It's like..." I stuck my tongue out and shook my head back and forth.

He chuckled and copied me, his own freaky face accentuated by his thick beard and wild hair. "I was goin' freaky as well," he said, "Freaky Fraochie."

I fell back in the dirt laughing. "Freaky Fraochie! Make the face again." He did.

"Awesome." I wiped my eyes from laughing so hard and he kept making the funny face. "Man, it feels good to laugh." I added, "You have a bit of cheese right here." I gestured on my chin.

He wiped it away, and then brushed his beard with his fingers modestly. "Dost I have it all?"

"Yeah, all cleaned up." I focused on the branches at the tip top of pine trees close to the sky.

"This place reminds me of going hunting with my dad, back in the day."

"Huntin' for what?"

"Deer."

"Och, tis big, ye would go? A woman?"

"I went as a girl, fourteen years old when I shot my first. I hated it actually. Not the hunting part, I loved being good at it, but to my dad hunting was a 'big big thing'. We would be away from civilization for the whole weekend and he always packed crap food. He seemed to think the fun of it was not having any fun at all. If you thought it was fun, had a bit of a laugh while waiting for the deer to walk by, he got sulky and mean. He would launch into these really long lectures on being a 'serious person'."

"I daena like lectures."

"God, me neither. I'm like, we can have some fun or it's boring. Later, I realized he was bored too, he just didn't like to laugh. His fun was lecturing everyone on everything. Part of the reason my parents got divorced."

"Divorced?"

"Yeah, they decided to break up, to not be married anymore."

"Och, they could decide it?"

"I guess that would seem weird to you, they had to go to court, divide up all their stuff, but yeah, my parents got divorced. You can do that where I come from."

His brow drew down in confusion. "Och, it sounds ghrua-mach, tae sin against the word of God."

"Goomag?"

He grimaced in explanation.

I nodded. "That's how I would have described it when I was growing up. But yeah, this is like hunting with my dad, except better food and company."

His mouth parted in a smile within his big full beard. "I am glad I was able tae provide ye with a meal, Madame Hayley. Dost yer husband take ye huntin' when he goes?"

"Huh, my — oh, no, he doesn't like to hunt. None of my friends like to hunt. Kaitlyn's never even gone."

I sat up and watched the sky. "Where is the storm? Why haven't they come yet?"

"I daena ken, but there is still enough light on this day."

"True. Yeah." I took a deep breath. "I'm just worried something happened to her. What if she isn't coming because she's *gone?*"

"She will be comin'. I haena known Madame Kaitlyn for long but if she said she would come tae get ye she means tae do it. Did I tell ye of when she came for me?"

"She did?"

"Aye, she marched ontae the docks of London amongst the pirates and the soldiers. Her hair was done up tae here," he gestured above his head. "Her dress was as wide as a door frame, and she was made tae release my chains, and a'cursin' God over it. She has a mischievous tongue if ye get her drunk enough."

"Oh I know it. Angry, she curses like a sailor."

"Aye," Fraoch chuckled. "The sailors were scandalized by the way she was carryin' on. She demanded I take her arm and I refused, I thought she had the words and actions of a witch."

"Well, that's the other thing about Kaitlyn, she has a nasty mouth but she's too sweet to be any trouble to anyone."

I watched his face as he watched the fire. "That's how you got here, to this time?"

"Aye, because I grabbed her arm though I was afraid tae. I am still nae sure twas a wise decision."

"You don't like 17— what's the year?"

"The year of our Lord, seventeen nocht four. Nae, Madame Hayley, this is nae the year tae like or not, this is a different family, and their different land. I daena have the ties I need tae be sheltered."

"I imagine that would be rough. After my parents split the only person I could count on was Kaitlyn. When she left to go to college I was pretty bummed for a long time."

I watched his face. "Do you know what I'm talking about?"

"Nae wholly, but I think ye mean ye daena like tae be alone either."

"Exactly what I mean." A squirrel entered the clearing. I watched it for a moment, coming closer and closer. I put out a hand, "Hey little guy, you looking for—"

Fraoch had moved from his seat around the circle with so much stealth I hadn't noticed him moving at all. He met my eyes, his meaning: *don't move.* The squirrel crept closer and closer to my beckoning fingers. My eyes shifted to Fraoch, a knife raised in his hand. I clamped my eyes tight. A moment later the twitching squirrel was right beside me, a knife through its side.

Fraoch had a wide smile inside his wild beard. He callously picked the squirrel up by its back paws and announced, "I hae a dinner for ye, Madame Hayley!"

I gulped. And forced a smile. "Perfect, Fraoch."

Night fell. There was something pretty awful about night falling on the second day.

I wanted to brush my teeth.

I wanted warm food without having to pick meat off bones, something I had never been that fond of doing.

I wanted ice water.

The squirrel had been good, but it was *squirrel.* I chased it with whisky.

I was having trouble — my anxiety was growing, like a subterranean panic attack, a lump growing in my throat, threatening to rise up and buckle me under.

As the night grew darker I felt like I couldn't breathe.

Fraoch accompanied me into the woods so I could pee. My chin trembled holding back my tears. I felt hopeless, sullen, and totally furious. I was here and no one was coming to rescue me. My friends had deserted me.

Back at the cottage I wrapped the blanket tight around my shoulders.

"Dost ye want a bit more of the whisky?"

"No." I slumped onto my side in the dirt and whimpered, "I just want to go to sleep. Will you wake me if there's a storm?"

"Aye, Madame Hayley."

There wasn't a storm all night. I could barely sleep. The breathing thing was worse. I tried to inhale and count and exhale and count but — I was stuck in the eighteenth century.

This was running through my mind: I had a vessel, a bag of vessels, but I was afraid to touch them. Kaitlyn never showed me how to use them, and I never thought to ask. What if I was zapped to someplace else, without the hope of Magnus and Kaitlyn? But then again, was there hope? What if some shit had happened in the future-future and I was stuck here until I saved myself?

It's amazing how fucking awful it is to have a panic attack and not have instagram to scroll through to calm down.

In the morning, Fraoch got up to fuss around the clearing, messing with the horse — I burst into tears.

"Are ye well, Madame Hayley?"

"No, I'm terrible. I don't think they're coming."

"It has only been a day."

"You don't understand, it's just numbers, a date. They know when I'm here. They can come to the day, the very next day. It's not dangerous. They could spend two years there without me if they wanted and still come here, the same day. They haven't." I pulled the blanket over my head and hid down inside. "And it was really dangerous what we were doing. We had all the vessels, Magnus was in an arena battle—"

"Och, was he winning?"

I pulled the blanket away, to shake my head. "I don't think so. We tried to rescue him, the arena was full of a storm and dirt and wind and this guy shoved me, grabbed my vessel from my hand, and I was running around looking for another one. It was life or death. As soon as I saw the one on the ground I jumped on it—" Telling the story, reliving that fear, was making my heart race. "I should have waited to make sure everyone else was safe but I didn't. I left while they were in a battle and they might all be dead. I might be the only person who knows where they are, what happened to them, what year they are... and I have all these vessels and no idea how to work them."

"Dost ye want to look at them?"

I sniffled. "No, they're too scary."

"Maybe ye can figure out how tae work it?"

"Kaitlyn and I have a deal, if you're lost, hold tight, let people find you. Just hold tight. Her Grandma Barb told us that years ago, because her grandpa got lost at Disney World, and ever since we kept it as an eternal truth — if you're lost, stay put, someone will find you. I just want to lie here for a while and feel sorry for myself."

"What is a disnie whirl?"

"Never mind. I can't possibly explain it." I curled up in the fetal position and stared at the dirt right in front of my face. I was wrapped in Fraoch's only blanket — he had been without one for two nights now. I said, "You were going back to Madame Greer's house, you can do that."

"I canna leave ye in the woods, Madame Hayley. I wouldna be able tae return tae m'man cave after because of the wolves."

"Why on earth...? Oh, because they would eat me and then want more?"

"Aye, and after they had a taste of lassie their wolf clan would come and they would all be wantin' more lassie tae eat. Dost ye ken how hard twould be tae explain tae the wolves I daena have any more lassie? I daena speak wolf verra well. I could hunt them, but one man against a family of wolves, would be a grave battle. I would perchance have tae just give them my braw castle."

I said, "Ha ha, very funny. Especially the part about your castle."

"Tis. Ye daena like my braw castle, Madame Hayley?"

"It's fine." I sat up. "I mean, don't get me wrong, you've been very hospitable, but it's really better as a wolf den than a man cave." I listed on my fingers, "You need some food, a mattress, some more blankets and some food."

He stood. "I will go get ye some food."

"You also need a security guard. It's really really scary when you go."

He accompanied me into the woods to pee, then led me into the hut and handed me the gun. He said, "Og Maggy and Madame Kaitlyn will be here verra soon, Madame Hayley, daena worry."

This time when he left I was thrown into a state of panic. I watched him go with tears rolling down my face.

My back to the wall, I prayed for help. I cried. Some kind of animal rustled outside and I begged the universe to help me, please please help me — *I'm not supposed to be here, this was an accident.*

FIVE - HAYLEY

Fraoch called, "Madame Hayley?"

I crawled from the cottage to see two horses. A woman was riding the second. She was dressed like she lived in the eighteenth century. Around her shoulders she wore a deep green wool shawl held in the front by a gold pin. Her long skirt was a deep blue wool. She asked, "Madame Hayley?"

I stood and brushed the dirt off my cargo-pocketed pants. "Yes, um, hello."

Her eyes were kind, though her back was stiff. She looked imperious up on her horse, even as she swung herself down.

Fraoch took her horse's reins.

"I am Lizbeth, Madame Kaitlyn's sister."

"Oh, I'm her friend, her best friend."

The woman nodded, her brow drawn down.

"Fraoch said ye are arrived mistakenly, that ye haena a way home?"

My blasted chin started to tremble again like I was a big baby. "I thought Kaitlyn and Magnus would come and get me by now." I devolved into ugly-crying.

She said, "Och, it has been verra tryin' on ye. Though we had Black Mac with us for some long months, twas half a year if I think on it, and he survived it. I daena think ye should worry much on a couple of days."

I sniffled and wiped my eyes. "I'm just scared and I'm very hungry."

"Fraoch, what does this mean? You have been keepin' this young lass in a lodgin' nae more than a pighouse, and ye haena fed her?"

"I have been tryin' tae discern what tae do, Madame Lizbeth. I kent Magnus was comin' and when he came he would take her tae the castle and would make it easy tae explain her, but I dinna ken tae explain her dress and manners tae the guards."

Lizbeth huffed.

"I came for ye the second morn."

"The second morn! Did ye consider the impropriety of it?" Lisbeth leveled her eyes on me. "Are ye unharmed Madame — remind me how ye said it?"

"Hayley."

"Madame Hayley, has Fraoch MacLeod, caused ye any trouble?"

"No, not at all. He's been... it's okay."

"Fraoch, you should have come tae me as soon as ye found her. If something or someone accosted her, or she was found alone while ye were hunting — there are many things that could have happened. We would have found her some dressing tae make her presentable. She should be at the castle."

Lizbeth yanked open a sack tied to the side of her horse and fished out a bundle of wool cloth. She held it out for me. "You can change inside there."

"Oh. Thank you."

I went into the hut to change into the clothes. Fraoch called in, "My pardon, Madame Hayley. I dinna ken."

I called out. "I understand. It made sense to me at the time too."

I peeled off my disgusting five-day-old clothes. Actually when I thought about it I had been wearing them for hundreds of years — gross. Then I tried to make sense of the fabric she gave me. There was a big nightgown, no underwear. I pulled it over my head. The skirt had no top fastener of any kind. I had a sweat going by the time I had it on, with a great deal of it bunched in my fist at my waist with no way to proceed. "Madame Lizbeth... um, I don't know how to?"

She joined me inside the cramped quarters. "Turn around." She gestured to raise my arms and pulled a bodice over them and tugged it around my chest and laced it up, pulling it very tight. She gestured again for me to pull my breasts up, tucked the skirt up into the waist, and then wrapped and cinched the whole outfit with a belt.

"There! Dost it feel better?"

"Yes," I lied, sort of. "I am glad to be out of those filthy clothes." She pulled my hair back and tied a string around the ends of it, then we emerged from the hut. Lizbeth had me join her on her horse.

Fraoch strapped my bag of vessels to our horse then climbed on his own.

Lizbeth said, "You winna need tae attend us."

"Madame Hayley's bag is full of valuable things, I..."

"Och, tis...?" She took a deep breath. "If that is the case, we do need ye tae attend us, Fraoch. I will take them intae hiding once we are in the confines of the castle."

So we rode to the castle and the ride was a little like being in trouble. Like I had landed in a foreign country and instead of going to the hotel in an Uber I had been sleeping in the airport. Now the police were involved and they had a lot of questions and were kind of pissed at my incompetence. Fraoch was in trouble too. His seemed to be more about not hailing me a taxi, but in some ways he and I were both in the same boat, stranded in a foreign country, unsure what to do next.

At the gate Fraoch slowed his horse while Lizbeth kept going. She said, "Thank ye for your service, Fraoch."

I asked, "Will you keep watch, Fraoch?"

"Aye," he said, "I will tell ye as soon as I ken." He called, simply, "My many apologies, Madame Lizbeth, Madame Hayley."

I called back, "No problem," as our horse trotted through the gates to the courtyard of the castle.

SIX - HAYLEY

I was inside a freaking castle. I had been in King Mags's safe house in the future-future. I had been on the roof of the castle in the future-future. I had sat outside this castle watching the gates in the past-past-past, but right now, this moment, I was on a horse, riding through the front gates of a real castle.

The men — scowling, menacing, unbathed — pulled the gate open and we rode through. Their gaze on me was like walking by a construction site, but with way more gaze. Way more. So heavy that gaze. I sank against Lizbeth's back to hide.

Her back remained straight and high though, proud and domineering. She guided her horse to a stone wall and a young man rushed up to take the reins.

She looped an arm in mine. "We will go tae my rooms tae discuss keeping ye safe. Daena meet eyes as we go."

We went briskly up two levels of dark stone stairs. They were unevenly placed and worn down in the middle. I stubbed my toe on one and almost fell on another.

She led me along long cold hallway. The floor was bare stone, but tapestries hung along the walls, but I couldn't really see them because it was too dark. Plus Lizbeth had made me promise not to slow down and get distracted and she was frankly kind of domineering.

She stopped at a big wooden door, opened it with a large key, and hustled me inside.

Dropping the bag, she pulled aside a tapestry on the far wall and, using a key from a ring tied at her waist, unlocked another door. She dragged the bag into the hidden inner room, then locked the door, allowing the tapestry to cover it again. She let out a deep breath and blew hair from her face. "Explain tae me again what happened?"

I considered. "I'm not sure what I'm allowed to tell you."

"I ken about my brother's travels. I ken my sister, his wife, Kaitlyn, is from the future. I am supposing ye are from there as well."

"Yes, I am. I was in the future-future in Magnus's kingdom. He was in this big arena battle and—"

Her brow drew down. "Did he survive?"

"I don't know. We stormed the arena. I was with Quentin who used to live—"

"Black Mac."

"Yes, Black Mac, me, another friend, and Kaitlyn, oh, and Lady Mairead."

"M'mum was there?"

"Oh, that's right, yes." Now I knew why Lizbeth was so unsettling. I had forgotten she would be Lady Mairead's daughter.

She watched me for a moment, then sighed. "Are ye married?"

"No, I mean, yes? I don't know what the right answer is. I'm not, but I told Fraoch I was married, just in case he got ideas. He didn't, by the way, he was very polite."

It was the first time she smiled, just a little, in the corner of her mouth. "Tis wise tae tell the men here ye are married and that yer husband will be comin' tae collect ye. We will tell everyone ye are the sister of Kaitlyn, and therefore almost a Campbell, and that I consider ye a sister as well."

She put her hands on her hips. "Ye daena have a man with ye though, twill be difficult tae navigate ye safely through the time ye are here. Ye canna be alone where one of the Campbell men might want tae discuss yer virtues. And I think it would be best if ye remained with me here in my apartments. I will tell Liam he should go on a hunt."

She tilted her head. "Now, we will get ye somethin' tae eat and become acquainted with each other."

Nearing the Great Hall we passed through a series of highly decorated rooms, each more elaborate than the last. Lizbeth slowed our pace. "This room is the Earl's favorite." There were long glass windows along one side. The ceiling was high and carved, the walls painted a deep red, accented with wood cornices and panels.

Along it were large painted portraits of old men, eyeing us as we passed. "Who are they?" I asked, my voice hushed because the room was opulently imposing.

"Some of the ancestors. There is Sir Duncan Campbell of Glenorchy, he was oft called Black Duncan. The portrait was painted of him in the year 1623."

"So old!"

"Aye, tae ye it is." She joked, "Tae us tis only a hundred years." She gestured toward another portrait. "This is Sir Colin, and along there, m'grandfather, Sir John." We walked farther along while I gaped at the ornately carved ceiling, the antiques, and the sculptures standing on pedestals in the corners.

We came to the big double doors at the end of the room. A guard opened them and bowed us through. "The Great Hall," said Lizbeth. I turned, taking in the ceiling, floors, the walls — a long table stretched down the middle of the room and smaller tables and chairs were clustered along the edges. Lizbeth said, "There are usually many people here eatin' but now tis between meals."

Two large trays with meats and bread lay in the middle of the main table. Lizbeth urged me to eat directly from the tray. I did, ravenously — I was so freaking hungry.

We made small talk while I ate. Other people came and went from the room while I ate and ate until I was able to truly smile and relax for the first time. My situation was still dire, but not nearly as much as when I woke up that morning in the dirt front yard of a hovel.

Lizbeth said, "I have only just met ye, but I think ye have yer color back. I imagine ye might survive Fraoch's hospitality if ye are fed enough."

I laughed. "He wasn't that bad. He tried to keep me safe, he just wasn't sure how to do it."

"He did keep ye alive, tis somethin' he accomplished. Though he should ken of the devilish tongues in the village and of keepin' your reputation. He has seen plenty of trouble since he has been keepin' house with Madame Greer."

I leaned forward. "Why, what is happening?"

"Tis nae for me tae say. He has been invited tae live in the warm home of the one widow in the entire village with the loosest tongue and the most interest in every villager's business. I do like her, truthfully. She is funny and kind, and I daena mind she is in all the business, she means well, and someone needs tae be mindful of the mischief, but now she has Fraoch in her home." She smiled and her eyes twinkled mischievously. "Many people are speculatin' on them, and speaking their minds about it. I warned her twould come tae this. She dinna heed me and now Madame Greer finds it difficult tae understand how they can be so interested in her life."

Lizbeth chuckled. "She daena see the humor that she is distressed by the verra meddlin' she is usually involved in."

I asked, "Is there something going on with Fraoch and Madame Greer?"

"I daena ken, might be. Twas a kindness of her tae take him in. He was grateful. For a time they seemed tae be comfortable. Now she is verra often tired of havin' him in her house, so he comes here for meals or goes on the hunt with the men. He lives alone verra often I hear, more than he lives with Madame Greer, but still the villagers like tae tell an entertainin' story."

"He does seem lonely."

"Och, I imagine he is. When I last conversed with Madame Greer her biggest concern was tae find him a wife. Tis trouble tae have young men about who are unmarried, they daena have the sense tae stay from deviltry."

Her smile widened. "Tis good ye claimed tae be married, ye wouldna want tae get caught up in that business." Then she asked, "So how is Kaitlyn?"

"She was doing well — but now... I don't know."

"And they haena found Magnus's son?"

"No, not yet—"

A large boisterous group of kilt-wearing men rambled into the room, hot but filthy, sexy despite their hobo-like appearances, how was that even possible?

Lizbeth glanced at them and back at me.

"Well, Sister Hayley, ye are married, thankfully, because those men will be circlin' ye, and I daena have the strength tae fight them off yer sweet unmarried self."

I joked, "As Kaitlyn would say, I ain't sweet."

She held up her beer mug and we clinked them together. She said, "Slainte," as the five men came toward us, yelling, pushing and jostling. Their accents were so thick, they were talking so fast, I couldn't tell if it was English, I couldn't make out a word.

In a weird way the night was fun, as if a shitty day had been redeemed by an acquaintance taking me out to lift my spirits. But also there were lulls where I stared off into space and thought, *what the fuck am I doing here?*

I should have been curled up on my couch watching Netflix instead of nodding and smiling while a guy who looked like a Viking, who had probably never had a bath, told a story about punching a fencepost on his way home from a pub.

Madame Lizbeth was jovial and fun and wore an easy smile. Occasionally she left me, but only for brief moments, and always made sure I was safe until she returned to sit with me again.

Halfway through the evening she led me upstairs to the nursery to introduce me to her two youngest children, Mary who was almost three, and the baby, Ainsley, who had been born with Kaitlyn's help. I was very impressed with my friend, in awe, actually — when she was young she had been a weak-stomached, nervous, silly girl. If I ever saw her again I would tell her I was proud of her. If.

Lizbeth's oldest son, Jaime, wasn't there, instead off running loose in the castle. She said, "Well, he is a boy he will be intae mischief because he has tae be."

She led me from the nursery back to her rooms. "I notified the Earl that ye would be visiting for a time. He would like tae meet ye, but daena feel up tae it today. His son went huntin' with

Liam and Sean, so we daena have tae suffer meetin' him. Ye daena ken how fortunate ye are, he is a bore, but is nae here verra often."

We stopped by the garderobe and I spoke to Lizbeth through the door as I peed. "Has Kaitlyn brought you toilet paper to try?"

"Nae, what is it?"

"Such an amazing thing, it's paper on a roll, and you use it to wipe your—"

Lizbeth said, "Wheesht."

I heard voices in the hallway speaking to Lizbeth and when I came out she was smiling. "I dinna want them tae hear ye, but I do like the sound of it? Tis soft?"

"Very very very soft. I miss it so much."

When we entered her rooms there was a fire in the hearth, making it warm enough for me to remove the heavy outer layer of my bodice and the thick skirt.

There was a small wooden bed at the end of Lizbeth's four-poster. Much like a toddler bed, like the trundle bed in my dad's office where I slept when I stayed the weekends with him after the divorce, except a lot more uncomfortable.

For warmth there was a thick linen cloth and on top a wool blanket, thankfully, because as the fire died down, the air turned freezing. I couldn't believe it was summer. It was cold down into my bones and my blanket was too short, I had to curl into a ball so my toes weren't exposed.

I got as comfortable as I could. "Thank you Lizbeth, for all of this."

"Tis nae somethin' tae worry on, Madame Hayley, I am sure they will be here on the morrow."

And then as I tried to sleep I cried, from fear, despair, being uncomfortable, but I tried to do it very very quietly so Lizbeth wouldn't hear.

In the middle of the night, this thought ran through my head: *tomorrow night, if no one comes for me, I will get one of the vessels and try to figure it out.*

EIGHT - HAYLEY

The next day was interesting, like a Saturday before a family holiday. Lizbeth had meet with the cook about food. That required walking to the kitchen and through all the storerooms. She had to go to the nursery to see about the children. That meant climbing the stairs to the second floor. We returned to the kitchen, and then we went to the wine cellar. After that we spoke to the women weaving the wool on the third floor. Then we were outside in the kitchen garden. I was exhausted from all the walking.

About mid-morning a group of four boys ran by us in a stairwell, and Lizbeth snagged the arm of a boy of about seven years old. She said to him, "Introduce yourself, Jaime, this is, Madame Hayley, a relation of Aunt Kaitlyn's."

He looked a lot like Lizbeth and a little like Magnus too. He said, "Tis nice tae meet ye, Madame Hayley, I am Jaime Campbell."

"You're Magnus's nephew?"

"Aye." He bowed a bit and then after a brief exchange with

his mother, was off, running down the halls to catch up to his cousins.

There were so many things to do, people to talk to about the things to do, a general bustle, yet also, a lot of the day that was fucking unbelievably boring.

Lizbeth and I ate our breakfast in the nursery with her babies and they were cute and all, but there was an awful racket the whole time we were in there. I rubbed my aching temples. "The bairns are carryin' on."

Lizbeth laughed. "When ye pass the morn listenin' tae the bairns wailin', the rest of your day will seem verra peaceful."

Sean's wife, Maggie, approached just then. She barely met my eyes as we were introduced. "I am glad tae see ye in the nursery this morn, Madame Lizbeth, after prayer this is our most important work."

Lizbeth said, "Aye, when I am about my many responsibilities of the castle and the lands of the Earl of Breadalbane, I am oft thinking, 'I should rather be doin' the important work of holdin' the bairns.'"

I clamped my lips in my teeth to keep from laughing.

Madame Maggie said, "As it should be," and crossed to the far end of the nursery to hold one of the wailing babies. Her whole demeanor, the act of picking up the baby, the way she sat there glancing at us was totally judgmental.

I glanced at Lizbeth, her back was straight, her look imperious, but that sparkle of humor remained.

It was a beautiful day when we left the nursery to walk a long path to the market. The sky was high with little tufts of clouds swimming across the bright blue expanse. Green fields to the left and right of us were dotted with pale white sheep, and gray, low stone walls stretched along our path. Thatch-roofed houses were settled along the route, more, and closer together, as we neared the village.

Along the way Lizbeth dished about the women I had just met, ending with, "And daena mind Madame Maggie, she has judged me tae nae be pious and matronly enough, and has included ye in on the matter since you're in m'company."

"Well, in my case she's not wrong, I am not nearly matronly enough."

"Och, ye seem tae be a better sort, wise in the way of the world. This is why I was pleased tae meet Madame Kaitlyn. She is verra kind and does nae make judgments, and she is also wise about the world. She has been a good match for Magnus. I am proud of him for choosin' her. And grateful she is neither unkind, silly, or overly pious like the rest of the wives."

I laughed, "Are those the only choices? You aren't any of them, how'd you get so cool?"

"If by 'cool' ye mean, I am nae unkind, silly, or pious, tis because of me mum."

My eyes went wide. "What — Lady Mairead?"

"She taught me tae pay attention tae the affairs of the castle, tae ken the maneuverings and strategies of the men, tae watch everything. I am too important tae be bothered with the rest of it."

I smiled at that. "That's a good sentiment, to be 'too important to be bothered.' I like that."

The village was holding a market day, tables set around the main square, bread, meat, and cheeses available for sale. A bustling activity, children racing by, chickens underfoot, a pig swishing its tail and ears to keep the flies from landing, not a few feet away from a table covered in slabs of meat. My ears were full of the sounds of yelling voices, animal grunts and squawks, and my nose was accosted by a mixture of baked bread and the stench of farm animal. Lizbeth worked the tables, bartering, discussing, arranging to have carts of bread and meat brought to the castle, and then she bought some food for our lunch.

After we walked back to the castle, I went to the room to lie down, because everything about the day had been exhausting. This was like living in a theater production, mixed with a family wedding, combined with a camping trip, and all I wanted was a storm.

This would be so much easier if Kaitlyn was here to help me get through it, if Magnus was here to protect me, if Quentin was here to joke about it.

After sitting by myself for a couple of hours, Lizbeth came to get me for dinner. We were having a mug of ale at the main table when Lizbeth's eyes drew to the door at the far end of the room.

Fraoch was headed our way — maybe there had been a storm?

He was smiling and he was alone, but I asked anyway, "Did it storm?"

"Nae, Madame Hayley, good evenin' Madame Lizbeth. There has been nae news, I am sorry about it."

His demeanor was awkward. He didn't seem to know what to do with his hands and finally settled on holding his belt. His hair was wet, slicked back from his face. His beard was trimmed shorter than before, not much, but a little, and looked cleaner. And there was a scent about him—

Lizbeth sniffed the air. "Master Fraoch, ye smell as if ye have gotten intae the rose-scented lotion Kaitlyn gifted tae Madame Greer."

He blushed red above his beard. "Aye, she leant it tae me, afore I came for dinner."

"Ah, I see." Her brow lifted. "As ye can tell tis a vast Great Hall without many men, most of them having gone tae hunt. Ye daena come for dinner verra often when they are away."

"Aye, I am usually acoompanyin' them on the hunt, but this

time I stayed behind tae see tae Madame Hayley, since she was needin' me tae watch the storms."

"I see, well, we are two auld wives, but ye may join us for the meal. We were just speakin' on children and their feedings." Her eyes glinted merrily.

Fraoch took a seat stiffly. He was a big man but seemed to be trying to compress his insides down into a smaller form. He wore the strain on his face. His unease was delighting Lizbeth.

I took a sip of a beer. I had been trying not to drink but this place had nothing but alcohol. Its saving grace was that there was no need to stay up partying. This vibe was more — get a buzz and go to bed early. Lizbeth told me it would get wilder once the men returned.

I felt a little bummed that my presence caused her to send the men away and now with the men away it was more boring-er here. Boring-er? Maybe I was a little buzzed.

I took another sip of beer. "What have you been doing since I saw you yesterday, Fraoch?"

"I have returned tae the village workin' for Madame Greer. A fox found his way in with the hens and has killed many of them. I had tae clean up after his feast and fill the hole it entered through. Twas an afternoon of work."

He leaned back, growing more comfortable. "What have ye been doing, Madame Hayley?"

I glanced at Lizbeth — what had I been doing?

Lizbeth, her eyes twinkling merrily, said, "She has been dutifully awaitin' her husband comin' tae collect her."

Fraoch nodded. "Och aye, yer husband. He is a big man ye say, Madame Hayley?"

Lizbeth batted his arm. "Tis nae matter whether he is big or small, he is what he is, her husband, ye daena have a reason tae ask her on it."

Fraoch drained his beer. "As I see it, he is nae here though, he is from — where is he from? What time?"

I laughed, truly enjoying his banter after a day of careful conversation. "Like three hundred years in the future."

Fraoch's eyes glinted. "Och, he sounds verra auld."

We all laughed.

Lizbeth said, "We should get our dinner, the Earl isn't here so we don't have to wait."

"Where is the Earl?" asked Fraoch.

"He has gone tae Edinburgh. There is a great trouble brewin' with the succession, he has a need tae be in the middle of the makin' of the trouble."

Fraoch squinted his eyes at her. "I appreciate yer astute eye on the dealings, I am nae used tae the fairer sex havin' so many opinions."

"Yet our Monarch is a queen? I would suppose she has many opinions on the succession, she has recently lost her son."

I asked, "Who is the queen?"

Lizbeth said, "Anne..." Her eyes looked off sadly. "She has lost all seventeen of her bairns. She must feel it verra deeply."

Fraoch waved a hand. "Och, she is a monarch, she haena a thought about it except the succession. Twill be goin' tae King George."

Lizbeth's eyes went wide. "You ken this tae be true?"

"Aye, I am from the future as well."

Lizbeth leaned back and looked from Fraoch to me.

"Are your futures much the same? My mother has told me of wondrous things. And I have seen them with m'own eyes when the flyin' weapons and the — I daena remember what Black Mac called them. He had tae train our men tae fight against them."

I said, "I remember the stories, I can't believe that happened here."

"They tore down the walls, I will shew ye in the morn. We haena fully rebuilt them yet."

I said, "Those weren't from my time, though we do have similar machines."

Fraoch said, "Sean has told me of the battle. Tis difficult for him tae guard these walls when he kens those weapons might attack again."

I said, "I think Magnus is doing everything in his power to keep them away."

Lizbeth said, "And what of your time, Master Fraoch, did ye have weapons like these?"

"Nae, in my time we still ride horses. I carried a sword along with m'gun. Twas much the same as this, though time has taken us further from our purpose tae have a Stuart king."

Lizbeth leaned back and sighed. "Och, tae think we are still arguin' on it years from now. How many years ahead were ye?"

Fraoch said, "It seems a lifetime though was about two score."

"And how many years for ye, Madame Hayley?"

I said, "Fraoch's future is long before my country was even a country, and my country has been a country for over two hundred years."

Lizbeth said, "Really?"

"Yep, we were founded in 1776 after we fought for independence from..." I chuckled, "Well, this is awkward — we fought for independence from England."

Fraoch said, "Och, this would have been after I was gone tae m'grave. I canna be blamed for losin' the colonies."

I said, "You wouldn't have been old enough to be in a grave. In 1776 you might have still been around to have a hand in it."

"If I live until I am three score auld I would believe m'self tae be graced by God, as I daena have the goodness in me tae deserve a long life." Then he added, "My apologies Madame Lizbeth, Madame Hayley, tis rude tae speak on my sins at dinner."

I smiled to set him at ease because though he was laughing, he was very uneasy, formal and stiff underneath. "Most people in my time live until their late seventies and doctors believe it's possible for everyone to live to be one hundred and five years old."

Lizbeth scoffed. "A century! I am exhausted just thinkin' on it."

Fraoch chugged some ale and swiped his arm across his mouth. "A man that can live that long has had nae real purpose. If he dinna need tae die tae protect his family — how dost he ken he was truly livin'? And if he is nae truly living, what is the point of continuin' on it for such a verra endless time?"

I watched him as he spoke. A rough guy, he needed a Harley, and would be home in any biker bar. He needed a tattoo: Live Fast Die Young.

I said, "Black Mac was in the military. He fought in Afghanistan to protect us. It is possible to put your life on the line in my time, just not everybody all the time."

Fraoch asked, "Where is Afghanistan?"

I thought for a moment before I admitted, "I don't mean to sound stupid, but I can't really tell you without a map, a pencil, maybe a computer." I sighed deeply, sadly. "Quentin fought in a war there. I'm going to need to make some serious amends when — *if,* I ever see him again."

Fraoch asked Lizbeth, "When will Sean and Liam return?"

"I think on the morrow."

He said, "The day after, Madame Hayley, could I take ye for a ride? Tae show ye some of the land?"

Lizbeth's eyes went wide. "I daena ken if that..."

I said, "I don't think I'll still be here actually. Thank you for inviting me, but Kaitlyn or Quentin will be here long before that."

NINE - HAYLEY

Kaitlyn or Quentin didn't come the following day. Sean and Liam returned later in the day and met me briefly before they set about unpacking from the hunt.

Lizbeth held onto me even more now, mindful to never leave me alone. There were many rough and dangerous looking men around, sexy in the way they strode through the castle halls, though many were short, ugly, and a few looked like real assholes. Like not at all the kind of guy you wanted to be stuck in a dark corner with — hence Lizbeth held my arm.

I understood her so much better now — I adored her. At first I assumed she was a married-woman-mom of the eighteenth century, like she was judging me, and that I would never live up to her expectations. But after watching the light at the edge of her eyes, the bemused smile, I realized she was joking about so many things. She was teasing, mischievous, and funny, almost a modern woman — only with a great many rules she had to follow.

One interesting thing was while she seemed at ease, jovial, her eyes continually scanned the room. There was a look to them, a guarded judging of her safety, or of mine, a watchful consideration of every person and their place in the room. There were things happening that I didn't understand — she would turn her back to people, or jump from her chair to manage them. There were people who made her laugh and some who caused her to scowl.

One night Sean came and whispered in her ear.

She said, "I already see him," and rose from her chair, grasped my hand, and rushed me from the Great Hall. "Vile Mac has come tae the castle. He is verra evil, ye canna look at him or he will try tae cause ye harm. He inna supposed tae be here unless he is invited."

"Oh, but the men will handle him, right?"

"Aye, they will, though he is dangerous and I daena like the idea of him bein' within the castle walls at nightfall. Young beautiful Mary was a lass when he took her away. We couldna prove it, but she has never returned, and some of the men take his side on it."

"This is awful, what should we do?"

She shrugged, "We will remain in our rooms until we ken he is gone."

So we went scurrying down the halls, and waited in her rooms all night. Lizbeth acted as if this was all completely normal, just life in the eighteenth century, but to me it was terrifying. I was at their mercy, a beggar for food, shelter, protection, and now evil men walked among us. I lay awake that night wondering if I should just hide forever in these rooms.

But when I woke the next day, hungry, Lizbeth was already dressed. She said brightly, "Tis all finished, Madame Hayley. Liam and Sean and the other men have delivered Vile Mac from the castle. I am verra relieved, are ye hungry? We missed our dinner last evenin'."

Fraoch was already in the Great Hall, his hair slicked back and smelling like roses and sweat.

"Would ye like tae go for a ride, Madame Hayley?"

I said, "Yes," because I was bored out of my mind, nervous from being cooped up last night, and desperate to do something besides this. Lizbeth was concerned, of course, but relented when I reminded her she would have the day off from guarding me.

She steered me to the wall to speak in private, "Madame Hayley, if ye spend the day with Fraoch MacLeod, the other men will be thinkin' ye belong tae him."

I chuckled. "Well, I don't belong to him, because I'm married, but also, that's probably a good thing, right? He's a big strapping guy, he can be in charge of my chastity for once, give you a break."

She laughed. "I daena believe ye should be allowin' Fraoch tae be in charge of your chastity."

I shrugged.

My horse was light brown and she rode well and listened to me about things, so we got along. It had been a couple of years since I last had ridden, and of course she was unfamiliar, but I felt comfortable and confident riding her.

About an hour into our ride, Fraoch told me about how war horses would bite during battles. I patted the neck of my horse. "Nicely done, you're like a princess *and* a monster."

Fraoch began talking about the real monsters, alligators. And by the end of the conversation I had nicknamed my horse Gatorbelle.

Fraoch and I talked, we talked and talked and talked. He

taught me names for the trees and the hills around us — weird words with barks and guttural sounds. Words that had been all around me for days, but I hadn't tried to learn them, because I wasn't planning to be here long. But now...

We passed by a pine that snagged in Fraoch's hair and he twisted around on his horse. "Did ye see it draw against me, Madame Hayley? Twas an attack on my person." He drew his sword and hacked at the tree branch until it was hanging broken then said, "Och, I was mistaken tae have fought it, I see now twas just a tree."

I laughed. "I read a book when I was young about a woman who lived at the very tip top of a redwood tree."

He looked up and down the trunk of the pine he had been whacking. "At the top, upon a branch?"

We started our horses walking again. "Yes, she built a little cabin on a branch and lived there for months and months. She used a long rope to pull up her food. She said the tree swayed in the wind while she was sleeping."

Fraoch arched back looking up at the top of the trees around us. "Och, a movin' house, I wouldna like tae be up so high."

"Me neither, but she didn't do it because she liked it, she did it to protect the tree. To stop the loggers who wanted to cut it down. She was what we call a treehugger."

"Och, she liked tae hug the tree? Why would she want tae embrace the fire logs?"

I laughed. "I guess it's a little like men here sword-fighting the fire logs, people do crazy shit sometimes."

He laughed. "Aye, that they do. Madame Hayley, dost ye think the tree I fought is still standin' in the time ye live in?"

"I came here once, near here, with Kaitlyn. She was following a storm, looking for a vessel, and there were woods still, but also many fields. A few roads. So I doubt this tree would still be here though we could pick one close to the castle, and measure how far away it is, and when I get home I can..." I let my voice trail off.

"Tae look for it?"

"Yes, but — it seems too hopeful to say it, I don't think they'll... you know."

"They will come, Madame Hayley. Remain hopeful, ye only must wait for them tae return."

I said, "Ugh. I'm not at all a waiting kind of person. I manage, I control, I make shit happen."

Out of the corner of my eye I saw him smile.

Fraoch asked, "What did ye mean by 'lookin' for a vessel'?"

"There were these storms. We saw them on the weather channel."

His brow drew down, so I explained, "In the future we can predict when storms are coming."

"Och, twould change the world."

"It would, wouldn't it? I never really thought about what a big invention that is, predicting the weather. But back to the story — Kaitlyn learned about storms over Scotland, over Castle Balloch, so we got on a plane and flew here in the year 2018, I think it was."

"Ye flew like a bird?"

"No, in those planes I was telling you about."

"Och, in the carriage in the air."

"Exactly."

"Tae find the magic vessel."

"No, these vessels aren't magic — they *seem* magic, but it's got to be science. It's just way, way, way in the future kind of science and I don't understand it at all. Like I said before, the vessels aren't from my time. They're as weird to me as they are to you."

"Och, tis the work of the devil. We should stay away from them."

"Well, maybe not that weird. I think it's just something we haven't learned how to do yet, we should try to understand them."

"Ye claimed there tae be storms over Bràghad Albainn?"

"Bridalban-what?"

"This area is the seat of the Earl, where the Castle Balloch stands on the strath of the Tay."

"Oh, yeah, right. Because of the storms Kaitlyn went to investigate, to find the vessel if there was one. We flew by plane and landed in Edinburgh, hired a car and drove, that's like a carriage without horses, to the grounds of Balloch. In my time it's called Taymouth Castle."

"Draws its name after the river." He looked thoughtful as he picked our horses' paths around a boulder.

We had been on an incline for a while, heading higher and higher into the hills. The trees had given way to open areas, covered in grass, with large outcroppings of rocks. Above us spread a cloud-filled sky. The day had turned cool. A wind was rising.

He pointed back over a gorgeous valley. "See the castle? And there is the Tay beyond."

"What a beautiful view." I shivered from the wind.

He said, "The tartan ye have wrapped there, around yer skirt, ye can pull it up and wrap it around your shoulders."

"Oh, true." I pulled the fabric from my belt and wrapped it around myself for warmth.

I watched him as he looked out over the vista — his face was worn, older, manly. Rough-hewn was the description I kept coming to, his eyes distant as he looked out over the landscape, taking the beauty in. His body was big and strong and even unmoving like he was now, he was in motion, a firm hand on the reins, powerful arm bent, ready for action, eyes sweeping the landscape.

He belonged here, as strong as the mountain, at home on the ridge, in the high sky and the fresh air, wrapped in wool, astride a horse, armed with a sword — this was his country, though to him, his belonging was to a different time. This was foreign to him — different mountains, different trees, borrowed people.

We began to ride again. "Madame Hayley, have ye heard the story of Balloch Castle?"

"No, I haven't."

"Sean told me Sir Colin Campbell of Glenorchy evicted all of the clan Gregor from these lands and built the castle here tae prove his strength. Sean said he was a brutal, violent man, so I expect he was."

"What year was this?"

"I have heard it said that the first brick was laid in the year of our Lord, 1550."

"That is so long ago."

"Aye, but the story goes, whilst making his way down the strath of the Tay, Sir Colin Campbell heard a blackbird sing. He stopped and looked around at the alders and redwoods growing in the woods around him, the river runnin' by, the loch glistenin' in the sun. That night he dreamt he should build a castle there in that same place."

"Where he heard the blackbird sing?"

"Aye, from the notes of a blackbird song a violent man built a castle that protected the clan Campbell through many a battle and now houses ye, Madame Hayley, tis a remarkable history."

"It really is."

His body rocked back and forth as he rode, a subtle shift of his shoulders, his feet tense in the leather stirrups. We spoke of stopping for a rest and directed the horses to a small stream and tied the horses to a tree and found a warm place to sit on an outcropping of rocks. Fraoch passed me some bread he had packed in one of the saddle bags.

It was dusty, so I brushed it off. It was also dry, but I didn't want to mention it.

I chewed and chewed and chewed.

He chewed and chewed. "Is the bread tae yer likin'?"

I burst into laughter spraying breadcrumbs all over my skirt. "It's so dry!"

He rubbed his jaw. "Aye, tis verra much stiffer than when I bought it." He added, "A day ago."

I teased, "This, sir, is five-day-old bread."

He laughed and leaned back then grew thoughtful. "Tis a much harder life than ye are used tae, Madame Hayley?"

"It is."

"Tell me something ye do that we canna do?"

"Let's see. Well, here's the first thing: when I'm hungry I can go buy food. There are stores, like markets, that have hundreds of things to eat, so many choices. Bread, so much bread. Also, meat and fruit."

"Madame Kaitlyn said she might be able tae have oranges every day if she wanted them."

"So true. Your scurvy would be cured right up. Actually you'd never have had scurvy."

He shook his head. "Twas so painful I thought twould end me."

"You're still here, and now you know — eat your fruits and veggies. I'm sure Katie told you to."

A wind rose, dropping the temperature about twenty degrees colder. I needed a parka, possibly mittens and a beanie, but all I had was a shawl.

We climbed on our horses and began the long descent back.

A distance from the castle, he pulled his horse short. "Dost ye need tae ride on m'horse? Tis verra cold."

My teeth chattered. "Y-y-yes."

He held my reins so I could climb down and then pulled me up behind him wrapping his tartan around us both, bundling me against his back. "Hold on tae me, Madame Hayley." And we rode very very fast until we drew near the castle, but then walked the horses the rest of the way.

Fraoch stayed at the castle for dinner again. He got along well with the men, Liam and Sean especially, and sat at their table, while I sat with Lizbeth at a table full of women.

There were a lot more men in the Great Hall and through the hallways and around the bathrooms, and as the day turned to night, many of them became staggeringly drunk. That meant I had to not drink too much because being On Guard Around the Barbarians was a thing I had to become used to in my new life here.

I wondered how Kaitlyn had managed her safety. Lizbeth explained, "Och, Kaitlyn has Magnus accompanyin' her, but even Magnus was nae always enough. Tis much easier when ye have a husband tae protect ye — without a husband it is a trial tae keep yourself from bein' a conquest tae every knave in the castle."

She teased, "We should have married ye tae Fraoch first day so he could do the protecting on ye."

I blushed to my hairline. "Marry Fraoch!"

And then I found my eyes settling on him down the table. The curl of his arm as he lifted his mug, his broad shoulders. The booming laugh and the cocky attitude. He was like a cross between a retired football player, full of swagger and bravado, and a lumberjack, full of independence and quiet, sometimes, plus that kilt.

They were all wearing them of course, but his was wearing so well — shit. *What was I doing?*

He turned to see me looking at him and his brow lifted in a laugh. The other men joined him.

I looked away kind of pissed.

I was Madame Hayley. A contemporary woman running a small family temp agency with a real estate hustle on the side. I did Cross Fit twice a week. I got my nails done. I drank mixed drinks and went to AA meetings occasionally because I was a modern woman and was trying for moderation.

I took a swig of beer.

I was not to be trifled with.

And definitely not by an almost homeless eighteenth century scalawag with a missing tooth. Even if he had been kind of swoonably hot when I pressed against his back on the horse earlier.

But there were lots of hot men in the world, and this one was not for me.

He came for my mug. "Would ye like another drink, Madame Hayley?"

"Oh, um, sure."

He went to the cask in the corner and when he returned, asked, "Would ye go for another ride with me on the morrow?"

"Um, yes."

"Good, I will see ye then."

He left to return to the men.

Lizbeth met my eyes. "He is layin' a claim tae ye," she said with that blasted twinkle in her eyes. "Imagine how much he would be claimin' and layin' ye if ye were nae married tae the man in the future?"

"That's why I'm not telling him. It's much better this way. If only Kaitlyn would freaking hurry up."

ELEVEN - KAITLYN

The first days were quiet and introspective and there was sleeping to be done. Magnus and Quentin spent many hours discussing our safety and protection.

Quentin was worried about Hayley's vessel — if she wasn't here, then she jumped with the vessel that had been loose on the floor of the arena.

Why didn't she jump with her own?

And if she dropped it, or if someone grabbed it — who?

They most assuredly would have jumped, probably to Florida, the year 2020.

Quentin hadn't seen whoever it was, but maybe the 'whoever' got here first.

Because none of them landed at the same time.

What if someone from the future was right now walking around Fernandina Beach, spying on us, watching us... It had happened before with General Reyes. So we were worried.

Magnus guarded a lot. He and Quentin made plans. More men were brought in for guard duty.

Archie and Ben played together all day the second day. They

had moments of tears or drama, but for the most part they ran and played together and chased and banged stuff.

And Emma had an idea — we moved a big mattress into the tiny office we barely used, and when the day and the boys were wearing down, we put a baby monitor in there.

After Archie fell asleep on my chest, the little spider monkey, sucking his two fingers with me singing softly to him, my lips pressed against his sweaty forehead, Magnus very gently, because my ribs still hurt, carried him into that tiny office and deposited him onto the mattress beside an already sleeping Ben.

I whispered, "It's like a little pile of puppies."

Emma high-fived me. Then she high-fived Zach. "Our bed to ourselves!"

Zach was practically giddy.

I kept the monitor close because if I heard a shift I would rush to Archie, making sure he didn't get scared. But earlier he napped and when he woke up, came and found me. He knew right where I'd be.

TWELVE - KAITLYN

*M*agnus and I went to our room. We brushed our teeth and I waited until I had a mouthful of lather before I said, as I liked to do, something along the lines of, "Mumphyleyfeeewll."

He lifted his brow and smiled, pulled his brush from his mouth, and said, "I ken ye do, mo reul-iuil."

I squinted my eyes. "Wait, what did you think I said? Just to be clear."

"That ye love me, that ye canna wait tae hae yer way with me. That ye have been conspirin' all day tae have some time with me and now tis here and ye canna wait."

I grinned. "Yep, you're exactly right." When I leaned over and spit he plunged a hand into my panties and poked and tickled while I giggled and squirmed. "Aye, I was right in my thinkin'. Ye are wantin' me."

I said, "I am, and if you aren't careful, Master Magnus, you're going to get me started on this bathroom counter again and all that work to get Archie happily asleep in another room will be for naught."

"Och, naught, I prefer ye naughty on our mattress made for a king."

He lifted me by my arse so I would wrap my legs around his waist, then used my butt-cheek to turn off the bathroom light, both of us laughing, and carried me down the hall to our bed.

"Is this hurting your side?" My lips were pressed to his.

"What side?"

I giggled as he sat on the bed and dropped my feet to the floor in front of him. He leaned over for the lighter and lit the two scented candles beside our bed and then clicked off the lamp. He lifted my shirt up and off.

"Dost your side feel painful?" He trailed his fingers over my bruise, causing shivers, then he kissed the center of my sore place, a full mouth kiss with tongue and oh god — *what side?*

I pulled his boxers down his legs and tossed them over my shoulder. I knelt in front of him and took him in my mouth, but only for a moment because that was plenty, this had been a long day of conspiring to have the bed to ourselves, and I wasn't going to spend a second of it in his pleasure at the expense of mine. I pushed him back on the bed and climbed on.

And hovered over him. "You really really like me don't you?" So tantalizingly close.

"Och aye, ye are a verra good wife."

I licked and nibbled his lips and wiggled my hips directly over him. "I am pretty great. Maybe the best."

His hands held my hips trying to center me but I held off and away.

"Aye, ye are the best wife of all time, I haena ever heard of a wife as good as ye, so randy and wantin' me even when ye are exasperatin'." He chuckled.

I laughed. "Oh, I'm exasperating?"

"Aye with yer arse too verra far away." His fingers pressed

into my skin as they tried to pull me down toward him. Our foreheads were damp as we pressed them together.

I put my mouth on his, a deep kiss, a wanting kiss, our lips wet, my tongue searching inside his mouth and allowed myself to be lowered down onto him with a shared exhale into each other's skin. At the low point of my breath, the deepest point of our touching — I groaned oh god and oh god that was — *oh god.*

We had the heater running, the blinds closed. The darkness of the room enveloped us. The small candles flickered light on our skin.

I held his hands needing that deep connection, his fingers wrapped in mine while our bodies worked together. The smell of amber and ginger and a little patchouli and spice drifting around the room. I rocked on him a little, our cheeks pressed, ear to ear, but then turned my head and he turned his to meet my lips again... we slowed... and kissed and slowed more... and it was very much intensely romantic and devoted and deeply deeply desirous and... *oh — god.*

He rolled me over, climbed on, and finished — in control, fast, deep, and desperate, then collapsed on me, gathering me up under him, holding me.

"You were saying I'm exasperating?" I whispered into his ear.

He chuckled. "I was sayin' ye are perfect."

"That's what I thought you said."

He rolled off and I rolled onto his side and we lay cuddling in the candle light. "You'll leave the day after tomorrow for Hayley?"

"Aye." He entwined his fingers through a lock of my hair. "I will bring her home but then I was thinkin' we need tae move again. I canna understand what Roderick kens about us. There is a man here, somewhere, we need tae prepare." He paused for a moment, then added. "I am only leavin' for a day, but Quentin will need tae be verra guarded."

"Trouble is we need Hayley for buying a new home, or mom, I could ask my mom to find us another house."

"Tell her I want it tae have stables for Sunny and a horse for ye and a horse for Archie."

"Beachfront, check, horse stable, check." I circled my finger around his chest. Thinking about moving again, the drama and how much we would have to do now and how important it was to keep Archie safe. "Speaking of Archie — we should have clothes on." I climbed from bed, got a pair of pajama pants for Magnus from his drawer, and tossed them to his chest.

But I went down the hall to our bathroom naked for Magnus's pleasure, he did love to watch me walk around our room with no clothes on. Afterwards, I dressed in a pair of sweatpants and a T-shirt, putting an end to all his fun.

I climbed back into bed, pulled up beside him, and we held hands as I fell asleep.

I woke up a while later, in the dark.

Magnus was climbing from bed. "I hear him wakin'." He lumbered from the room.

I heard his thudding footsteps through the living room and heard, through the monitor, the door swish open. I saw Magnus crossing on the monitor's screen, and heard his whisper, "Och, wee'un ye awake?"

Archie held up his arms and Magnus lifted him from the mattress.

Ben shifted and woke too. "Mama?" Magnus put out a second arm and Ben climbed to Magnus's other side and then Magnus hefted both boys up and left the room.

I heard him as he crept up the stairs and gently knocked on Zach and Emma's door. Magnus's low rumbling voice sounded and then Zach's as Magnus dropped Ben off with his parents. Magnus's footsteps were soft as he returned to our room.

He dropped Archie onto our bed where he sweetly cuddled against my front and Magnus climbed in beside me, and a moment later, both Magnus and Archie were asleep.

I lay awake for a while longer though, thinking about how full my heart was and how much I needed to do to keep my men safe.

THIRTEEN - KAITLYN

The next day was for enjoying time together, but also readying Magnus to leave. Zach packed a cooler bag with food and drinks with a smaller bag full of more scurvy remedies: a big bottle of vitamin c pills, orange packets for drinks, plus some orange juice and a bag of oranges, too.

Magnus needed a sword and a dirk and Quentin was grumbling about how often he had to replace those on short notice, and Beaty was feeling so much better. She joked, "Tis the cloudy weather makin' me feel better, I canna abide all the sunshine, twill be the death of me."

Quentin said, "The sunshine is the only point of living here, Beaty, we damn sure don't do it for the culture."

She continued the joke, "Tis the summer though, right Quenny? Once it is winter, twill be dreich every day like home?"

Quentin said, "This is the winter."

"Och, tis a dreadful place. So much sun! Today is verra nice and cloudy though, I will have tae make do."

Over a breakfast of pancakes, omelets and bacon, Quentin and I discussed a new house. Archie and Ben were playing with a 'busy toy' with blinking lights and spinning parts, and so many beeping, squeaking, shrill sounds that it made our skin crawl and our ears ring. They had a game going where Archie would push a button, make it squeak, then make a squeaking noise in reply, and Ben would laugh hysterically.

Quentin and I, discussing over the cacophony, decided we wanted to find a house on the south end again. We weren't certain whether it should be on the beach side or the marsh side, either might work, though I would miss easy access to shark teeth hunting. It would have to be a really great house for me to give that up.

Mid-morning Archie and Ben were looking overwrought, so Ben was carried up to his room for a nap before he pissed everyone off. Archie found me sitting at the table making lists and climbed into my lap, curled up, and quietly watched us as we made plans.

"Will you need water treatment?"

Magnus said, "Aye, for Hayley, and some extra food for both of us."

I said, "I was thinking about the date, if you jumped to a few days before she gets there. You would be waiting for her when she arrives. You could save her any drama or excitement. Plus, if she's injured you could get her home really fast."

Quentin said, "But I kind of really like the idea of her spending a few days with this Fraoch guy, he sounds like a lot of fun." He stifled a laugh.

Magnus said, "Och, he is fun, he is also a great deal of trouble for a young woman, even someone as bold and uncompromisin' as Mistress Hayley. I agree with Kaitlyn, I will arrive a couple of days ahead. If she daena come I will return and we will take men tae the future tae find her."

Archie said very quietly. "Where Da go?"

My eyes met Magnus's. It was the first time Archie had called him Da since he arrived. "He's going on a small trip, he'll be back the very next day. You and I will be so busy we won't even notice." I looked at Magnus sadly. "Not really."

"You no go?"

"No, I'm staying here with you."

His little hand sweetly twisted in my hair. I kissed his knuckles.

A few minutes later and he had fallen asleep against my chest. And I knew my butt was going to be in that chair for awhile, because I wouldn't dislodge him. Ever. Ever-ever.

Zach and Emma went to the store. Quentin was guarding. Beaty was watching television.

Magnus brought me a Coke.

Surrounded by lists, things circled and underlined, he held my hand at the table. Our view was of the cool day beyond the sliding door, the windswept dunes and white-capped waves farther on.

"He called you Da, my love."

"Aye, tis a good sound. I am happy he is here and that we have the monitor above us tae watch for trouble."

"Me too. Speaking of trouble, we need to talk to Lady Mairead. I was thinking, we know there was a tracker, there is also the way that you set the vessels to 'homing'. But also there is a way, if I remember correctly, to dismantle the vessels so they only go where we want them to go. We need more information about the pile of vessels. If we can, we should dismantle the ones we aren't using, and hide them."

"I agree with ye, where dost ye think Lady Mairead is?"

"I have an idea. But we can wait until after you rescue Hayley."

"*M*adame Hayley, dost ye want another?" Fraoch held out a crusty bread, smeared with butter and a bit of berry preserves, slathers of goat cheese. Delicious. This was my favorite meal here. Most food in this time tasted like deep dark winter in a hovel beside a ditch with no salt. Except this. Crusty bread with enough butter and goat cheese was almost like something from home.

Fraoch had seen me delight in it, ravenous for anything that tasted sweet and savory, that *tasted*. After that he brought it to me every afternoon.

Because he did come visit me every day. And he asked me to ride with him if the weather was good enough. I asked once, "What's your job? Don't you have something you have to do?"

"What dost ye mean, Hayley, my job?"

"How do you work, make money, to buy the food you bring me?"

His brow drew down. "I have the work of Madame Greer's land. She has me up early tae do the work of ten hen-pecked men. In exchange she feeds me and kens ye like this bread so she has me deliver it for ye."

"That's nice. Thank her for me. This is delicious and it's the only thing keeping me happy right now."

"The only thing?"

The horses were eating grass nearby, a slow chew, gentle tugs at the blades. A beam of sunlight warmed my face and my guess was it was almost seventy-two degrees, practically sweltering, though I still needed a tartan around my shoulders.

He had his shirt open, his thick legs stretched in front of him bared to the knees, his kilt draped across his thighs. He was lounging in the grass, basking in the sun like it was a full blown summer. Imagine if he saw Florida — he'd be sweltering, heat-stroking, whining like a baby.

A rose-scented baby-man.

I chuckled to myself.

"What is funny?"

"I was imagining you in Florida. After you recovered from the shock of the tiny dresses on the women, you'd succumb to the heat, so hot, hot hot hot. Sweat rolling down, panting hot." I mimed panting and collapsing in the heat.

He grimaced. "I wouldna like it much, but I could eat oranges, ye say?"

"You can pull them right off the trees. Peel it, pull a slice, and eat it with sticky juice running down your chin." I acted-out that one, too, and he laughed at my theatrics.

This was what we did now, one-upping each other with stories of our past, or in my case, our futures. We compared and contrasted and laughed a great deal about it all.

He said, "Och, but, Madame Hayley, I can pluck a squirrel from a tree, slice it through the middle, cook it over the fire, and —" He licked his fingers. "Tis delicious."

"Tis why I daena want to find it. I daena want tae deal with it when tis the devil's work."

"I get that, and you're right. It makes me furious Kaitlyn and Magnus never taught anyone else how to use the vessels, hence why I'm stuck here, so we should probably leave them alone, right?" I sighed the sigh of someone completely irrevocably lost.

FIFTEEN — MAGNUS

Zach was preparin' dinner and we were gathered around the kitchen island havin' a drink and sharin' stories and laughin'. Kaitlyn stood in the kitchen proper, smashin' garlic cloves for the bread, havin' been pressed to work while Emma had Ben on her lap.

Archie came tae me with his arms raised and I brought him up so he could see what Kaitlyn was workin' on. He looked down at the rows of bread on the pan, buttered, awaiting the garlic tae be spread upon them and reached for one, hungrily, his hand opening and closing, "Mammy, I want."

Kaitlyn stopped in mid spread. "What? I mean... Oh." Her eyes brimmed with tears. "*Oh.*"

She picked up a piece of bread and put it into his waiting fist. He ate hungrily, intent on the slice, while she stood stock-still her gaze intent on his face. "He just..."

We all nodded.

"Is that okay?" Her hands shook. "I don't know if it's okay." Her chin trembled and then tears spilled over.

Archie looked up at her. "Mammy cry?"

Kaitlyn said, "No, honey, I mean, kind of... I'm crying but it's okay, I do that sometimes." She dabbed at her face with a kitchen towel.

She met my eyes. "Is that okay? He should call me Kaitlyn, right? I don't know the rules." She dropped the towel to the counter.

We were all watchin' her as she burst intae tears. "I never know the fucking rules." She touched his arm. "I'm sorry I said the f-word honey. I know it doesn't seem like it but I'm really okay. I'm going to my room for a minute. I'll be right back." She rushed from the kitchen.

"Och."

Archie placed a butter-covered palm on my cheek and looked in m'eyes. "Mammy okay?"

"She will be okay, it means a verra great deal tae her that ye have named her Mammy, and she feels verra strong about it."

I dinna ken how tae handle it, or what tae do, but I kent I couldna put Archie down. Not while he was worried on Kaitlyn so I followed her, carryin' him with me.

I knocked. "Kaitlyn? Tis me and I have Archie as well. We want tae speak tae ye on it."

Her voice called, "Come in."

I smiled at Archie as we went through the door so he wouldna be worried.

She was sitting on the bed holdin' the photo of us when she had been pregnant.

Archie reached for her so I passed him tae her arms.

I asked, "What are ye feelin', mo reul-iuil?"

Archie tucked his head tae her chest.

"I'm scared. My heart hurts and it's so full of love at the same time. I think I've never had so much and that means I have so much to lose, right? Too much. And do I get to be that? Can I?

Do I? No one told me I get to. What if it all... ?" She was guardin' her words tae protect him, even in fear.

I sat down beside them on the bed. "I think ye have taken him intae yer heart Kaitlyn and I daena think ye can worry about havin' done it. Dost ye mean to love him all your days?"

She nodded.

"And we mean tae do our best tae keep him safe and healthy, daena we, wee'un?"

He nodded as if he was a part of the conversation.

She asked, "Is it fair for me to let..."

"I call ye Kaitlyn, I am the only person tae call ye by yer true full name. Dost ye let me, or is it what I call ye?"

She sniffled. "You just do."

"I call ye mo reul-iuil, and sometimes I call ye mo ghradh, and ye answer tae all of it because ye ken tis my heart speakin'. Ye dinna let me, I canna help it."

She nodded.

"Wee'un, what dost ye call her?"

He twirled her hair with his butter-sticky hands. "Mammy."

"I ken ye feel it through and ye have a million emotions about it, but he has named ye, tis naethin' tae do but say thank ye."

She cried while smiling and said to Archie, "Thank you sweetie, I love the name so much. I'm honored you think of me that way."

Archie said, "Want more bread," and dropped off her lap to run from the room.

I dropped my hand to her thigh.

"I'm sorry I got emotional."

"I ken it, Kaitlyn, I understand it."

"That was momentous." She looked down at the photo still clutched in her hand and then put it away in the drawer. "I didn't realize it would make me go so untethered, but that was really awesome."

"When he called me Da this morning, I cried too."

She playfully pushed my arm. "You did not."

"I kept it all inside," I joked.

"What happens if she comes back for him? Or what happens if I'm not that great at it? Or what happens if there's a custody battle across the centuries?"

"What would we do, tell him he canna love us because we are worried about what might come? Och, we are braver than that — we are Kaitlyn and Magnus Campbell. We have fought against madmen and kings. I daena think we should worry on what might happen. We will raise our swords and meet what comes."

She leaned her head against my shoulder. "So I've been raised from Kaitlyn to 'Mammy'?"

I grinned, "Ye went tae bed m'randy wife and woke up on this day a mammy. Tis a verra fast alteration of yer person. I hope ye winna forget in all yer mammy-ness tae be randy for me, I do like it verra much when ye are."

She stood. "I am Kaitlyn Campbell. I have battled madmen and kings. I can be hot for you and I can be an excellent mammy. I am all that and more."

"Good." Then I joked, "but first ye have tae clean the butter the wee'un wiped in yer hair."

I followed Archie tae the kitchen while Kaitlyn straightened herself for dinner.

SIXTEEN - MAGNUS

The next mornin' I said m'farewell tae Archie on the back deck of the house. I crouched down, "Dost ye ken I will be home on the morrow?"

He nodded.

I hugged him. "Kaitlyn will take verra good care of ye, tell her ye get an extra bowl of ice cream if ye want it, tell her that Da said it was okay."

He asked, "What this?"

"It's my sword strap." I shewed him the buckle and then twisted my shoulders tae shew him the sword down m'back.

"Big."

"Tis. And verra heavy."

I stood. He touched the hilt of my dirk. "What this?"

"Tis my dirk, wee'un. I wear it for protection, but also tae make me look m'part, a Highlander, ready tae fight. I'm a barbarian king. From long afore ye were born I have strapped them on so that someday ye winna have tae."

"Why?"

"Because they are too verra heavy." I ran my fingers down his cheek. "I will see ye on the morrow."

"On the morrow, Da."

I smiled.

I said m'farewell tae Kaitlyn at the house. We dinna want Archie tae see the storm and we dinna want tae take Kaitlyn from him when I was leavin', so we embraced beside the Mustang. Her arms wrapped under mine, pullin' us close taegether.

She looked up in my face. "Tell Hayley I love her, and bring her home. Will you tell Lizbeth that I'm sorry I didn't come. Tell her about Archie, tell her that someday I'll bring him. I don't know how, but somehow and she can meet him, but tell her that I miss her and..."

I smoothed back her hair. "I will tell her all that and more. I will tell Sean that the presents are from ye and I will give Madame Greer the chocolate and I will force feed the vitamins tae Fraoch." We both chuckled.

"Then you'll be here tomorrow with Hayley."

"Aye."

We kissed and then I dropped into the car beside Quentin.

She pressed her hand to the window before she walked up the steps tae the house.

Quentin drove me tae the south end and I stood in the sand surrounded by sacks filled with gear and presents.

"I wish I was going with you, Boss."

"I ken, but this is the easy part. Hayley came tae rescue me, I will go and rescue her. I plan tae get there afore she even needs tae be rescued though, so there will be nae difficulties. She winna even meet Fraoch. He winna have a chance tae vex her with his roguish behavior."

"What's the date? Just in case, you know — something?"

"The sixth day of July the year 1704 is the date Kaitlyn put in the vessel in the arena. I will go tae the fifth day tae be early enough tae meet Hayley."

"All right then, Boss. I'll be watching the skies for both of you tomorrow."

He crossed the sand tae stand by the Mustang and I set the vessel tae jump.

SEVENTEEN — HAYLEY

We were on a trail in the woods when we noticed the wind rise. Fraoch shifted in his saddle and looked behind us. "Tis a storm."

"Wait, what?" I looked back behind us. Trees, nothing but trees, barely any sky showing. And I was a little turned around anyway — "Is that the direction of our…?"

"Aye. Tis. Follow me."

He turned his horse and I turned mine to fall into line behind. We rode at a fast pace and through the trees I could see a sky full of banking clouds, a flash of lightning. "How long will it take us to get there?"

"Nae long."

I had forgotten that he would not talk in minutes but in vague passages of time.

God I missed having a sense of passing time.

How long had I been here now? A month? At least? So long that I had forgotten to hope there would be a rescue, forgotten to watch for the storms.

And then here one was.

~

Gatorbelle wouldn't go closer and I was worried about forcing her. The wind was still raging and though this horse and I worked together really well, against this storm she seemed likely to throw me off.

I yelled over the wind for Fraoch to go on without me.

Instead, ignoring my direct order, he came back. "Ye will be good here? Daena move, I will return for ye."

"Yes, of course, just go meet them, hurry!"

He raced off to the clearing.

EIGHTEEN - MAGNUS

*H*orse hooves were thuddin' the ground beside me. I opened one eye, twas all I could do. "Och, Fraoch MacDonald?"

He swung down tae the ground. "Tis nae MacDonald, as ye ken, tis MacLeod now that I live on Campbell lands. And what are ye doin' writhin' in the dirt like a worm?"

I slung an arm over m'eyes. "I am bein' a hero. I have come tae rescue m'friend, she will arrive on the morrow."

"Madame Hayley? She is already—"

"Magnus Campbell!"

I looked up tae see Mistress Hayley, dressed in the clothes of the time, ride a horse intae the clearing. "Magnus Campbell, where is Kaitlyn? Oh my god, I'm so glad to see you. What took you so long?"

I sat fully up with a groan. "I daena ken, I thought ye would be here on the morrow. Kaitlyn told me ye were tae arrive on the sixth day of July."

Mistress Hayley groaned. "I'm going to kill her. I've been

here for a month." She climbed from the horse, holdin' the reins as if she was used tae the horse.

"I came the first I believed I was needed. A day early tae save ye the trouble of findin' your way."

She stamped a foot. "'Save me the trouble'? I've had to find my way for a freaking month! I have been literally starving! I haven't had a shower in days and days and I am at the castle to sleep but then have to leave during the day because the Campbell men are not to be trusted — ya'll need a whole bunch of lessons on manners. And Lizbeth, who is lovely by the way—"

"She is verra—"

"She has to guard my chastity! What the fuck is up with that? I have no idea what the men here think is appropri—"

Fraoch said, "I have been lookin' after her until her husband could come tae collect—"

Hayley interrupted, "Yes, Mags, my *husband*, why isn't he here? Fraoch has been protecting me every day to keep my sex parts unviolated for my husband. How is he by the way — is Michael well?"

I wondered if she had hit her head, but guessed her lie was tae keep Fraoch from advancin' on her. I looked from the one tae the other. "So ye have met?"

Fraoch said, "Aye, we have met."

Hayley said, "Of course we met, he has been trying to keep me alive. I'm so furious at Kaitlyn, I want to kill her! I'm glad you survived by the way."

"Thank ye for your part in rescuing me, Madame Hayley." I climbed tae my feet. "I am sorry I dinna save ye the trouble of fendin' for yourself. My deepest apologies. Kaitlyn has been verra worried on ye and she sent me as soon as she could."

She squinted her eyes. "How long did she wait?"

"From the arena we rescued Archie and brought him tae Florida. We have nae been there long."

"She found Archie?"

"He had been left at an orphanage, abandoned, three years auld. He has been verra afraid of bein' alone so I had tae make him feel safe afore I could leave. Kaitlyn canna leave him or she would be here."

She humphed. "Well, thank god he's out of the baby years. Is he cute?"

"Aye, but when we found him he had verra many bruises on him. Twas verra heartrendin'. We have been worryin' over him but if Kaitlyn kent ye were alone she wouldna have left ye waitin'. Ye ken she loves ye."

She sighed. "I wasn't alone actually. Fraoch and Lizbeth have taken very good care of me."

"I thank ye, Fraoch, for the care and attention." He nodded while looking at the ground. I asked, "Madame Hayley, dost ye have a bag of vessels?"

"Yes, Lizbeth has hidden the bag in the castle."

We all stood together in the clearing. Hayley stared at the ground, then huffed. "Fine, I'm happy for Kaitlyn that she found Archie and now she can be a mommy like she's dreamed of, without suffering the babyhood part. Yeah. Fine, so I forgive her."

"Thank ye, Madame Hayley."

Then tae Fraoch I asked, "Why dost ye smell like an overripe rose garden?"

NINETEEN - HAYLEY

*B*eing in the castle sitting between Magnus and Fraoch, with Sean and Liam around us, Lizbeth across from me, it was like belonging, like being safe. I enjoyed drinking ale while listening to their stories. I could relax. Magnus told the men all about his arena battle and Sean was angry he wasn't done battling for his crown. "Brother, what became of yer mighty fightin' skills? You hae been trained in the warfare of a Campbell. Has yer wife made ye soft? You have allowed a usurper tae take yer kingdom?"

"Aye, it has fallen, Sean. I wasna soft on it, but I wanna there, I had another battle and while I was away I couldna keep it from fallin' tae Roderick." Magnus shook his head.

Sean waved his hands. "This is nae the Young Magnus I ken. You are a king and a warrior, what are ye speakin' on? Ye were away and yer kingdom fell? Ye should raise an army and win it back." The men all raised their mugs and yelled in agreement, a giant cacophony of manly men words.

While Magnus talked, I peeled oranges and passed slices

around the table. Many of the Scots acted as if they'd never tasted orange before, grimacing and smacking their lips. Magnus also had a few cartons of orange juice and sparkling water, so I mixed up orange sodas and passed them around, making sure Fraoch received extra.

He and I sat shoulder to shoulder and he was attentive to me, I hadn't noticed how much before. He was polite and considerate, then when he returned his attention to Magnus and the other men he was loud and funny and like the worst, most eye-rolling example of All-Man. Or the best kind. Depending on my mood.

Magnus passed around chocolate and meat and cheese. There were a great many people circling our table for the next taste and the next. Magnus presented it. I would serve it up.

For some it was as if I had just arrived. "Who is this then?"

"Tis Madame Hayley, a sister tae my Kaitlyn Campbell." I was offered drinks and women smiled at me, conversations included me.

It was shocking, really, how much I needed a man to introduce me or I wasn't even seen. Even Lizbeth, one of the important members of the family, wasn't able to truly provide me the proper introduction I had needed.

With Sean and Liam and Magnus together, beside him, Fraoch was treated with more consideration too.

It was an odd thing, but on deeper reflection, not much different from a party in Fernandina. If someone was vacationing and found their way to an island party, there would be locals — if they knew James or Quentin or Michael, they'd be in the in-crowd. If they knew me or Katie, they'd want an introduction to James. It was odd how much the world kept being the same.

The night wore on and the Great Hall got wild. Magnus being in town was a big event. His stories were exciting and it had been boring around here. He told Lizbeth about finding his son — Kaitlyn picking Archie up in the tent city of the orphanage and bringing him to Florida, and I did fully forgive her then.

The look in Magnus's eyes when he spoke about it, he loved her so much, it reminded me how great she was.

We heard some stories from Sean too while the chocolate was passed around.

And then late in the night we all headed to our rooms. I was in Lizbeth's for one last night. Liam and Fraoch and Magnus and all the other men slept somewhere else.

I couldn't believe I got to go home.

I also couldn't believe I was about to leave. What the hell was up with that?

Ninety-five percent of me wanted to get the hell out.

But that five percent?

Or to be honest maybe like eleven percent?

That part was not in a hurry about leaving. When I got home I would need to unpack that with a therapist after some jalapeño poppers, a margarita, and some street tacos with extra street. Not the dusty medieval street, the cosmopolitan kind of street.

The fire in the hearth was dying down, a soft red glow that I stared at because the rest of the room was pitch black.

The air felt thick with smoke and dust and that rock-wall smell — mildew and wet. My mattress, not much more than straw and a few feathers, on boards, under a wool blanket, was so uncomfortable but now familiar, would I miss it too?

As we were falling asleep, Lizbeth asked, "May I speak tae ye on something, Madame Hayley?"

"Of course."

"I have been watchin' Fraoch and he is wantin' ye for his wife. I was wonderin' what be your intention with him?"

"I don't — I... do you think so?"

"Aye, I daena ken how it works in your time, but here he has made his intentions plain. He is nae intent on ye, twould be a sin, of course, as ye are married. He is fearful of sinnin'."

I watched the embers in the hearth. "I shouldn't have lied to him about it."

"Och, but ye did, and twas sensible tae do it. If ye haena, would ye have married him?"

"No, definitely not. I mean, what would that even...?"

"Then tis good he thinks tae pursue ye is a sin. While ye have been here he has spent a great deal of time in prayer."

My eyes went wide. "Really, over me?"

"Aye. I like ye verra much, Madame Hayley. I wish I could say ye are always welcome, but I daena think ye should return. Twill be too difficult for Fraoch. We will see tae him tae find a wife. I have been leavin' him tae Madame Greer's care, but I see he is verra alone much of the time. I will apply m'self tae findin' him a young bride and we will get him settled. Sean is glad tae have him around tae ride intae battle, he will be a strong warrior, a good hunter, but without a wife he is apt for causin' trouble."

"Yeah, he deserves better, he's a good guy."

"Aye, I am glad ye see it that way as well. I believe I ken a young woman tae place him with. I will begin once ye are gone."

"Perfect. Yeah, that makes sense."

Magnus spent the morning with his brother. He thought he would have more time with his family, but once he knew the length of time I had been here, he was going to turn around to take me home.

I said, "You could stay, as long as you want, I'll tell Katie you'll be home tomorrow."

"Nae, Archie is still new tae this and Kaitlyn is nervous about our family's safety. I daena want them tae worry. I will go home."

After saying our goodbyes, we met in the Great Hall.

Fraoch arrived to accompany us to the clearing and bring our horses home. He was wearing a clean shirt. His hair slicked back, wet at the top, oily. Magnus smirked and said, "Ye look as if ye have fallen in the lard."

The scent of roses about him was very strong.

I knew in my heart he was doing this for me, but I had been doing my best to ignore it, or to think of it as just something all men might do with women, but then Lizbeth had used the word 'wife' and... I had grown heavy about leaving.

We galloped from the castle gates, our horse hooves thundering on the dirt, a cloud of dust behind us. Green grassy fields stretched around our path, the smell of the stables, the thick dark woods beyond — I would miss this place. If it had hot showers and decent bedding I might never leave. Maybe antibiotics. Spices. Chocolate and coffee.

I rode behind Magnus, Fraoch behind me. I could feel his eyes on me. Hard.

We arrived at the clearing. Magnus swung from his horse and began unbuckling bags, setting sacks around his feet.

Fraoch swung from his horse and ambled over to help me slide down from Gatorbelle though we had long ago established I didn't need help. His hand brushed mine as he adjusted a buckle.

I glanced away. Standing very close, really close, he said, "Could I be speakin' tae ye in private, Madame Hayley?"

"Sure."

He wrapped Gatorbelle's reins around the branch of a tree.

I glanced at Magnus, pretending to be busy at something, purposely not watching us.

We stepped to the side. Fraoch looked uncomfortable like he

wasn't ready to know what to say. His eyes swept the space. "Tis where ye landed many days ago."

"True," after a pause, I asked, "was there something you wanted to say?"

Another very long, painful pause — he wore a struggle on his face. Finally he said, "Nae. I am pleased for ye that ye get tae go home."

I met his eyes and held them, looking into mine. "Thank you for taking care of me."

He broke our eye contact to look at the ground. "Aye, I dinna mind the work of it."

I watched him standing there awkwardly. "Yeah, I... yeah. Take care of yourself, okay, Fraoch? Don't forget to take your vitamins and... Just, please, take care of yourself."

"Aye, I will."

Then Magnus, glancing at us, said, "We should leave now, Madame Hayley."

"Yes, of course." I tried for a regal, straight back, strong and sure as I crunched through the leaves in my trainers to stand in front of Magnus.

Fraoch asked, "Og Maggy, dost ye need anythin' else?"

"Nae, I will return soon, Fraoch, thank ye for your help."

"Then I will go." Fraoch moved slowly to the edge of the clearing.

Magnus asked me, "Are ye ready?"

"No. Not at all." I added, "Will Kaitlyn mind if I put my forehead right here?" I pointed just above his pec.

"Nae, tuck in, Madame Hayley, we have tae get through it taegether."

I leaned forward, my forehead on his chest, staring down at my feet while Magnus held the vessel between us. He twisted and turned it. I was scared about the trip, and very excited to be going home, but there was something else...

Wind and storm rose around us. I turned my head to see if Fraoch was okay.

He was walking away, through the forest, headed not toward the castle, but the other way, toward his man cave. I closed my eyes because tears were threatening to come.

*M*y phone buzzed on the nightstand. I glanced over — Quentin.

His text read: Get to the closet.

Shit. I jumped up, slid my arms around Archie, pulled him up, and raced with him down the hall. I pressed into the dark closet, tucked in under clothes, behind the shoes, and held Archie as he began to squirm awake.

"Shhhhh, shhhhh. Don't wake up, stay asleep, I've got you," I whispered, gently rocking him. And then — *fuck*, realized I hadn't brought my phone.

I had no idea what time it was, who or what or why. I didn't know where anyone else was or literally anything...

Long long long minutes passed.

Footsteps.

Coming down my hallway.

My heart raced, fear stuck in my throat. Archie was sleeping but I held my hand on his cheek, thinking, *stay asleep baby, stay asleep, let me figure out who this is.*

James's voice whispered, "Katie?"

I sobbed, "Yes."

The door opened. He blinded me in the light of a headlamp, held out his hand to hoist me up, his other hand held a gun. Without a word he led me, carrying Archie, through my room and across the living room. Then we crept down the steps to the garage.

Emma was there, holding Ben, awake, writhing, wanting to get out of her arms. Beaty was beside her. We were all in our pajamas — yanked from sleep, thrown into a panic. Not one of us had on shoes. Why didn't I get shoes while I had been in the freaking closet?

James pressed his finger to his lips then led us through the side door to the outside, cool winter, windy air, dark and brisk. He whispered, "At the end of the road, my truck — hustle."

We ran the hundred feet or so. Emma grabbed the door handle, yanked it open. Beaty jumped into the back seat. Emma shoved Ben into her arms and scrambled in behind him. They all slid across as I passed Archie up and climbed in last.

All these movements hurt like hell — my bruised ribs were not ready for this kind of panicked activity. I winced as I lurched myself up onto the seat. James asked, "Clear?"

"Yes."

He slammed the door then ran around the truck and dove into the driver's seat.

"Keep your heads down," he ordered.

We hunched over and sat quietly, not moving.

A few moments later the passenger door opened and Zach jumped in. "I'm here, go go go."

James roared the truck to life and raced us away from our home.

Beaty, Emma, and I huddled with the kids in the back seat. I kept my eyes clamped shut, but had to keep checking to make sure everyone was okay. The boys were great considering I wanted to scream my head off.

"What happened?"

James careened the truck around a corner. "Quentin called me, said the monitor lit up like a Christmas tree. Told me to get you to safety. He's following the storm."

"It wasn't Magnus? It could have been Magnus."

"No, it wasn't Magnus, Quentin's sure of it."

"Can I get up now?"

"Yeah. Shit man. That was intense." James called Quentin. "Hey, we're on Atlantic. Yeah man, all of them. I'm headed to DJ's house. You remember, he bred the Weimaraners? Yeah, there's a trailer ... I know, it's just temporary."

Beaty asked, "Where be Quentin?"

Zach said, "He's headed with the other guards toward the center of the storm."

To all of us he said, "He'll meet us at the trailer in a bit."

He turned on some country music and we drove over the bridge, off the island, headed to Yulee.

The trailer was cramped and dark and cold. I lugged Archie up the steps and down the length of it and dropped onto a threadbare, disgusting couch.

Zach asked James, "Best you could think of?"

I said, "We should be at a hotel." The couch had a ripped arm and a gross stain. I didn't want to complain but this was not...

It was not much longer or bigger than an RV. Zach had to stoop because he was so tall.

I raised an arm so Beaty could tuck in against my side and curl around her legs. Archie fell asleep against my chest again.

Ben fussed, but Emma got him settled at the other end of the couch. Zach said, "Well, look on the bright side, if we need to get out of here we can just hook our hiding place to the truck and drag ourselves to a proper hiding place."

"Very funny, it was all I could think of quick-like."

I said, "I left my phone, I know it sucks, against protocol, but I didn't realize we were evacuating."

James said, "I'll tell Quentin."

And then we sat there, in a stifling, dusty, moldy trailer, with only the light in the bathroom on. "What time is it?"

"Four a.m." James went out to stand in the long grass and watch down the road. Zach joined him.

Beaty said quietly, "Tis verra scary here sometimes."

I whispered, "You lived through battles before though, men fighting outside the castle walls, right?"

"Aye... but this is different. Here I daena ken who is comin' or when."

I asked Emma, "You cool?"

"Not really. Tired of being scared. I kind of thought the monitor would mean we'd be safe at our house, not locked in a trailer in Yulee."

"Me too."

I must have fallen asleep — head lolling on the back of the couch. The door opened and woke me up, the sun was rising, light streaming in the broken-ass blinds. I looked groggily at James as he passed me his phone.

Quentin's voice, "Katie, sorry about this. You cool?"

"Not really." Something caught my eye, a cockroach scurrying past my feet. Ugh. "Can't we do a hotel until Magnus gets back?"

"There were storms last night, not predicted. The monitor

picked up a vessel on Talbot Island and then another one in Savannah. We checked the one south of us but by the time we got there—"

"No one."

"Yep. No one. No vessel. The monitor has nothing."

"What if it was just someone checking on us? Maybe they left?"

"Sure, but more likely since they came from the north and south, it's not just a 'checking on us.' They've hidden the vessel somehow. My guess is right now they're surrounding us... There's something else you need to know."

"That sounds ominous."

"Your phone is getting text messages."

"Uh oh."

"Yeah, they say scary shit. So don't worry about—"

"What do they say... tell me. It'll be better than my imagination, I promise."

"The gist is 'I know where you are.' Also, 'you're under arrest' and 'you need to turn yourself in'. They're coming to your phone about every three minutes."

"I'm so glad I don't have it now."

"Me too. They're definitely tracking it. I dumped it at the warehouse, but I would guess our house is gone."

I said, "You won't let Magnus go there, right?"

"Nah, I've still got the monitor, I'm watching for him. There's another thing..."

Archie climbed down from my lap and said, "I hungwy."

I covered the phone with my hand. "I know, sweetie, we'll get some food," to Quentin I said, "What?"

"They sent a video, Katie. You — placed under arrest for murder. You're surrounded by future-soldiers. You're in handcuffs."

I put my head in my hands. "I've never been arrested before."

"Yeah, I didn't think so."

"So they have a future video of me. They're fucking taunting me with a video of themselves arresting me — that happened? God, I can't breathe."

Quentin's voice, "Keep calm, Katie, we have you hidden, you're safe. This is just a thing they have, it might even be photoshopped. It was probably photoshopped or, like, staged. It looked like you, but it was probably that tech that puts your face on someone else's body."

"Yeah, of course, we're always writing a new story and all. Did you watch the video? Do you remember what I was wearing?"

"Yeah, sweatpants, green, and a T-shirt, it was funny because it read: Team Edward, on it and—"

I looked down.

Yep.

"I'm wearing that right now."

Quentin faltered. Then he simply said, "Shit." Then he added, "Put Zach on the phone." And then that was it. I looked at Archie, trying to figure out how to talk, to act normal, to be brave and strong and motherly.

I went for simple. "Need potty?"

He nodded so I held his hand and took him to the tiny disgusting bathroom.

"I'm so hungry."

Zach said, "I've got cash, I can go get something."

We all decided on McDonald's and Zach left to pick up our order.

It took forty-five minutes and we were all hot, tired, stir-crazy, and hungry by the time he returned.

I was famished but also too nervous to eat. My hands shook as I opened the wrapper around Archie's breakfast sandwich while he bounced up and down saying, "Good, good, good!"

James yanked open the door and stuck his head into the trailer. "Quentin called again, still no news."

I asked, "Did he tell you about the video?"

"Yep. That's bullshit, Katie. I don't know how they're doing it but don't worry about it." He glanced around the room. "Maybe everyone should turn their phones completely off in case we're a part of it."

I groaned. "You know, here's the thing, they shouldn't be a part of it. We should get Emma and Ben and Zach out of here. Beaty should go with them."

Zach shook his head. "We don't know anything yet, we need to stay tight until we have a plan."

I thought for a moment. "I need Hayley to find us a new place to stay. In lieu of that, Emma, will you call my mom and tell her you want a house for Beaty? At least four bedrooms, tell her the paperwork should be in Beaty's name or Quentin's or... Crap, I don't know. Does that make sense?"

Zach shook his head. "We don't know. We just have to wait. I don't know if the island is safe for you anymore. At all. Ever."

"Crap." I leaned back on the couch and tried to be the kind of person who could take care of Archie while completely freaking out.

About an hour later, Quentin's text to James read: Storm.

Someone shifted beside me. I raised my head.

Quentin said, "Boss, got a situation."

I opened an eye tae see Quentin standin', facing away, gun drawn, speakin' quietly tae me over his shoulder.

"What is it?" I tried to sit up but it was painful and took a moment.

"Shit's going down and every minute here is a dangerous minute. As soon as you can walk we—"

I pulled myself tae standing with a groan.

"Good." He thrust a gun in my hand. It took me a moment to understand what it was. He leaned down and lifted an unconscious Hayley up drapin' her across his shoulder.

I grabbed all m'bags. "Is Kaitlyn all—"

"She's safe, but move to my truck, fast."

He lugged Hayley tae the truck, and shoved her in the front seat. I tossed the bags intae the trunk. "Get in the back seat and keep your head down."

When he climbed in the driver's seat he strapped a belt

across Hayley's sleeping form, started the truck, and drove it ontae the road headed north. He pushed a button and spoke, "Call James."

A moment later there was James's voice. Quentin told him, "I got Boss and Hayley — yeah. Be there in about twenty minutes."

Then he ran his hand over his head as he careened us down the road.

I found enough strength tae speak. "What happened?"

"I don't know, not really. There were storms last night. In the north and the south. James got everyone out to safety while I chased the storms. I didn't find anything or anyone, either they were testing us, or they—"

"Are here, hidin'."

Hayley woke up and said, "The future-future guys might be here?"

"Yep, and they're sending messages to Katie's phone. They say she's going to be arrested for murder. They sent a video of her being arrested."

"Och. Tis true?"

"We're dealing with the laws of time and physics here. I don't know if it's true. It might be bullshit, but I described to Katie what she was wearing in the video and she's wearing it right now."

Hayley said, "That shit is freaky — she must be terrified."

I asked, "How long until we arrive, Quentin?"

I jumped from the truck and raced intae the small building, duckin' under the low ceiling. The house smelled of burgers, and damp walls. It took a moment for my eyes to adjust on Kaitlyn's fearful expression.

She flung herself intae my arms.

"Are ye frightened, mo reul-iuil? Daena be scared." I tried tae soothe her worries, while she clung tae my shoulders.

Finally calmed from a big cry, I noticed Hayley. She looked as distraught as I felt.

"I'm so sorry I'm crying, Hayley, I really am so glad you're home. I wish it was under different—"

She was frowning a frown so big it was almost cartoonish. She stared at the far wall of the trailer as if she couldn't see it.

"Hayley, are you okay?"

Her chin trembled.

I asked, "Are you crying? Hayley what happened?"

Tears streamed down her face. "I don't know. I think — I think I made a big mistake."

"What do you mean?" I pulled her down to the couch beside me. "Tell me."

"I can't, there's so much going on here. Just — there's plenty of time for me to tell you my whole sob story another day."

"True, but how did you have a sob story? It's only been—"

Magnus said, "Madame Hayley was there for a month afore I came for her."

"Oh. Oh no. That does sound like a sob story in the making.

Are you hungry?" I dug through the closest bag of cold fast food. Zach dug through bags, collecting enough fries for both Magnus and Hayley.

Hayley dabbed at her eyes with a napkin. "I don't want to talk about it right now. We have this to deal with." Then she noticed Archie. "And I didn't want to mention it before but Mags is holding a strange child who looks just like him."

Archie had been watching Hayley intently, now he dropped from Magnus's arms, scrambled onto my lap and hid his face in my shirt.

Hayley joked again, "I suppose he's with you?"

"This is Archie."

He pulled my shirt from his eyes to peek at her.

Hayley said, "Nice to meet you, Archie. You'll have to excuse me, I've been through an ordeal. Would you happen to have any whisky?"

I groaned. "Hayley, he's a little boy."

"He looks old enough to me, plus he's the son of a Scot, don't tell me they don't know where some whisky is..." She laid her head back on the couch. "Fine, I agree, Aunt Hayley is being inappropriate again. I will never learn, right Ben?"

Emma and Ben were returning from the bathroom and Ben ran into Hayley's arms.

"Hey, little Ben. No I didn't bring you a present. It was the freaking eighteenth century, and they have nothing, absolutely nothing." She sighed. "Except they have everything."

My eyes went wide. "What the hell? I can see you are in a mood, and I do want to hear all about it, we all do. I've never seen you cry this much or sigh this deeply."

She sighed again.

I said, "We do have some big shit to deal with."

"I see you wore your Team Edward shirt, Twilight is so last decade, honey, plus, you have Magnus."

"Magnus knows he's hotter, plus it's super comfortable." For the hundredth time that day I regretted my pajama choice.

Quentin stood, which meant he was looming. There were too many giant men in this tiny trailer — Zach bent over, Magnus hunched, James in the doorway blocking the light, Quentin looming. He said, "You weren't shitting me, that outfit you're wearing down to the stupid T-shirt about vampires, is the exact one in the video."

Zach said, "Fuck, that's not good." He opened the curtain and glanced outside.

Emma said, "Archie, come down the hall with me and Ben." She led the boys away to distract them, saying, "See this... isn't that cool?" about something that wasn't cool at all.

Magnus said to me, "We must get ye from here at once."

Quentin looked down at his phone, scrolled, typed, and then winced. "Find My Phone says someone is moving your phone. Shit, I put it in the warehouse, someone broke in and has it."

Zach asked, "The warehouse in Yulee?"

"Yeah, I thought the lock and the security guard would slow them down at least. Could this be your mother, Magnus?"

"Nae, ye said there were two storms. She does like tae arrive unannounced but she wouldna hunt us like this. Plus, she daena want tae arrest Kaitlyn. She wants me tae be king. She kens arresting the queen would end her hopes. This is Roderick and involves his army."

Quentin said, "Well, you have to get her out of here."

Magnus nodded, "Aye, we need to go."

I asked, "Where, what do you mean? Like a hotel, right? Just like, in Savannah, or Atlanta. We could take Archie to Orlando, see Disney World while we wait."

Magnus shook his head.

"Why can't we?"

"They ken too much of us, mo ghradh, our houses, our

friends. If we go away we will be hunted and we winna ken when they are comin'."

"But we have the monitor."

Quentin said, "They're already here. The good news, we know they're here. We're a step ahead of them. But if you drive out of here you don't know if they're right at the end of the road."

I looked up at Magnus from my seat on the couch. "I can't leave Archie."

"I ken, we will take him with us."

"It's too — no, we can't jump with him, no."

"What would ye have me do, Kaitlyn? I have tae get ye tae safety. If they find ye, and they will, they will find him as well."

"It will hurt him. He might hate me. I can't. Don't make me."

"Last time I was surrounded by an enemy I couldna protect ye, and it took a verra long time tae get home. I barely survived. Dost ye want tae put everyone at risk for it?"

"No, but—"

Magnus said, "Master Quentin, what's your plan?"

"I will stay here. I'll find these fuckers and kill them. Then Beaty and I will move to a new house. I'll add to our security, because this is bullshit and I'm not allowing it anymore. You should go, but don't tell me where, in case I'm captured."

I gulped. "You could be captured?"

They ignored me and kept conversing.

Magnus asked, "Mistress Hayley, what will ye do?"

"How long's it been? I think I have to go to work... my mom doesn't know what the hell she's doing."

"Aye, but daena make any new friends."

"Very funny."

"If anythin' seems off, tell Master Quentin immediately. What of you, Chef Zach?"

"Emma, Ben, and I will head to Austin like we talked about.

Visit her aunt. We'll lay low until you're back. When will you be back?"

"I will speak tae Lady Mairead, she has knowledge of the tech. More information would be another layer of protection. I will ask her tae advise me on it. Kaitlyn and I will return in six weeks. Quentin dost this sound—"

"Yeah Boss, give me six weeks. That'll be enough time."

I said, "Can't we figure something else out? I promised Archie I wouldn't hurt him."

Quentin interrupted, "Find My Phone says your phone is headed this way."

James said, "Everyone to the trucks. We have to leave the back route, north." Everyone stood to rush from the trailer.

Panic hit me. It felt a lot like a safe falling from a ten story building crashing onto my head, like in the old cartoons, flattened. "What are we doing? I can't—" There was no way I could get up from this couch.

Emma crouched down to speak to Archie. "You're going to go on a trip, and when you come back, Ben and Chef Zach and I will make you a feast of all your favorite foods, and I'll take you to the park like we were talking about."

Zach tugged her by the hand to the door. "We've gotta go, Em."

Magnus said, "I need ye tae get up, Kaitlyn. I see ye are scared, but we need ye tae rally."

He pulled Archie up into his arms.

Archie burst into tears and reached for me but Magnus carried him away, striding from the trailer, sword slung down his back, accentuating the danger — headed outside.

Archie's cries grew louder and louder — shit. I was going to hurt him. I was going to break my promise to him. I promised him no pain and now, *god...*

They were after me. They had my arrest on camera. I was wearing this stupid fucking shirt and...

I walked out of the trailer, and down the steps. Blinded by the sun, I shielded my eyes with my arms. The scene was otherworldly, trucks pulled up on the grass. Pine forest surrounding us. One road, in and out. Everyone I loved rushing, yanking open vehicle doors, scrambling inside.

Archie's screams filled my head.

James's truck sped from the yard, kicking up a cloud of dust. Quentin dropped the bags of vessels at Magnus's feet. Magnus twisted one while Archie writhed in his arms trying to get to me.

As Quentin wrenched the door of his truck open he yelled, "Fucking A, Katie, go with Magnus!"

I clutched my chest. "Please don't." My panic was a full-blown, completely out of my mind, unable to think, awash in the hormones of fear, attack. I couldn't do this.

People were hunting me. Hunting. If I just locked this door on this weird little trailer, I would be fine. I was too scared and it was painful and Archie was screaming, and, "Please don't, we can..."

"Kaitlyn, come here, right now. Ye have tae rally your courage. We canna do this without ye and if ye let them take ye, I winna be able tae—"

Archie was back-bending almost falling from Magnus's arms, screaming, "Mammy!!!"

I tried to pull in air as my feet moved forward, *no no no no no no no*, the storm rising above us. The last thing I remembered was clutching around Archie and Magnus, gasping in a last wrenching bit of air, *I'm sorry I'm sorry I'm sorry*, again, not enough, not enough of a mom, not enough of a protector, a freaking murderer, wanted for murder — not enough air — for a jump—

TWENTY-THREE - KAITLYN

*I*t was scalding hot pain in every fiber and then like clawing my way from deep underwater, I grasped for the top, drew in a deep necessary breath, *drowning. God I'm drowning.*

Magnus's face swam into focus.

On his knees, reaching, splashing, trying to grasp — he begged, "Kaitlyn! Please, Kaitlyn!"

The pain in my chest was unbearable, the pain that snaked through my every tissue, muscle, bone and sinew. I was slid onto a board and lifted through the air.

Two strange men at either end of me, carrying me up a dock, up a grassy slope, they shoved me into the back of an ambulance. Racing up the slope after us, Magnus, with a wailing Archie in his arms, and beside him a couple that I barely recognized — their faces a blur that was jogging a memory. Familiarity mixed with strangeness. The doors of the ambulance closed.

~

I woke in a hospital room. Like clawing my way up from a time jump, I came conscious through pure force of will and determination and want and then it was shock and pain and awful, but also calm, dark, quiet, a bed, beside my bed, my grandma, Barb, only younger, much younger.

It was incongruous and I stared at her for a while wondering where and why and when and especially how old was I? Had I died and if so what was this? And why did it hurt?

And where was Magnus?

"Magnus?" His name croaked from my dry unused throat.

The young lady who was wearing my grandma's unlined face leaned forward. "Magnus is out in the lobby."

To another person in the room she said, "Jack, do you want to let Magnus know she's awake?"

I turned my head. A man wearing my grandpa's hair and build and body left the hospital room.

"Where am I?"

"The hospital. You were on the dock and slipped in. Magnus got you out right away but you weren't responding, so we brought you here. They thought it was a drowning, but thankfully not."

The man, my grandpa Jack, younger and no longer passed away, slipped back into the room, and I still wasn't entirely sure this wasn't heaven or some other unexplainable thing.

Time travel, sure, but — was I sure? That back there had felt a lot like dying.

A tear slid down my cheek, tickling my skin, convincing me I was alive.

I couldn't move my hands to wipe my tears though, reminding me I was definitely dead.

I stared at the tile ceiling. "Is Magnus coming?"

My grandma said, "Yes, but here's the thing. He's told us an unbelievable story. Before you see him, I want you to tell me your side of it."

She leveled her eyes on me. Familiar eyes, the eyes of the matriarch, eyes I had been looking into since I was a baby. Her hands folded in her lap, waiting for what I would say.

"You're my Grandma Barb, and you're my Grandpa Jack. My parents are John and Paige Sheffield and my name is Katie. I'm a time traveler. Where I'm from it's the year 2020. Magnus is my husband. Is Archie okay?"

She looked up at Grandpa Jack and they met eyes. "Yes, the boy is okay."

Grandpa Jack said, "He's asleep, Magnus has him."

She said, "Explain the time travel. Is that possible in the year 2020?"

"No, not at all. There's a year in the far away future-future where it's been invented." I smacked my lips. "Is there some water?"

She passed me a cup of room-temperature water. I drank, filling my parched mouth and then dropped my head back on the pillow. "These vessels allow people to jump through time, they are the property of Magnus's kingdom in the year 2383."

Their eyes met again.

I continued, "As you can imagine they're very dangerous and very powerful. Ever since I married Magnus we've been trying to keep them under our control."

Grandpa Jack asked, "How did we meet Magnus?"

"In the beginning, when we were first married, we didn't know how to work the vessels. One night just before he was going to time travel and I taught him all the names and addresses I could think of, my whole family tree. I taught him your names and your address. He got stuck, ricocheting around in time and ended up here — I don't know when..."

"About eleven months ago."

"Oh, yeah, he stayed with you and you helped him figure out how to work the vessels because he was trying to get home to me."

Grandma Barb's brow drew down.

I said, "Please don't hold it against him. I know he lied, but he didn't have a way to prove the story to you. I don't have any way to prove it, except—"

"Except you look a great deal like your grandma did at your age," said Grandpa Jack.

"You believe me?"

"Well, no, it all sounds like a lot of magical malarkey actually. I need some hard scientific proof or it's just a leap of faith and I'm not prone to—"

Grandma Barb said, "Your entire thesis was predicated on a leap and you've been defending it for years now."

Grandpa Jack said, "Yes, but it wasn't time travel: unknowable, unbelievable, unreal."

Grandma Barb said, "Your granddaughter is in front of you telling you it's the truth. Name one other explanation."

"Phffft, now I'm fifty years old with a grown-ass granddaughter giving me an old age complex." He added, "I suppose the boy is my great-grandson?"

"Not really, he's my stepson. You aren't connected to him by blood."

Grandma Barb humphed. "You claim to be my granddaughter and you've opened your heart to be his mother?"

"So much."

"Then that's good enough." She said to Grandpa Jack, "He is your great-grandson, old man."

Their eyes met once more.

Grandma Barb said, "Their stories seem to check out."

Grandpa Jack asked me, "Tell me something only my granddaughter could know."

"One summer, you and I were canoeing, I was about six years

old, and you told me a story about when you were about to get married to Barb. You were both turning in your thesis papers. One of your professors called you into his office and warned you against marrying a woman who was in the same field. He told you Barb wouldn't be content to take care of your house and your kids and that you were making a mistake. You told them you were looking forward to the intelligent conversation, it would be a lot better than the dumb..." I searched my memory but it was hazy. "I can't remember what you said, but it was something."

His brow drew down. "I said, 'Better to have intelligent conversations with my wife, than fucking idiotic conversations with a sexist doctor of physics.'"

I chuckled. "I don't think you used the f-bomb when you told me the story, but Mom and Dad say I have your mouth."

"Well, I am sorry about that."

"I'm not, it served me well, and is one of the reasons Magnus fell in love with me. The way I speak my mind."

Grandpa Jack asked, "What color canoe were we in?"

"It was a wooden Old Town canoe, your pride and joy. Cedar. You got it before I was born. You always had it. There was another one in your shed, a green one, but this one was wood."

He smiled. "You heard that, Barb? You let me get one — it's my pride and joy."

"I heard it, I guess you do convince me eventually."

I said, "Oops, did I already tell you your future?"

"Yes you did, this is going to be a tricky visit. Let's keep the information to a bare minimum, unless of course you brought me lottery numbers."

I said, "You have a lottery? Isn't this the dark ages?"

He said to Barb, "She seems legit and she looks just like John."

"She does, it's uncanny."

Grandpa Jack asked, "You got any questions for her?"

"The young boy, Archie? He has a bruise on his head, faint, but I saw it. Would Magnus hurt him, would he hurt you?"

I shook my head, "No, not, it's not in his nature. Besides, I warned him from the beginning that I'm the motherfucking matriarch and he better not ever lay a hand on me. He wouldn't."

Grandma Barb's mouth curved up in the corners. "She does sound like one of us." Then she added, "Good, because I liked Magnus a lot and I've been very sad today while I considered all that he might be lying about."

I said, "He honestly is from the eighteenth century. He doesn't understand these vessels. He uses them, knows how, now, but he prays for guidance. He believed they were an act of God and that he — he's trying to do the best he can. He had to ask me, like you just did, if time travel exists in my time, because cars blow his mind. So I'm very sorry he lied to you, but he was trying to get home to me with a very small working knowledge of how the world works."

Grandma Barb patted the back of my hand. "Okay dear, I'll go back to thinking of him as part of the family. What do you call us in your future world?"

"You're Grandma Barb and Grandpa Jack. Most of the time Grandma and Grandpa. But now that I think about it, I should call you Barb and Jack. How about we let Archie call you grandma and grandpa and do our best not to screw up the time-line at all."

She sighed. "You up for this, Jack? You might be old, but I'm only forty-eight!"

"Barely. But what are we going to do, put our granddaughter out on the street?"

TWENTY-FOUR - KAITLYN

They sent Magnus in to my bedside where Archie wiggled from his arms to my bed, and curled up beside me, his head on my shoulder. "Mammy."

I pressed my lips to his forehead and held him as tightly as I could.

Magnus sat in a chair, elbows on his knees, looking down at his hands. "I am sorry, mo reul-iuil. I ken ye dinna want tae come, twould mess up the history of ye, but I had tae..."

"I know." I tried to reach for his face but he was about six inches off and Archie was on my arm. "Come closer." I waved my fingers.

He pulled his chair closer, with a loud screech, and pressed his cheek to my palm. I pushed a lock of loose hair behind his ear. "Was it pretty frantic?"

"Aye. Twas difficult. I thought ye were lost."

I stroked a hand down Archie's shoulder and pressed my other hand to my husband's face. "I'm not lost I promise. I'm right here. I'm sorry I froze back there, but I'm here, I promise."

"Good. Because I told Archie when ye woke up ye would hold us and tell us ye loved us and make us feel all better."

"God yes. Come here." I waved my arm and he rose up and folded across us, holding Archie and me in his strong arms, nuzzling his face to my chest with his nose close to Archie's nose.

Archie giggled.

Magnus chuckled. "Told ye she would put her arms around us."

"Did I tell you today how much I love you?"

"Ye haena had time tae say it properly."

"I love you."

"I love ye too." He kissed me and then nuzzled against me again.

Grandma and Grandpa took us home to their lake house. Grandma bought us some clothes from Kmart and food for the night. I helped Archie dress in warm clothes because it got very cold and while I dressed him I heard the murmuring voices of Magnus and Jack and Barb as he explained more to them — the deeper story, how we were being chased. Hunted actually. Through time. And had barely escaped.

Magnus and I would need to rest and decide what to do. He was asking if we could stay for a while.

Because they were my grandparents, they were saying yes.

The problem was, as we stayed, that I was a little problematic.

Magnus was a close friend, someone they knew. He got along with both of them eagerly and was an invited guest. When he woke up, he bounded out of bed to have breakfast with them, with shared stories and conversations.

I was two things, one, the plus one, the wife of the friend. Everyone was very pleasant, but it was 'pleasant', a little standoffish.

Because I was also, two, overly familiar, plus a foreign entity. Any conversation with me was awkward.

Our manners were formal and stiff.

It was just as well. Too much talking was going to make me cry.

We spent the day letting me rest until near dinner time when I declared I was done. Done. Done not feeling good.

We had a big dinner, chicken and dumplings because I asked for it and then we played cribbage, and then went to bed.

Lying in bed that night Magnus and I whispered to each other — *Do you think they're okay?* and *I think so* and *where do you think they are?* and soothing each other with *they are fine.*

They have hidden.

They moved somewhere new.

We will see them soon, mo reul-iuil, and we will know.

Quentin will take care of them.

Aye, Master Quentin will handle it. As we slowly fell sleep.

The following day we all donned bathing suits. Archie wore inflatable floaties around his arms and we met at the end of the dock.

Barb jumped in and floated on a lounging raft. Jack climbed down the ladder and began kicking and pushing a large platform-dock farther out from the shore.

Barb yelled, "Not too far!" Kicking her feet to trail behind him on her raft.

As she passed the end of the dock, she held her arms out to Archie. "I'll hold you on the raft, sweetie." He shook his head.

I said to Magnus, "You first. I want you to be on the receiving end of my epic cannonball splash."

He jumped into the lake, came up with his 'fwish' sound and I tossed four pool noodles to him.

He stuffed them all around his arms and legs and said, "Tis warm!"

Barb said, "Exactly, it's a balmy seventy-four degrees."

"Says the people who live in Maine and the Scottish man, to this Florida girl that's freezing."

I said to Archie, "Do you want to jump in, your Da will catch you?" He shook his head.

"Okay, I'm going to jump in, don't be scared, this is fun." To Magnus I said, "Ready, Highlander?"

"Och aye, tae see the little cannonball," he joked. "I have been in the water with real cannnonballs fallin' around me, I daena think I need tae be ready for yer tiny little—"

I backed up and pounded down the dock, bam bam bam bam, juuuuuuump, with a truly gigantic and epic splash all over Magnus, Barb, and even splashing Jack too.

When I emerged from the water, there was applause and cheering, and just in time I turned around to little Archie, his arms and legs flailing, leaping right after me, landing on me, puffing air from the cold.

Magnus yelled, "Twas a perfect cannonball, wee'un!"

I found a pool noodle and all of us lackadaisically swam, floated, and kicked to the larger inflatable floating dock and climbed up to sprawl in the warm sunshine.

. . .

The rest of the day was spent playing in the water, swimming and jumping from the docks. I was bossy about how to do it and everyone laughed and agreed I was the best.

Grandma and I went into the kitchen to make some hotdogs for everyone and I was getting things from the cupboards like I lived there.

She said, "You know your way around, which tells me I never rearranged my kitchen in thirty years."

"True. Plus I was here every summer for as long as mom and dad would let me."

"Oh." She added, "I'm very glad I'm the kind of grandmother a child wants to spend time with," as she pulled the ketchup and mustard from the refrigerator.

We sat at the picnic table outside, eating under the pine trees at the edge of the lake.

Jack asked, "Every now and then, Kaitlyn, you seem to go wistful and sentimental, as if you're missing us, I've done the math and—"

Barb said, "Jack, don't go asking the future, you don't want to know it."

"You might not, but me, this is a once in a lifetime."

She put her hands over her ears. "La la la la laaaa."

I said, "The truth is, now that I'm here, we don't know if it's going to be the exact same story or not. Even if I tell you, you won't know. Like I might tell you that you were an astronaut and that you died during the flight of Apollo 79 on an expedition voyage to Mars, and yet by telling you, I might set a whole lot of other stuff into play, and therefore you might not die then."

He leaned in. "Do I die on my way to Mars?"

Barb laughed. "Of course not! Have you ever in your whole life wanted to go to space? Plus, I'll remind you, you're too old to be an astronaut."

To Archie, Barb loud-whispered, "He likes me to drive when

it snows because it scares him when the tires skate on the ice. He's an excellent mathematician, but would be a terrible astronaut."

Archie giggled and stuffed a hunk of hotdog in his mouth with ketchup dribbling down his chin.

I said, "Either way though, I really don't think I should tell either of you—"

Jack said, "But do either of us end up alone? Wait, don't tell me — do, am I gone? Don't tell me..." He deeply sighed.

I frowned, "I'm so sorry I came. I'm really happy to see you, but this is unprecedented and probably very very very difficult. I'm a literal Pandora's box."

Jack said, "That you are."

Barb said, "I only needed to know one thing, that in my whole life, from beginning to end, my granddaughter still wanted to come see me, that means a great deal."

Magnus joked, "I want tae see ye as well."

"Exactly! If our grandson-in-law, king of a future land, jumper of time zones, bearer of heavy swords, wants to see us, that means a great deal too, that's enough for me."

Everyone grinned.

TWENTY-FIVE - KAITLYN

*L*ater that night after blueberry cobbler, and after Archie was fast asleep, we brought out the bags, placed them on the carpet, and arranged the vessels in rows on top of them.

Jack asked Magnus, "You haven't fully investigated them yet?"

"Nae, I dinna have time, twas a great deal of... I have been told this is my weakness: my desire for peace and security. A life with Kaitlyn. I am told I daena worry enough or plan on what comes next."

Magnus clasped my hand on his knee. "I daena like tae be weak. I should become better at guardin' against danger."

I brought his hand to my lips and kissed the back of it.

Grandma said, "And how many days of peace and quiet have you had?"

Magnus smiled sadly. "Perhaps only three since I married her."

"Then don't mope around here about your weaknesses. You have the right to expect a moment or two of peace and quiet, a chance to think about one other thing than time-traveling and danger. You're human, not a god."

I grinned. "We say that all the time."

We had eighteen vessels. Most had rings around them similar to the ring Lady Mairead had added to ours so we could go to whenever we wanted. A few were without rings, we put those together. They were the broken ones, the ones with training wheels, or able to be controlled. We had another set that was exactly like the monitor we had over our house in Florida. Not that it did us a lot of good.

We turned things on until they buzzed. Talked about the numbers and speculated about the science.

One vessel at a time had always seemed mostly magical. Seeing them arranged before us turned them commonplace. These were the product of someone's imagination, an invention, created to do the freaking impossible. And yes, magic, because none of the thousands of steps that led up to their invention had occurred yet.

We had leapfrogged past the inventing of the invention.

Like cavemen looking up to see a satellite coasting past their beloved stars, we were dumbasses looking down at a mysteriously perfect unexplainable object.

Grandma asked, her voice full of awe, "What do you think when you see them laid out in perfect rows?"

Magnus said, "I don't think God would want me tae have this much power."

I said, "I think, 'Whoa humans are amazing — look what we can do.'"

Barb smiled. "Jack, how would you like to be a fly on the wall while these two figure out how to navigate their marriage?"

He looked up from one of the vessels, "It's hard enough navigating a marriage between two numbskulls with almost matching doctorates." He started to twist one.

Magnus said, "Careful Jack."

"Oh, yes, of course." He put the vessel to its row. "You know, I haven't been able to stop thinking about the numbers on the equation you were working on last time you were here. I thought it was an interesting, yet basically useless exercise. But now I know it's related to this and I want to know their origin, what they're doing here, how to deal with them. I might never be able to turn off my inquiry. I'm worried my curiosity might change the timeline."

I said, "I'm still here. But yes, this seems very dangerous, we should tread carefully." We sat quietly. "I grew up in Fernandina Beach. Are mom and dad... I mean, John, is John there?"

Barb said, "Yes, John and his wife, Paige, have recently moved to Fernandina. They're hoping to start a family as soon as she gets her real estate license going."

"Good, perfect."

Jack asked, "Since my head is full of information, and I don't know what it will be like to meet you when you're young, how will I act? I will second guess everything I think. We should stay here in Maine?"

I said, "God yes."

"Is there anything in particular, anything at all that we need to say or do that is important?"

I sighed. "It's all so freaking important. Everything you ever said to me."

I kind of felt like crying.

Jack looked at Barb and shook his head, "Uh oh, she's talking past tense."

Barb said, "Well, this we know, you're going to die, I'm going to die. You can't stop the march of time, dear. Well, maybe Magnus can stop the march of time, he can apparently drop in and out of time all he wants, but you and I, we're stuck in the endless march. You've learned nothing new except that our granddaughter loves us. This is a good thing. We should live our lives accordingly."

I said, "Magnus can drop in and out, but he's promised not to, because it sets shit too kerflooey. He has to be linear in his actions, not try to redo things. So in a way, though he can be creative, he has to deal with the march as well."

"Aye, many time periods marching forward, side by side by side."

"And there is a shit storm in each one to deal with."

Barb said, "This is a lot to bear on your shoulders, Magnus, a great deal you have to do. Remember to focus on what is important."

"Aye, Kaitlyn."

Barb beamed. "The good news is that though life is linear, we are in a time loop and not much has changed, has it, Katie? You still have the love of your life, his son, your family, you haven't lost anything, right?"

I looked from one to the other. "There is one thing, a really big thing. It might seem inconsequential, but it has influenced my life so much. It also influenced my friend Hayley, I told her about it and somehow now, almost every pep talk she gives me relates to it…"

Jack said, "Uh oh, this sounds big."

"Not really, but it's important. There was this time, when I was six, that you and Barb took, I mean take — god this is weird — you will take me to Disney World. And halfway through the day we lose Grandpa, I mean Jack. Grandma and I look everywhere for him and finally found him at the 'lost children station'. He was wearing the mouse ears and had a sticker and a balloon. The lesson I learned was that if you're ever lost, stay put, let the person who isn't lost search for you. It was a very influential lesson."

Magnus said, "It saved your life in Scotland when ye were kidnapped by the men."

"It's saved my life so many times, and anytime I get heroic about something, Hayley reminds me, stay put, wait for Magnus to solve it. You're the one who's lost. She's usually right."

Barb said, "Well that should be easy enough, Jack does have a terrible sense of direction."

"Do not, I'm just usually thinking of other things, but this once I will make sure to be very lost." He added, "Have you considered, you two, that there might be more vessels? And that it's imperative you find them? You have the homing sequence — which one of these lets you remotely turn on the vessels? Perhaps you can use the homing sequence to find the ones that are still missing."

Magnus pointed at three pieces of tech that we didn't know what the hell they were. "Could be one of these."

"Does anyone in the world besides you know how to work this tech?"

Magnus and I both said, "Lady Mairead."

I added, "Great, we apparently have to see her again."

*A*fter a bit more conversation Jack and Barb went to bed and after repacking the vessels into the bags and then hiding them in the back of the shed behind the Sunfish sailboat, Magnus asked, "Would ye like tae come sit with me on the dock?"

"I'd love to. I'll check on Archie first, make sure he's sleeping. Bring the blanket."

We donned coats. Magnus carried a bundled blanket, but as we were sneaking through the door that led down to the lake he whispered, "Shew it tae me."

I smiled. "You know me so well." I spread my arms wide. "This, my love, is my grandparents' lake house. If I think of paradise, it's exactly like this."

We crossed the sloping yard to the dock stretching about twenty feet into the lake, our feet thudded on the boards. The faint sound of water rippling was all around us.

From horizon to horizon spread a pitch black sky with stars flung across it and glowing high above us a pale moon.

"There are always the same stars, mo reul-iuil."

"Always."

Then I said, "There is the east. Way over there, past the horizon, beyond what you can see, is a castle. It's called Kilchurn, and a boy was born there. He grew up in the shadows of a mountain named Ben Cruachan." I glanced at him from the corner of my eye.

He smiled, staring out across the lake. "Och, say it once more."

"Ben Cruachan, my love."

"Ye are verra sexy."

I continued, "I've been there before, at Kilchurn Castle, at the edge of a loch, with that man, the grown up boy. He told me I should imagine that this lake and that loch were connected. That our childhoods were close, almost no distance at all. Imagine: I am six years old here, he is six years old there and we are destined through time to love each other more than anything else in the world."

"He told ye that?"

"Aye. He did. And now I'm telling you, so you know it too. Sometimes memories are here," I tapped my forehead. "Sometimes they are held here." I pressed my hand over my heart. Then I reached out and pressed a hand to his heart too. "It doesn't matter that we weren't both there. I will tell you — you and I, we stood on the top of Castle Kilchurn and you told me that my home in Maine was across the lake and that I should take you there someday, with our children. You said we should teach them to cannonball into the lake. So this is me fulfilling that promise to Old Magnus."

"I love ye, mo reul-iuil. I can see it, but I also feel it as if twas an echo. I hold the memory inside."

"Good. Because holding some memories while allowing others to leave is part of being human. 'Not a god,' as we always say, you aren't a god, you're a man, you have to hold onto what's important. And earlier you said you were weak. I disagree, you're the strongest man I know. And it's not your muscles I'm talking about, it's your heart. Though now that I think of it, that's a muscle too. Your desire to be happy, it isn't a weakness, it's a strength. I've never met anyone less involved in petty arguments and less inclined to hate or want revenge, though you would maybe deserve to want it, to hate, because so much terrible shit has been done to you and the people you love. You somehow manage to stay full of love and protection and I don't know..."

I stared for a moment up at his face, my palm still pressed to his chest. "Sometimes I am as full of love for you as I think a heart can hold and then there is a moment like this — where I'm reminded of the strength of memory and love, but also of the vulnerability of memory, the ties and entanglements that bind us and that might stretch and fray. I love you—"

"I love ye too."

"Yeah, I know, I know it so much. And now, I am standing here on my grandparents' dock, years before I am born, with my husband, a man from centuries ago, here, flesh and blood, my helpmate and lover. We are together staring out on the horizon of our worlds at the point in the distance where your time entangles mine and your home meets my own. And just inside this house lies your son, sweetly sleeping, the past, present, and future, and god I want to fuck you." I grinned.

He chuckled, grasping my hand, looking down into my eyes. "Twas nae how I thought that story would end, but I liked it and will join ye in the effort. There has already been a great deal said on your love for me. I have enjoyed the words, but would prefer some action tae prove yer heart and mind."

"Oh you would? Well, yes, I suppose we could..." I spread my hand down his chest enjoying the form and curve of his muscles. "But we've only gotten to the first of the directions. Now we have to turn this way, to the north." We turned that way.

"I'm not sure what to say about this direction except that there lies the North Pole and I don't know if anyone has told you yet, but the ice is melting, and some days, if you're listening, you'll feel like it's all going to fall apart, but to focus on that means to not focus on love and happiness and our strength, so instead turn here, west: Los Angeles. The place where you passed me that red envelope. And then turn here, south: Our home, Magnus, your home and mine. We've been building it together against great odds and though we might need to move again, we'll keep our family together. Our fear is nothing but a thing."

Magnus stared down the dark lake shore. "Tis more than a thing, they are wantin' tae arrest ye and try ye for murder."

I shrugged. "We'll figure that out."

I spread the blanket on the end of the dock, sat down, and brought it up and around my back to warm my arms. It was quite cold out here.

Magnus sat down beside me, and then I lay back and looked up at the stars. "It looks like that night at Balloch when you took me on the high walls."

"Here I have only the lowly dock risin' and fallin' on the water instead of the high strong stone walls of a castle."

"Stone walls crumble. It might be better to float."

He was leaning on an arm looking down at me.

I said, "You should look at the stars, it's beautiful tonight, high and clear and..."

He shook his head and slowly lifted a side of my shirt exposing the breast closest to him, looking down on it with what could best be described as joy. "Nae, I have seen the stars. I haena seen your breast in ever long."

I softly sang a few lines from the Foo Fighter's song by the same name. While my breast was cool, his gaze intense, the breeze causing me to shiver slightly.

He said, focused on my breast, a breath away from kissing me there — "Tis beautiful, what dost it mean?" His words were warm on my skin. I arched toward his mouth.

"It's a Foo Fighters song, a love poem."

While I stared up at the tiny pinpoints of light on a jet black sky, he kissed my breast, lips and sucks and gentle nibbles. "Ye are wrigglin', mo reul-iuil."

I arched more and my legs spread. He chuckled. "Ye are an easy magic, tae open wide for me with a kiss."

I gasped, "It's the where of the kiss."

I am guessin' ye are ready for me. Ye are a verra accomodatin' wife." His hand slid into the waist band of my pants and played between my legs.

"Accommodating, like easy? Alas, I'm dreadfully insulted." I added "More, more." I arched higher.

"I wasna speakin' for me, twas m'cock speakin' his heart, he daena mean it as an insult."

I pulled the other side of my shirt up and turned so he could suckle that breast too. I whispered. "I don't think your cock has ever spoken his heart before, why has he been so quiet?"

Magnus chuckled. "M'cock prefers the action tae the spoken profession of love."

I giggled and raised to shimmy my pants down my legs and laid them on the dock above our heads. I rolled the blanket up around me and started pushing the waistband of Magnus's sweatpants down. "I accept it as a compliment then, Master Magnus."

"Good, m'cock meant it as the highest compliment." His pants were off, he pulled my hip to his waist and his hand rubbed up and down the inside of my thighs. I was so ready for him and he for me. I pressed closer and closer as his breathy mouth was on my neck and down my shoulder. He shifted forward, rolling me to my back and—

There was a noise.

Magnus went still. Then in one fast move he slid off me to his stomach on the dock. Pressed there, but every muscle on his back rippling, tensed, ready — to leap up. I turned to my stomach and went as flat as I could.

"What is it?"

A big dark bear shambled through the yard between us at the end of the dock and the house.

Magnus, full of stealth and quiet, reached beside him and without taking his eyes from the bear, got his hand on a long pool noodle. He drew it from its strap and crossed it in front of him, raised, as if it was a sword. It arced gracefully up, neon yellow, loose and wiggly.

I tried to stifle my giggle.

The bear kept shambling. It rocked the trash can. Luckily Jack had locked the lid down.

Then the bear stood on its back legs, still and giant and ferocious in its silence, and looked out at us on the end of the dock.

Magnus stared at the bear. The bear stared at Magnus.

The pool noodle wiggled in the cool breeze.

Then the bear dropped to all fours again and shambled away.

Magnus watched it go, tense and focused, then as soon as it was out of sight he collapsed down with relief. "Och, he was eyein' me."

I giggled. "What were you going to do with the noodle?"

"I daena ken. I needed tae draw a sword and twas the only thing I had close. I was a half-second from tossin' ye intae the lake."

"That would have been surprising. Man, my heart is racing."

"Och, mine as well, tis fear and danger and starin' at a battle, I need tae—" He shoved aside the blanket, nudged my legs aside, and climbed onto me. I wrapped around him as he thrust inside me.

He was fast and hard and deep, no longer the slow romantic,

fondling, teasing, and relishing of moments before — this was his battle fuck. We had been here before. This wasn't wanting, this was needing, desperate and forceful, taking his adrenaline, his battle-ready, fear-hardened body full of the wash of hormones, out of his mind, and allowing it to use my body, also with adrenaline coursing — riding the wave of it, together, *ohgodohgodohgod,* with low moans rumbling through us, until he came and there was — *release.*

And then collapse.

And then the sweet fondling that came after. His gratitude made plain with his mouth on my skin and his sighs of relief in my ears.

I was pretty sure if his cock had words they would be — thank ye.

My response would be — you are always welcome.

But Magnus didn't have words. He held me tight and when he rolled to his side he brought me with him, front to front, cuddled. His lips on my forehead, the deepest sigh of them all into my hair.

I love ye.

I heard it inside my heart.

I turned my head to look up at the stars. The Milky Way stretched across the sky, boundless and infinite, at least to me. I was sure there was a limit, to strength and time and space — I ran my hand down his arm, loose and relaxed now that the danger was over. Sex had released the pressure on him.

I hadn't really thought that much about that part of being his wife, accommodating his needs. If you had asked me three years ago about being this receptacle for him, an old-school man, I would have told you to fuck off. My strength was my independence, or so I thought, but here, cuddled in his muscular arms, I was strength. Strong enough to live through danger, to take what needed to happen, to help him meet what's next. To receive and hold and love.

God I was a stereotype — wife.

But also, so freaking proud of myself that I was this terrible arse of a wife to Magnus. Accommodating him.

His cock liked me.

I giggled softly.

He murmured. "What is funny?"

"I was thinking about your cock talking to me earlier."

He put his hand over his cock. "Wheesht, he will hear ye laughin', he is verra insecure when he is sleepin'."

"You are cracking me up. But speaking of sleeping, we should dress. We need to go to bed."

We crept up the dock to the house and snuck through the door to the guest room, shifting little Archie to his own bed in the corner, and climbing into the double bed, not nearly large enough for the three of us.

I fell asleep wrapped in Magnus's arms, with the sweet sounds of Archie sleeping beside us.

*a*t the first ray of sunlight, Archie climbed intae bed with us, laughin' and happy. I snored loudly, pretendin' tae be asleep.

Then, hearin' the sounds of work in the kitchen, Archie crawled across us and dashed through the door tae see, "What Baba make?"

Kaitlyn filled his space, nestlin' beside me. "He calls her Baba."

I said, "Aye, he has fallen for her as well."

"What are we going to do?"

I trailed a finger up and down on her arm. "Ye mean, after breakfast?"

"Definitely, after breakfast, I can hear your stomach rumbling."

"I have been thinking on goin' tae speak tae Lady Mairead if I can find her. I could use her advice on how best tae protect ye."

"That sounds like a risky business."

"She kens the future, she tries nae tae see it, but she has seen it. I feel sure she will tell me. And she kens how tae use the tech.

She owes ye now that ye have saved her life. She will be forthcomin'."

"Where will she be?"

I said, "You tell me."

"I think she is in Paris. I believe she is in the year 1904, there's a love letter with the paintings. I believe she went there to rest and recuperate."

"I canna go alone. I need ye tae come with me, mo reul-iuil."

She raised up to look down on my face. "You need me?"

I nodded. "I do, though how can ye come? Ye canna leave Archie."

She looked thoughtful for a moment. "We'll give him a few more days and then we can go at night, right after he goes to sleep. We'll tell him to have breakfast with Jack and Baba and that we'll be back later that day. As long as we're back before the next night, which we can do, as long... He'll be fine."

"Aye, true. He is verra strong and happy and healthy, ye have already built him back from the lost boy we found."

"We have, my love, we did it together. He took the jump in stride. He's building resilience. He will be a strong warrior..." She paused a beat, then said, "Like his mother."

"Ye are a terrible arse."

"I am, and now my love I need breakfast. Then we will cannonball, and maybe go to Bar Harbor, eat a lobster, more cannonballs. I rather liked watching you pounding down the dock in your wee bathing suit."

"'Tis nae wee."

"Smaller than your kilt, more thigh, quite sexy that." She kissed me, threw the covers back, kissed m'stomach, and climbed from the bed. "See you in the kitchen."

∾

We were washing dishes, Kaitlyn and I, when she asked, "So tell me more about Hayley, you found her a month after she got there?"

"Aye, ye had remembered the dates wrong."

Kaitlyn groaned. "She must have been furious."

"She was verra upset with ye, questioned yer loyalty, but I believe I smoothed it over with her. And she daena hold it as rough as I thought she might. I think twas because of Fraoch."

Kaitlyn shook her head. "Fraoch MacDonald? He is missing a tooth."

"He is still verra charmin' when he wants tae be, and a scoundrel when he daena. But whether his charms worked upon her or nae, her charms had him verra afflicted. He reeked of rose and was attentive in a way that made his attentions clear. All the men were speakin' on it."

"I can't believe he was wearing Madame Greer's rose water perfume."

"I told him twas verra strong. He said Hayley told him he had a stench and he dinna want tae bother her with it."

Kaitlyn groaned. "So he's hot for her?"

"Och aye, and sufferin'. He believes she is married. That tae act on it is a sin. He would watch her in a way that..." I shewed Kaitlyn that Fraoch was almost crosseyed with love.

She laughed. "I mean Hayley is very awesome. He should love her. But also, she is a handful. Like she would be a handful for a modern man. Opinionated, bossy, a woman like her would be a nightmare of a wife for any eighteenth century Highlander."

"You have a great many opinions."

Kaitlyn said, "True, I mean, yeah, though I've always been willing to see the other side in things. She believes her opinions are facts, indisputable. There's a subtle difference, I suppose. I'm still a modern woman, sure, but our saving grace is that you aren't actually a true Highlander. You have grown into a very fine modern man."

"My sword is still verra big," I joked.

She returned the joke, "Och aye, tis the one thing ye have retained from your homeland, the awesome sword." Her eyes glinted mischievously and she continued with the Scottish accent, "Your sword was verra wiggly the other night on the dock though."

"Wasna speakin' on my weapon, my own sword was big enough."

She sighed. "Man, I am so horny. You must be too, all we're talking about is your dick." She blew bubbles toward me.

"Tis only one solution that I can see."

"Yep. But we might have to wait, we have things to do."

TWENTY-EIGHT - MAGNUS

*A*rchie, while we washed the dishes and straightened after dinner, was nestled on the couch beside Baba, who was readin' tae him from large books, full of pictures and poetry and stories that were written for his young ear. Kaitlyn, on seein' the domestic scene, looked up at me. "We can go tomorrow."

I agreed, with as much certainty as we could ever have. We could go. Archie was becomin' a great grandson of Jack and Baba. Baba was becomin' his great grandmother.

Kaitlyn tucked him in bed and sang him tae sleep.

I kissed him goodnight and followed Kaitlyn tae the living room. She said, "Jack, I need to Google something, where's your computer?"

Jack squinted his eyes. "My IBM is at the office. What is a guggle?"

Kaitlyn's eyes went wide.

I stared dumbly from one tae the other, though I was used tae bein' on the outside of conversations in the future.

Kaitlyn opened and closed her mouth for a moment. "Wait, what? But... What do we do if we need to know something?"

Jack and Barb looked tae each other in confusion. Barb said, "Tomorrow you could go to the library and use the reference section?"

More indignation from Kaitlyn. "The *library*? What even — like an *encyclopedia*? How did you know anything before Google?"

"Maybe it would help if I knew what you wanted to know."

"Picasso. Anything about Picasso. I assume his early years."

"I have a book about him, let me see..." Barb left down the hall.

Kaitlyn said, "Jack, seriously, when Google stock goes on sale, make sure you buy it. Promise... wait, forget that. I don't want to ruin my life."

"How would it ruin your life?"

"You'd be massively wealthy."

"You mean in the future I'm not? I really thought this whole college professor thing was going to work out better for me."

Barb returned with a large book with the word 'Picasso' printed in gold on the front. She opened it on the table between us all.

Kaitlyn dropped to the floor and began flipping through it. "See here, this painting, this is a lot like the one we have—"

Barb asked, "You have a Picasso?"

"More than one." Kaitlyn flipped through some more. "They won't be in this book though. They've never been seen before, because she got them directly from the artist."

"Who did?"

"Lady Mairead, Magnus's mother, this is where we're going to find her, I think."

She drew along the page with her finger. "Here it is, his address!"

Barb passed her a paper and pen.

Kaitlyn copied long passages upon it. Next she asked for an atlas and we spent some time poring over the maps, discussin' the best area tae land.

Kaitlyn asked, "Now what kind of clothes would we need to wear?"

Barb brought forth another book, saying, "See, who needs Goodle?" as she opened it on the coffee table.

The next day we were driven tae what Kaitlyn called a 'thrift shop', tae buy a dinner jacket and pants for m'costume. Kaitlyn purchased a long skirt and a verra large hat for herself. We found everythin' we needed for our trip and though we were nae authentic we were close enough tae pass.

Kaitlyn joked, "And no one would suspect us of time travel, because time travel doesn't exist."

We swam in the lake all afternoon, enjoyed a delicious dinner, and then we said goodnight tae Archie, explainin' tae him we were goin' tae be away from the house in the morn and he was tae awaken Baba for breakfast.

He put his hand on Kaitlyn's cheek. "Mammy be right back?"

"Yes. I am always coming back."

We gave some last instructions to Jack and Barb. I spoke tae Jack about protectin' the house, watchin' over the vessels, and being on guard. We collected a few of the vessels and other gear intae a bag, and then Kaitlyn and I walked tae a secluded spot farther along the lake road.

Kaitlyn said, "I'm nervous about leaving Archie and my grandparents, what if something happens?"

"Jack has a firearm, he kens how tae use it. I spoke with him on it, they will be fine."

"Grandpa Jack has a gun?"

"Aye, more than one. There is the one just over the door, ye ken?"

"Oh, I thought that was decorative. Weird, grandpa Jack has a gun."

"He lives in the woods, he might need it for the bear that comes hungry."

"Shit, now I'm worried about bears." I laughed, "But of course they have the pool noodles for that."

"Aye, that they do, they will be verra safe." I added, "The first one of us awake will wake the other."

Kaitlyn said, as she pressed her face intae the front of m'coat, her fingers pressed tae the chest strap that was holding m' broadsword down m'back, "It's usually you," she clenched her eyes tight. "I'll try to wake up." Then her voice from right by my heart, "I love you, I'll see you on the other side."

Her arms slipped around m'waist and held on.

I twisted the vessel and set us intae a jump.

I awoke with all the pain of a time jump crampin' my muscles and achin' my bones and opened my eyes tae see Lady Mairead. She stood straight and tall, starin' down at me, crumpled in the grass of a public park.

There were people everywhere, shoes passin' on a path verra near my head, horse hooves clattered on cobblestone close by, and the city sounds of markets, yellin' men, children squealin', and running feet.

Lady Mairead wore a wide brimmed hat upon her head, a long dark skirt, a frilled white shirt. She stared down at me, one eyebrow lifted.

I groaned and rose tae sitting. "How did ye ken...?"

"The entire world, or at least this area of Paris, has seen your storm, Magnus. I kent it was nae a natural occurrence."

I jostled Kaitlyn's shoulder. She moaned. I leaned tae see her face, tae make sure she was breathin' well and nae... "Are ye well, Kaitlyn?"

"She needs be up."

"Give her a moment, her last jump was verra dangerous. She was in the hospital after."

Lady Mairead read her pocket watch, attached tae her waist on a delicate gold chain. "Tis worrisome that ye have arrived here, Magnus, I was nae expectin' ye."

"I ken, I have come tae see if ye are well after the rescue. Also tae speak tae ye on other matters."

She huffed. "I am relieved tae see ye alive. I have been considerin' going tae see if ye lived through the arena battle but I couldna raise my will enough tae learn of your fate."

"I am alive and the rescue brought me tae safe haven. M'apologies for yer worries. Have ye been here the whole time?"

A couple walked by Lady Mairead jostlin' her as they passed. She stepped from the path. "Aye, I have been restin' and recuperatin' here... there is something, Magnus, I need ye tae be quiet on me as your mother, twill make me older than I would like. Picasso would prefer me tae be a younger woman."

Kaitlyn raised her head, looked around dazedly, and noticed Lady Mairead. "Oh. I didn't..."

I asked, "Can ye stand, Kaitlyn? We are exposed tae the whole city of Paris."

She got tae sitting, patted her hair, groaned, put her head on my shoulder for a moment, then said, "I can get up."

I helped her to standing and we brushed grass and dirt from our clothes.

Through all of this Lady Mairead kept a watchful eye on the crowds and also spoke in French tae passers by. "You will need tae remove your sword, ye canna wear it on the streets of Paris, tis nae..."

"Will we be safe?"

"I am nae foolhardy, keep it close, but daena wear it prominently."

I unstrapped my sword and carried it wrapped in the bag. Finally she judged us as 'adequately presentable,' and led us from the park.

The streets were cobblestone, the buildings close taegether, everywhere crowds, much like London. I had visited France when I was young, crossin' the channel in a ship tae stay at a grand house with m'uncle John and his family. Twas a blur tae me. In my youth I hadna cared much for the city, twas foreign, and I remember feelin' verra far from home. I had enjoyed the grounds of our vacation home with the cousins, but the gardens had been small, and not as friendly as the gardens of Ham House. And this Paris was a couple of centuries away from the one I kent.

We pushed through crowds. A group of boys rushed towards us. Lady Mairead urged, "Hold your bag, Magnus, they mean tae..."

I was jostled by one of the boys, so I turned on him with a growl. He raced away intae a crowd, weavin' across the busy street, around carts and trams, shovin' as they ran.

Kaitlyn was still groggy, requiring a hand on her back for forward momentum. "Paris?"

"Aye, tis a — what are those machines?" Three vehicles rode

down the street, weavin' and careening through pedestrians. Another went the opposite direction. A fifth crossed their path, honkin' a horn, causin' another tae swerve away. They were small, with large spoked wheels, and open on the top.

Kaitlyn stood gaping. "What the — what? The first cars! Holy cannoli, do you see that Magnus? Those are the precursors to the Mustang. Wow. I wish I had a camera. Why didn't I bring my...? Oh, yeah. I left my phone in Florida during our big escape." She sighed.

Lady Mairead asked, "Ye had tae leave Florida?"

I said, "Aye, Roderick's men have chased us from our home."

Kaitlyn said, "I really hope everyone is okay."

Lady Mairead sighed, "I am sure they are fine, Roderick only wants the two of ye... ye have time tae stop his—"

I said, "We have found Archie and have him in our care."

Lady Mairead stopped. "You went and got Archie?"

"Aye, he is about three years auld. He is now with Kaitlyn's grandparents in the year 1991."

"Och. Well, I daena agree with your decision, Magnus. But I am glad he is safe." She directed us down a passage, a small street, tae the door of a storefront. "This is my gallery, I live on the floors above."

TWENTY-NINE - KAITLYN

*L*ady Mairead led us through a large room with paintings all along the walls. I gawked as we walked through it and wanted to investigate, but knew Magnus needed me in their discussion. She led us up a staircase to the second floor, where a maid bustled about a room that was a mixture of Victorian decor combined with modern loft. It looked as if a bohemian queen decorated for a New York hipster out of an Anthropologie store from the early twentieth century.

Lady Mairead pulled pins from her hat and tossed it onto the rack in the corner.

Magnus and I sat on the pale pink velvet sofa, with our bag on the floor. He placed the vessels one by one on the coffee table in front of us. We hadn't brought them all, only a selection, because what we really wanted was information about the extra pieces in the bag.

Magnus asked, "How many vessels dost ye have in yer possession?"

"I have one. I am nae happy with this fact, Magnus, I want at least three tae feel comfortable."

Magnus's lips curled up in a smile. "I will take that intae account after we discuss how tae work what we have. Kaitlyn has risked her life tae have these vessels in her possession. We want tae understand how tae use them."

Lady Mairead sat opposite us in a floral-patterned chair. "First, would ye like some tea?"

"Nae. We have our own tae drink." He passed me our water bottle, having decided to never, ever drink what Lady Mairead offered us again.

Magnus began, "You have told us there is a way tae track the vessels. Donnan was able tae turn on a vessel remotely so he could locate it and bring it home tae him. Show me which of these is for that work."

She leaned over the table, pulled up the piece that was alike in size to a brick and said, "This one." She twisted a dial that ran across the middle and it activated. She picked up one of the vessels. "See this marking here?" She pointed at the bottom of the vessel. "It's different on each. You must find the corresponding marking on this piece." She pointed it out on the brick piece—

"What do you call it?" Asked Magnus.

She shrugged. "I daena ken, the locator?" She added, "Donnan only told me of things when he was feelin' patronizing, and wantin' tae impress me with his power. I listened tae him, kept it in my memory."

I said, "And now here you are holding the pieces."

She ignored me and continued looking down at the pieces. "Aye, after ye killed him and have now stolen the vessels, tis now our power tae hold."

Magnus said, "Careful..."

She sighed. "Oh I am verra careful, Magnus. I wouldna dream of harmin' Kaitlyn. She has saved m'life, gathered m'vessels, and is motherin' m'grandson. She has kept ye in Florida and..."

"We ken ye wanted me tae be king, daena pretend tae have given up on it. We ken ye are always deceiving—"

"Magnus, it is clear that the time for my wants and wishes is past, is it nae? Ye daena have a kingdom anymore, ye have taken your son intae custody, ye winna negotiate with his mother or battle the king, so ye have decided tae live as a humble man in Florida. It daena matter tae ye about honor or duty, or my wishes, ye have thrown it away."

Magnus said, "I haena thrown anythin' away. I have the possession of most of the vessels and with ye advisin' me, I can plan what comes next."

She huffed, deeply. "I daena ken everything, but if you—" The two pieces she held hummed awake, surprising her. "I suppose ye daena have tae find the markings, they will speak tae each other on it."

Magnus asked, "If I set this one on, usin' the markings on the other, I can locate it?"

I said, "We should make a list of all the known markings. When we use a vessel we can mark it as being used, track it, and locate it if it goes missing."

Lady Mairead's eyes glinted as she leveled her gaze. "Ye already possess the list of markings."

"What?" My brow drew down under her gaze. "Oh." I gulped as it occurred to me the list was in the book.

"Aye, 'oh.' Ye ken where the list is, because ye have the book." Magnus looked from her face to mine.

I shrugged. "Think what you want."

Magnus intervened, "Kaitlyn daena have the book, she daena have the list. I will make the list from what we ken and we will gather all the vessels around us."

"Except for mine. I winna allow for ye tae 'locate' me. I have things tae do, business, and need my secrecy."

Magnus said, "Fair enough."

I said, "Our other question is about this ring, most of these vessels have a ring around the middle, except this one, it's like the one Magnus was using in the beginning."

"Aye," she picked up that vessel. "When ye twist it," she showed me the glowing lights, "it's missing the middle system. It canna be directed on its own." She pulled up the brick-sized 'locator'. "From this locator you can see this vessel has been activated, the markings across here have the numbers and symbols that are bein' used. Ye can add tae them and misdirect the jump tae a different time or place. As I pulled ye here that time tae negotiate with ye."

"Tae put the shackle upon her throat."

She asked with a faked sweetness, "And where are those, Magnus, there should be three?"

"I dinna bring them."

"Pity, I would have liked tae shew ye how tae work them. I believe ye might have use for them. Bella, for instance, could have used—"

I said, "God, you are so freaking evil—"

Her brow raised. "My daughter-in-law daena think her husband's mistress deserves tae have her freedom curtailed? What about as the woman who deserted Archie? You daena want tae see her suffer?"

I shook my head. "No, I mean, yes, I would love to... but no, no way am I going to harm her, she..."

Lady Mairead said, "She would put it upon your throat in a second."

I tried to keep my voice steady. "Well that's one of the many ways I am a better person."

"A deceased person, perhaps."

Magnus groaned. "Lady Mairead, dost ye see that I am visitin' with m'wife nae a full hour and already ye have threatened her life? How dost ye want me tae deal with this? I tell ye, I have tried tae be civilized. I have told Kaitlyn that ye are only expressin' yerself, that ye daena truly mean it, but it causes her, and therefore me, a great deal of worry tae have ye threaten her."

He shook his head. "I ken ye winna kill her, because tae draw a weapon on her would be the last thing ye do, and ye prefer yer life tae nae life at all. Why else would ye be scramblin' so tae live it? I have threatened ye tae behave. I have tried tae compromise and negotiate, but ye are seemin' tae be unmoved in this matter. Kaitlyn is my wife. You are tae speak tae her with respect. I have nae patience for discussion on it and will do what comes next if I am pushed."

"Very well, Magnus, I have heard ye on it. Kaitlyn, my apologies."

A bell rang. There was a clattering of footsteps up the stairs. Magnus shoved the vessels into the bag and still had two to hide as three men sauntered into the room. Their clothes were simple: wool pants, linen shirts, vests, and coats, like many of the people I had seen on the streets, dingy and dirty.

The man in front, with greasy hair, dark over his forehead, smirked. He spoke in French to Lady Mairead and she answered him languidly, with a flirtatious smile I hadn't seen before. He kissed her cheek while keeping his eyes on me. "Who is this, Lady Mad?"

She said, "Friends, Pablo, this is my friend, Magnus, visiting from Scotland, with his wife, Kaitlyn, an American."

"Ah, Monsieur Magnus!" Magnus and Picasso shook hands.

Then Picasso said, "And the beautiful Madame Kaitlyn." He kissed me on both cheeks. He reeked of alcohol. There was a hotness to his breath and an insistence on being the only one in the room that mattered that made me worry Magnus might kill him and then where would the modern world be?

He straightened after leaving a bit of wet on my cheek and announced, loudly, a little slurringly, "Mes amis, Guy and Max, this is Magnoose." He drew the name out long. "And Madame Kaitlyn, his beautiful wife." He added, "Nous adorons une belle femme."

His friends all laughed. Guy and Max shook Magnus's hand and then slumped into chairs to round out our circle. Picasso took a seat on the coffee table directly in front of me, knee to knee. "Have you posed for a painting before, Madame?"

Flustered, I said, "No, never, I..." I glanced over his shoulder at Lady Mairead. Her head was tilted, a smile spread across her face, enjoying my discomfort.

Magnus was looking from my face to Picasso's.

Picasso lifted my chin and turned my face from side to side speaking to his friends in French.

Magnus said, "She is m'wife."

Picasso let go of my chin and banged his palm down on Magnus's knee. "Of course she is, friend Magnoose! I am paying you a compliment with my admiration. A man like you!" He patted Magnus on the shoulders. "You are the kind of man who can love a woman like this." Guy and Max stifled their laughter.

Picasso sauntered to the bar-cart in the corner, chose a bottle of Lady Mairead's whisky, pulled the cork with his teeth, spit it to the side, shoved the bottle under his arm, grabbed five glasses, and brought it all to the coffee table. He poured, with spills and splashes while laughing drunkenly, a shot for each of us. Swerving, he directed his ass onto the arm of Lady Mairead's chair and perched there, swigging from the bottle. "Will you be entertaining tonight, Mad, or would you come out with us to the restaurant?"

Lady Mairead tilted her head and smiled. "I daena ken..." She focused on her wrist as she languidly turned a hand. "I have Monsieur Jacques tae meet with this evening, he has promised tae bring more paintings."

Picasso scowled, swigged some more whisky, and said something in French that sounded a lot like, "That guy's an asshole."

Guy and Max laughed, they laughed at anything Picasso said, apparently.

Picasso said, "I will give you another painting, Mad. We do not have anyone to buy dinner, please come buy us dinner."

She seemed to consider it for a long time to make him suffer.

Picasso said, "If your guests come to dinner you will have to come as well."

He splashed whisky into Magnus's glass. "Magnoose! Accompany your friend, the Lady Mad, to dinner. Bring your beautiful wife, her visage will whet our appetites." He pointed at me, leering, as if Magnus needed a reminder who I was. "Mad has promised she would come to dinner but only if you will come."

Without waiting for our reply, he turned to Lady Mairead. "They said they would, Mad, but only if you are going as well."

Lady Mairead laughed. "Aye, I will go, I will take everyone tae dinner. Ye will owe me a painting, Picasso, I rather like the portrait ye did this week of the young harlequin."

He yelled, "We have a fairly struck deal!"

Lady Mairead stood. "Kaitlyn, we needs tae get ye ready. You canna go in your current state."

Lady Mairead brought me a piece of jewelry from her collection but passed it to Magnus to place around my neck, along with a pin for my hair, twisted up. And a scarf to tie around my waist to make my skirt and blouse pretty. Magnus straightened his coat and vest.

She swept from the apartment following Picasso, Max and Guy as they clattered down the stairs drunkenly yelling and singing.

Magnus's eyes twinkled. "Tis verra awkward for m'mother tae have a drunk makin' love tae her in front of me."

"That drunk is the most important painter of the twentieth

century, almost any century. *Please*, whatever happens, don't hurt him, or we really will change time."

"I could rearrange his face tae match his senseless paintings."

I groaned. "Just be on your best behavior. We all know you can kick his ass, but not kicking his ass is just as heroic."

"Tis why I haena yet. Like a true hero."

We swept from the house following them as they staggered down the street, with Lady Mairead in their midst.

THIRTY - KAITLYN

*A*bout three blocks away we came to a very, very crowded restaurant. Every square inch was packed with revelers. A clown juggled, somehow, just within the front door, and I ducked to miss getting walloped by a ball. He laughed and pinched my chin, "Tu es la plus belle fille," then he turned away to juggle somewhere else.

I pushed through the crowd following the back of Lady Mairead's head, as she followed the men. Picasso was in the lead, stopping to speak and kiss and greet all the characters, because the restaurant was filled with characters — women were barely dressed by the standard of the day, their shirts much lower than mine in the front, their dresses long, pale, and gauzy, a little like wearing corsets and nightgowns. Women pressed against Magnus's chest as he pushed through the crowd, easily the tallest man in the room.

I was expecting Picasso to ask for the table, but instead Lady Mairead arranged it through the owner. We were led to the best table in front of the stage where dancers with a shocking lack of clothes were performing. *Holy cannoli this is decadent.* Then I wondered how the fuck I became such a prude.

The music was loud, people stood all around our table pressing in toward our seats. This nightclub was without any rules about overcrowding, obviously, the women, the crowd, the cacophony, and laughter — a glass was passed my way, a green liquid poured from a fancy bottle. I took a sip. *What is it?*

My brain thought, *Absinthe,* though I had never come across such a thing before. I took another sip, and went completely warm all over.

A laughing woman sat down on my husband's lap, her arm around his neck. "Oooooh!" rubbing a hand all up and down his chest.

He stayed completely still, chuckling, but not moving, so she grew bored and climbed from his lap to twirl away to sit on Guy. He enthusiastically returned her affections.

Magnus leaned forward. "Ye okay?"

I took another sip of absinthe. "Aye, Master Magnus, I am perfect, this is delicious!" I giggled. "Be careful, I think tis alco-holicky..."

Across from me, Lady Mairead looked beautiful, flushed and laughing. Picasso kissed her cheek and said something sexy, turning her cheeks a high color. Platters were brought, plates passed around, amazing rich sauces — a cassoulet, braised beef, a chicken dish with red wine, oysters and roasted vegetables.

I ate enough to take the edge off the alcohol a little, a very little. There were pastries delicately coated with powdered sugar and filled with pear, and loaves of bread. I smeared fresh butter on a slice and chewed happily.

I scanned the room. It was lot like a giant raucous frat party, a little like an LA party, mixed with costumes and then some oddities like — the crowd parted and a man rode through on a unicycle, stopped at the stage, grabbed the hips of one of the dancing girls and rubbed his face in the back of her pantaloons.

I announced, "I think I'm drunk."

Magnus followed my eyes. "Everywhere I look is a sight of wonder."

Another underdressed woman slid her arms around Magnus's neck, holding on, kissing and whispering in his ear.

I tugged his elbow. "Come sit with me."

He shrugged off the woman, laughing. "But ye have a wee chair."

I wobbled up to standing. "We can stack."

He slid over and I sat on his lap, took another bite of sweet sugary pastry, and kissed him, full lips and tasty tongue.

He said, "Ye taste of a delicious dessert."

I glanced up, Picasso was watching intently. My face flushed. I reached for my drink.

Picasso leaned across the table, yelling to be heard over the revelry. "Mad has amused me with stories of time traveling, have you ever heard these outlandish tales, Magnoose?"

Magnus said, "I have heard her speak on it, seems she has a talent for tellin' tales that arna true."

Picasso grinned. "Ah, but Lady Mad has the best stories, told in such a way that though they can not possibly be true, they certainly seem to be. She tells me about the future, a land of planes, and automobiles and..."

He asked Lady Mairead, "What did you call them, Lady Mad?"

Lady Mairead stroked his hair back from his forehead. "They will be called computers, ye can ask them for any information and they will answer ye."

Picasso stood and held up his glass. "To a future of certainty, all the answers to every question — the end of religion, of philosophy. We will be left with only truth and equality!"

Everyone held up their glasses, most having heard not a word, or not understanding most of it, but cheering anyway.

The roaring music ended, the dancers left the stage, a pianist played a quieter song. Picasso's head wobbled as he turned to me. "Ma belle, you must be a time traveler as well, are you not?"

"What on earth makes you say that?"

"You have a glow, as if you emanate light." His fingertips stroked down my cheek and down my arm, only inches away from Magnus's arm. He clutched my chin and peered into my eyes. "I would like you to pose for me, I could—"

Unable to think of what else to do I pushed myself across Magnus's lap and slid butt first onto an empty chair. I giggled because I was almost upended, my feet across Magnus's lap, almost in Picasso's face.

Picasso laughed. "La fée verte has taken Madame Kaitlyn!" He leaned back against Lady Mairead, opening his mouth, waiting for her to offer him another slice of pear.

I kissed Magnus again and then we were interrupted once more by Picasso. "A question for you, Mangoosey."

"Aye, I will attempt tae answer ye."

"If your friend, Lady Mad, is a time traveler and has arrived from the year... what year are you traveled from, Mad?"

Lady Mairead said, with a sexy lilt, "Monsieur Picasso, tis verra rude tae ask a lady her age."

Picasso nestled his face against her neck kissing her there. He said, "I do not see a lady."

She laughed. "Fine words from a scoundrel, careful or you will have tae buy the dinner tonight."

He jokingly straightened up. "I have to carry myself with the manners of a statesman around Lady Mad or she tires of her poor

Pablo." He swigged straight from one of the bottles then turned his bleary eyes on Magnus. "I think you are from an ancient time, Mangoose, from long ago, a time of barbarians. You have the difficult work of pretending to be civilized, no?"

The jaw muscles on Magnus's cheek tightened, but he kept his smile. "I have cleaned up well enough." He drank from his glass.

Picasso returned his focus to me, "So, ma belle, I have a question. Here are your friends, from a time of barbarism, darkness, and superstition. If I ask them this question, they will have an answer that will not surprise us. Here is Pablo Picasso, a painter, with my friends the poet and the philosopher..." He waved to the men at the end of the table. I was too drunk to remember who was Guy and who was Max.

He continued, "If I ask us this question, we might not have an answer, we would argue about it for the rest of our lives, but then there is you, a beacon of beauty waiting for us in a bright future of promise. If you are tired of the bright lights, and you could travel to any time and place in the world, where would you go?"

"That's an easy one, I would go to my husband's bed."

Picasso held up his glass. "To the future! Not a time of harlots and wild women, but of beautiful wives wanting to fornicate!" Picasso held up his bottle and his friends held up their glasses. They drank. He slammed his bottle to the table and leaned on it. "It must be very hard, Beautiful Kaitlyn, to have all the times in history laid out behind you and before you, a long straight line of days."

"Not really. It's not really like that at all..."

He leaned forward, "What is it like?"

I leaned on my hand and considered. "I believe it's like this — time is not a straight line, but strands, past present future, and all the times in between. I think they're all happening at the same moment, lives in each, though the 'years' are different. I go from one life, family in the year 1704, a child is born, an uncle passes away, then I go to the year 2400 and there is a war, and then I go to the year 2017, and there are friends there. In each of those places the story of their lives carry on, like fragments of a whole. Time is a lot like different planes of the same shape." While I had been talking, my cheek stretched on the heel of my hand. Picasso leaned on his own hand and it stretched his face too.

"Time, for you, mon chérie, is at the same time, just in different places?"

"A lot, kind of, exactly. I think I just blew my mind."

Picasso asked Lady Mairead, "Is this the way it is for you, Mad? When you are visiting me and you have been here for... How long have you been visiting me this summer?"

"Long enough to be bored with your endless questions."

He laughed. "Lady Mad is bored with her Pablo!" He kissed her neck. "I will need to be careful on the discussion, no?" Then he instantly forgot to be careful and said, "I think Mad has been here for three decadent months. How long has it been since you saw her last, beautiful Kaitlyn?"

"A couple of weeks, I don't really remember, but not long."

Picasso applauded. "Time!"

He turned to Lady Mairead, "I want you to take me with you on your next travels."

"Maybe someday..." She sat up straight in her seat dislodging him from her lap. "I am tired of your questions and ready tae go home. You should find yourself somewhere else tae sleep tonight."

Picasso grabbed a bottle off the table and tucked it under his arm. "I am sure there is a lady here with a warm bed to share with Pablo." He weaved down the chairs to slump beside his friend Guy, a moment later there was a woman on his lap.

I slurred, "That sucks, he should at least come home with you."

Lady Mairead said, "Tis nae matter in it, he will come tae my bed afore the morn. He always does."

"Whoa..." I said, as Magnus helped me up to leave.

Lady Mairead walked a block ahead of us.

I staggered on the way home, bumping Magnus, and giggling. He put an arm around me to keep me straight, but then we were both weaving.

Magnus laughed. "We should nae have drunk so much."

"I barely drank anything!" Then I laughed and doubled over. "I drank everything. I'm lying. I drank sooo much." I looked down at my feet. "I could walk straight if it wasn't cobblestone. It's tooooo faaaarrrr to walk!"

Magnus leaned over, grabbed me around the waist and hefted me to his shoulder.

I squealed in indignation and a little in delight.

"Ye have tae have braw man feet for the stones." He strode through the crowds, dim lamps lighting our route, drunken people along the path, someone peeing on the curb, a couple totally making out — *wait...* "Oh my god, Magnus, they're having sex, right there."

"Och, tis nae the first time I have seen it this night."

"Paris is a trip. This is like Mardi Gras. And it's what, like a Saturday?"

As he strode along, me bouncing comfortably over his shoulder, I watched the revelry and decadence. "Are we the only people who didn't have sex tonight in public, is it because we're married? Do you not lust after me anymore?"

"Tis because ye arna a harlot."

My eyes widened. "These are prostitutes? I don't think I ever saw one before."

My husband's pace, as he carried me home, lulled me into a

daze. I put my head against his. Then we were at the front door. He let me down and I leaned against his chest while he opened the door. "Ye have tae get yer self up the stairs."

"Push me, I'm already asleep."

Magnus helped lift me up the stairs and then we spilled, laughing, into the living room.

Lady Mairead was curled up in pale blue silk pajamas at the end of the pink velvet couch. A very dim lamp beside her. The sounds of the street party floating up through the windows.

"Ye made it home? The streets are full of revelers."

"Och, tis the usual manner of the city?"

"Aye, most nights."

"This is a level of decadence I dinna think ye would enjoy."

She sighed. "I enjoy it verra much, there is a freedom tae Paris that I appreciate."

Magnus slouched down in the chair across from her. I dropped to the floor in front of his chair and leaned my head on his thigh. His hand drifted over to rest on my hair.

He said, "This is where ye always come, here, tae live when ye arna dealing with the future?"

She nodded. "I have my gallery, and the respect of—"

"The Picasso man is verra young and a scoundrel, ye shouldna—"

"He is nae a scoundrel, he is the most important artist in the modern world. I provide for him and he paints for me. He comes tae my bed when he wants the company. It is a good arrangement, mutually beneficial. He is verra attached tae my good graces."

"I just want tae make sure ye..."

"That I am careful? I am."

"Will ye be livin' here then?"

"It depends on whether ye need m'help in the kingdom. Dost ye need my help?"

"Nae, I daena."

"Well, then this suits me."

"Thank ye for tellin' me how tae work the rest of the vessels."

"I am sure ye are aware, there are more ye daena ken of, Donnan had more sons, your uncle had more sons. There are vessels in the world that haena come intae play yet."

"I guessed as such."

She gestured toward a door. "Your bedroom is through there."

Magnus nudged me lightly, but as I was groggy and near sleep, he hefted me into his arms and carried me through to the guest bedroom. It was decorated with an ornately carved four poster bed. The bedding was all in a crisp white linen with lace.

He dropped me to the bed and pulled my shoes off.

I sprawled back on the bed. "I can't believe this is her happy place."

Magnus removed his vest and unbuttoned his shirt. "I canna either, I am often surprised by her reasonings." He pushed his pants down to the floor, like a super sexy man.

I, on the other hand, unbuttoned my skirt and floundered it off, like a drunk person, kicked it to the floor, and pulled off my white frilly shirt, getting trapped in it for a moment, giggling, as he climbed into the bed. I crawled under the covers and shoved in beside him, curling up against his chest. "Remember all that stuff I said about wanting to lustfully have sex in public? I'm too drunk to have sex in private."

"I ken ye are. Go tae sleep, mo reul-iuil."

THIRTY-ONE - KAITLYN

*S*till dark in the room, middle of the night, or near morning, by the sounds, or lack of sounds, through the windows — the streets had finally grown quiet except for one man yodeling in the distance, and a dog barking nearby. I couldn't figure out what woke me. But then — clattering footsteps on the stairs.

A man's voice, Picasso, called loudly and drunkenly, something that sounded like, "Mad, let me in!"

Lady Mairead was at the door. She said something in return and then they both whispered at the top of their voices, coming into the living room while bantering with each other, and collapsing on the couch.

The sounds were unmistakably: drunk guy coming home for the night, and then, though I couldn't make out the words, it was broken by what could only mean kissing.

I had been asleep on Magnus's chest and raised my head to see if he was awake — yep, listening.

"Is this weird for you?"

"Och aye."

I said, "I never would have believed this is what would make Lady Mairead happy."

"Aye, the tiny man-child with the terrible disposition."

Picasso's voice from the living room rang out, "Beautiful Kaitlyn, come out come out wherever you are!" He laughed, then must have done something grabby to make Lady Mairead squeal.

Magnus asked, "I canna kill him?"

I twirled my fingers on his chest. "Of all the things we've done throughout time, that would be the thing that would send the whole history kerflooey. He's only twenty-three years old he has to live to be ninety-one. He has to paint a shit ton of paintings. He has to become a cubist or else we won't have..." I raised my head to look down on him, my eyes wide. "Uh oh — I think I just explained multiverse theory and time travel to the guy who will invent the modern age with cubism. Fuck, did I blow it all?" I nestled into Magnus's chest. "Of course it's already happened, too late now. It's so hard to know what to do or say, everything is liable to change something else."

We sat quietly for a moment. I asked, "So she's going to live here in her happy place, give up her desire to be queen mother?"

"Aye. I have never seen her so contented. She is pleased tae protect the important man-child and provide for him and at least for a time daena want tae involve herself with us."

"Do we like her enough to let her stay here and be happy?"

"Nae, she daena deserve it. I ken she has helped us verra much but she has also done a great deal of harm tae ye. I daena want tae let this stand." He considered for a moment. "Tis useful though that she wants tae stay here. She is out of our way. If I could relieve her of the vessel, she would be trapped in a perfect place."

"We could visit her once a year on a holiday."

"Aye, tis a nice dream."

Their voices grew louder as if Picasso had left their place

together on the couch, his voice carried through the door. "Take me with you, Mad, I want to see it."

"I will someday, I will take ye tae Scotland and—"

"No, I want the future, the limitless, boundless future. I would learn about what lies ahead, see the art I will make, my studio, and—"

"Twould be a mistake. Tae see the past is a solace, tae ken the future is tae bring a dark wanting a'grip on your soul. I canna—"

"I will force you to. You will never have another painting from me. You will be ruined."

"Och, ye are drunk and irritatin'. Without me feeding ye, ye are nothing but a penniless street artist. You wouldna be able tae pay your prostitutes, what kind of life would ye have? I will take ye at m'own discretion wherever I care tae take ye. Daena forget yourself."

"I want to see it, Mad."

"Nae, tae travel tae your own future would be a—"

"Kaitlyn said our lives were moving at the same time, side by side, our past and our future, I am only asking to visit it, no? Only as an observer. You can do this much for me, Mad. You have it in your power."

"Nae, daena ask me anymore. I am tiring of your insistence."

"Magnus is a thug. How can you allow him to go but I can not? He is too dim to understand philosophy and art, but you have allowed him to see the future. Let me."

I reminded Magnus quietly, "Can't kill him."

Lady Mairead said, "He haena seen the full future. There are a great many terrible things about tae happen tae him. I hae sheltered him from what is coming."

Magnus threw aside the covers and jerked on his pants.

I said, "Where are you going?"

"I am discussin' this matter, instead of listening furtively, like a child." He pulled a shirt over his head and stormed out of our room, booming, "What dost ye mean, Lady Mairead? What are ye hidin' from me?"

I followed to see Picasso standing, wobbling, in the middle of the room, just before he collapsed onto the couch at Lady Mairead's feet.

Magnus was glaring.

Lady Mairead remained lounged, seeming unperturbed. "Tis none of your concern, Magnus. I told ye nae tae change the future, but ye wouldna listen tae me. You insisted on allowing time tae pass and rescued your son, thereby setting the passage of time as permanent. I warned ye tae intervene earlier—"

"Tell me."

Picasso stared from Magnus to his mother.

Lady Mairead sighed and flicked a piece of dust from the leg of her blue silk pajamas. "You and Kaitlyn will spend the rest of your lives on the run from Roderick and Bella. They want ye tae die so they winna stop chasin' ye. For a long time they are only a step behind and when they catch up tae ye..." She shook her head. "You will pay for nae dealing with them from the beginning."

Magnus dropped into the chair, his mouth resting on his hand, watching her. His expression — fury, barely held in check. "I demand tae ken what happens, and when?"

"They find ye, what does it matter how?"

"It matters because I might be able tae change course."

"In one future they find ye because they obtained real estate documents signed by your mother-in-law's hand. In another future they find ye because they lay in wait and meet ye at a restaurant. In case ye are wondering, the restaurant is in Los Angeles. There are many possibilities tae your hiding, but there are as many possibilities tae them finding ye. You ken this, ye ken it. I told ye I have seen the future and I dinna like it. I begged ye tae change course. You winna listen."

"We might have changed the future, we are always over-writin' it."

She shrugged. "Ye haena done anything different than what ye ever do, try tae live in comfortable obscurity, but it is nae a life for ye. You were raised tae be a king. Tis your fate. You must ken denying your fate leaves a terrible destruction around ye. Tis the same for Pablo, neither of ye can change what ye are destined tae become. By forcing your will, by changing your destiny, ye have unfurled the world."

Magnus took a deep long breath. "If they find me, do I always lose the battle? This daena sound like my fate. I hae trained my whole life tae protect m'family and take m'kingdom."

"Even Magnus the First canna fight when his wife and son are held captive. Or should I say, especially, Magnus the First canna. You either need tae be the king or live in hiding. You will bring danger tae all the people ye hold dear. I will remain here, so I winna have tae be in the middle of it, and I daena want tae live in a future where Bella has won."

"Aye, she is a problem."

"She winna rest until Roderick has finished ye."

Magnus said, "Kaitlyn, we should prepare tae leave, we will need tae go for Archie."

Magnus remained in his chair, but turned his attention to Picasso. "Master Picasso, ye are askin' Lady Mairead tae do the impossible, shew ye the future. You canna ken of it because twould change ye, and my wife tells me ye are too verra important tae change. This is the one and only reason why I haena called ye from the room tae speak on your behavior. Because your future may well hold your true size, right now ye are behavin' like a verra small and unimportant child."

"Says the barbarian thug."

"I am a barbarian, yet I have somehow managed tae control

m'anger. You are pretendin' tae be a civilized man yet ye haena shewn any self-control at all."

I spun around, headed to our room to get dressed for travel. Magnus followed me. I hugged him briefly, and then we readied to leave.

*I*t was just before dawn, the light barely breaking. The vessels and other gear were in our bag, Magnus's sword wrapped in it.

We entered the living room to find Lady Mairead leaning against the arm of the couch, Picasso passed out, face down on her chest. Her arm was draped protectively around him.

"We are leavin'. I canna continue tae leave Kaitlyn's grand-parents in danger."

She whispered, "True," and waved her arm to the wall of the living room. "Take those paintings with you, have them appraised."

I said, "Are you sure?"

"Of course, they are never before seen — very important. Tell Jason at the London Appraisers that I gave them tae ye."

I pulled one off the wall, "This one is of you."

"Pablo paints me often. He is as in love with me as Pablo can be. He will find someone new, verra soon, but until then I will have a verra extensive collection of his work. He has friends as well, of course, who are artists. Not nearly as troubled, rather boring actually."

Picasso spoke in his sleep, "No no..." He said something in Spanish, then passed out again.

Lady Mairead smiled fondly down on him.

Magnus huffed. "We shall leave then."

Lady Mairead said, "Oh, there are some papers in the top drawer, a deed and some patents. I have a safe deposit box at Coutts, I will continue to add tae it." She sighed. "Take care, Magnus, remain guarded."

"I ken. We have tae go."

I put the last stack of papers from her drawer into our bag and Magnus swung it to his shoulder.

We left Lady Mairead in her upper-story apartment on the edge of Montmartre, in the middle of Belle Époque Paris.

We didn't talk as we walked through the dawn streets of Paris. Merchants opened doors, lifted shades, carts pushed through streets, in many ways not a lot different from London a hundred fifty years earlier, but also different in so many ways — more, faster, louder. The noises surpassed man-made, they were machine noises — iron, steel. The air was smoky and thick, but through it, like through clouds of coal fire, would be ladies in finery and men in suits, but not right now. Now, most everyone in the city was still sleeping, probably sleeping off their hangovers if that party last night was any indication, not yet busy at the work of the morning. Now was dawn for the lower classes, their labor building the day.

We came to the park where we would jump to get to Archie, but what next?

I pulled Magnus's hand to a stop. "I need to rest before we jump."

172 | DIANA KNIGHTLEY

We sat on a park bench, Magnus's bag beside him, his arm resting on it. A bag of paintings at our feet. His hand on the hilt of his sword. We faced ahead — the wide avenue, a crossroads. "What are we going to do?"

We held hands, loosely between us. Magnus's eyes watched a man on a tricycle pulling a cart piled high with fabrics, jiggling up and down as he maneuvered the cobblestone streets.

"We are goin' tae get Archie and then... I daena ken."

I watched the workers pass busily before us, then I climbed over, pulling my skirts aside, and straddled Magnus's lap, nestling my face against that warm spot between his shoulder and his throat — the steady thrum of his heartbeat beside my lips.

He chuckled. "Ye are randy in the dawn on the busy streets of Paris?"

"No," I whispered against his skin. "But we need to plan to jump and I need to concentrate. It will be easier if I'm holding onto you. Everything is easier when I'm holding onto you."

"Aye," he said. His hand went firm and tight and comfortingly around my back.

I whispered again, "What are we going to do?"

"We are going tae get Archie and keep him near tae protect him."

"We can't stay at Barb and Jack's?"

"Nae, twas lackin' in judgement of me tae take ye there. There is a chance of changin' your history and I like ye the way ye are."

"Thank you. And you did what you had to do, the only thing you could think of to do."

"Well, we ken we are a danger tae them. I daena want tae take a chance."

"Me neither." I kissed his neck, lingering my lips there. His skin up-close. "So where do we take Archie? The past? The castle could be a good place, it—"

"If Roderick brings an army there, they canna fight against him. They daena have the weapons, and I canna arm them. You remember how it changed their lives. And there winna be ice cream. What kind of life would there be without ice cream?"

While he spoke his face was close to my cheek, his breath by my ear. I could feel his warmth. We were in public, outdoors, crowded streets, energetic work all around, but this was just me and him, mouth to ear to mouth to ear, only our words from me to him and back again...

"We can't go to the future-future. Roderick is king, everyone recognizes you. The drones... we don't have an army, it..."

"Aye we have tae go tae your time. Tis our only option." I could feel his fingers rubbing back and forth on the fabric of my skirt, a thinking move, while he worked through all the angles.

A large crash sounded behind me. I twisted to look. One of the cart pushers had tilted his load, dumping scrap iron onto the street. Three men rushed over to use shovels to scrape it back to the cart.

I nestled back against him and whispered, "Will we be safe there? Do we need to move to a different town? A different state or country, I mean, we should, right? Go into deep hiding?"

He paused for a few moments. "Nae, we have the monitor, you have the book with the codes for the markings, we can create a master list of vessels and begin tae track them. We have most of the vessels in the world, we have an advantage. Where dost ye have the book?"

"It's in our safe."

"Good, and Quentin kens the island, he has men tae work as guards. He can hear when things are amiss. We will tighten security. We need a house, much more like a fortress. Dost ye think we can find one such as this?"

"Yes, there are some on the south end, secluded and big.

We'll get mom on it — or better yet, Hayley can get us one. Do you think Zach will come back?"

"I daena ken. I will ask him tae, but I will understand if tis too much of a concern for him."

"We'll have to turn off all our computers, our phones, go dark. Maybe I can hire a consulting company that shuts down trails of money, we need offshore accounts and maybe aliases — this is a lot to handle." I rested my chin on his shoulder and sighed.

"Dost ye agree on it?"

"Yes, I agree. But how do we move Archie there?"

"We will take him and then after we will tell him we are sorry on the pain of the jump and that we love him."

"I love you so much," I said into his skin.

"After that we will give him a cookie and he will begin to forgive us for it. He will miss Baba but he will have the memory of her."

And then grief welled up from inside me, grief for my grandmother and my grandfather — they were gone. I was walking around inside their lives, a place I wasn't supposed to be, living with them as a stranger, and I hadn't had time to consider it yet, how awful it was to play with my memories of them, their memories of me, and they were both going to die and...

Archie would miss them.

I wrapped my arms around Magnus's neck and cried, for loss and fear and despair, and all the dangerous things we were afraid of, and the people we were in charge of and all the things we didn't know how to do and overwhelmed by it all.

Magnus didn't even need to ask me about it. He just knew, and he held on while I cried in his lap on a park bench in Paris.

She said three lives, she knew him...

I ken, she knew him, she knew you.

God, I wish I could talk to her about it.

He held me tighter and I cried more.

.   .   .

Finally I calmed and he wiped my face with his fingertips. "We have only left tae jump."

"Yes, that's all, except for the million other things we have to do."

I climbed off his lap and he took my hand and led me to the park, a quiet place, a private spot, so that we could jump.

THIRTY-THREE - KAITLYN

The jump this time, from Parisian park to Maine backcountry was painful, and awful, and so bad, but also uneventful.

This time we landed in a field in a pile together, surrounded by wildflowers and buzzing insects, dappled light splashing and twinkling on my eyelids. I batted a little flying thing away and opened my eyes to see Magnus sitting above me, his hand on my hip, guarding me the way I loved.

"Hello love."

"Good morn, mo reul-iuil. Are ye ready tae see Archie?"

"So ready, I missed him." I pushed the hair from my eyes and got groggily to my feet and then we walked up the road to the lake house.

Archie was eating waffles. "Mammy! Da!" He shoved his chair from the table and bounded to us and I lifted him into my arms and got the little baby boy hug I was needing desperately.

"What have you been doing?" I asked.

"I waked up. Went walk with Ganpa. Baba made waffles."

"Perfect, and you weren't sad at all?"

Barb said, "Nope, he was a perfect soldier."

"Good," I said and then I asked Magnus, "Do we have time for a swim before we go?"

Jack walked in just then. "Where are you going?"

Magnus said, "We have tae leave, Lady Mairead told us how tae work the vessels but she also warned us that we arna safe. We have tae leave, we daena want tae bring danger tae ye."

Barb dropped the oven mitt she was carrying. "So you're going to be on the run? What kind of life is that?"

"Nae, we will continue tae live on Amelia Island, with more precautions, we will be always on guard."

"That doesn't sound like any life at all. Magnus, can't you do better than this?"

"I canna, I have tried tae leave tae keep Kaitlyn safe, but I canna bear tae be away from m'family."

She softened and patted his cheek. "Well, dear, that does sound awful."

To me she said, "Your husband is doing his best to keep you safe. You will need to be strong and live as if you aren't in danger, it's all around us, you can't stop living, you must be the mother-fucking matriarch and live bravely. The only thing you can do, the most important thing, is to make memories with your family. If you have memories of good times then you have everything you need."

"Thank you, Barb," I said, "that's good to remember. And yes, you're right — I'm going to demand a swim and lunch before we go. We can go at Archie's nap time. Danger is always imminent, but the lake is calling to me, it deserves a proper goodbye."

Our morning swim was full of pool noodles and cannonballs off the dock, and swimming games and floating moments, and then we had lunch, a simple fare of bologna and cheese sandwiches and chips, and then, Barb and Jack walked Archie over to the field and showed him the wildflowers and butterflies while we packed our belongings. We all skipped rocks, one... two... three... into the lake, a traditional ceremonial goodbye to it for now, then Baba told Archie how much she loved him and Jack hugged him. After all of that, Archie sat on my lap and we watched as he slid his two little fingers into his mouth. His eyes glazed over, his lips turned up in his sleepy smile.

Magnus went to our room and emerged with our packed bags. I hefted Archie up to my shoulder and we left the lake house and walked down the road to the field. By the time we reached it Archie was asleep.

I was nervous.

Magnus was going first, six weeks after we left. Then I would come the following day. He would protect me when I landed.

And we would hope, really really hope, that we would survive what came next.

THIRTY-FOUR - MAGNUS

I awoke with Master Quentin standing afore me. "Boss, you up?"

"Dost it look as if I am up? I canna tell, my teeth hurt too much tae stand."

"Very funny. Is Kaitlyn coming tomorrow?"

"Aye, with Archie. Is everyone safe?" I pulled myself tae sittin' and then sat there unable tae move.

"Yep, there were three men. Dead men. I killed them, jumped them to 1682 Scotland, because I could. Left them in a bog, with all their stuff, because someday an archaeologist is going to find them and have their whole world view blown the fuck apart and then I jumped back here. We haven't had a visitor since. I hired a security consulting firm to make sure that keeps happening."

He added, "We've also got a *new,* new house. Zach wants you to call him as soon as you get back."

He helped me climb tae my feet.

Master Quentin explained on the way tae the house that Hayley had found it for us. It was nae far from where we liked tae jump and included so much property we would hae our own place for landin'.

We pulled up tae a security gate and I kent that it was already a better house, havin' more layers of security than we ever had afore. Down the long drive, lined by oaks covered in hangin' Spanish moss, we came tae a paved circular drive. The main house was large, encompassin' two thirds of the circle, and another smaller house stood across from it. There was also an enclosed swimmin' pool and a pool house beyond.

"Och, tis a fortified town."

"If this isn't perfect for us, what is?"

Master Quentin turned in his seat. "Something I want to mention, Boss."

"Aye."

"Beaty is... well, she's gotten really modern. I just want you to be ready. She has embraced the New World. First thing you'll probably notice, her hair is bright blue."

"Och, blue? How dost ye...?"

"It's a hair dye, also she is going to be so excited to see you, she needs people to talk to about all the stuff she's learning." He grinned.

"What kind of stuff?"

"Mostly makeup and clothes and shopping. She's keen on driving lessons, but we need to get her a birth certificate, first. She's barely recognizable, though she does say she misses the food back home, I think because we haven't had Chef Zach in a month."

I chuckled, "Och, tis a mistake tae be missin' what inna worth rememberin'. We will ask Chef Zach tae come home soon."

· · ·

AGAIN MY LOVE | 181

When we got to the door Master Quentin called in, "Beaty?"

She came bounding out of a back room wearin' verra short shorts and a shirt that exposed her stomach. Her feet were bare. She wore a great deal of makeup around her eyes, colored lips, and her hair was a verra bright blue and loose around her shoulders.

"King Magnus!" She hugged me hello. "Welcome tae the house!"

"Madame Beaty, ye have become a Campbell blue."

She smiled and preened, flippin' her hair over her shoulders. "Dost ye like?"

"'Tis verra bonny." I looked around at the walls and high ceilings of the house. "The house is verra braw, have ye been enjoying it?"

She grabbed a camera and took a photo. "I'll call this one 'King Magnus sees his castle for the first time.'" She bounced on her feet excitedly. "You are home from exile? We really hope Chef Zach will come home now, the food here sucks, daena it, Quenny?"

He chuckled. "Och aye. I'm not known for my cooking and apparently Beaty isn't either."

"King Magnus, we are verra happy tae see ye."

Master Quentin said, "Come with me Beaty, let's show King Magnus the house." Beaty bounded ahead of us, pointin' and talkin' endlessly.

The two of them guided me, showin' off the rooms and bathrooms, all furnished grandly, with thick walls, and fewer windows. Master Quentin shewed me the roof with a view for miles and already with the monitor installed.

Then they took me down tae the grand kitchen. Beaty happily shewed me how tae work the ice and water in the refrigerator.

Master Quentin said, "We should call Zach."

. . .

Chef Zach's image and voice emitted from inside Master Quentin's phone. "Magnus you're back! Are Katie and Archie okay?"

"She has delayed her arrival by a day, and they are both verra well. We have been worried. I am glad tae hear yer family is unharmed."

"We are, we're laying low in Austin. Great place by the way and it worked out well for us — we were fucking gone while Quentin moved into the new house. James and Michael helped him and I got to be on vacation."

Master Quentin said, "The new house is amazing, I told you about it, there's a whole wing with your name on it. It's got a bedroom, a bathroom, an office. All the things."

"Sounds great, when do you want me, boss?"

I said, "Tis a good question, if I ask ye tae return, would ye? Tis nae too much tae ask? I have taken yer protection verra seriously, but I have also brought danger tae ye. I ken ye need tae keep yer family safe and...." I was sitting on a barstool at the kitchen island with my head in my hand. I wanted tae beg him tae return but I also kent it was too much tae ask. "I have more protections. Master Quentin has fortified the house."

He said, "Yeah yeah yeah, turn the phone around, let me see the kitchen."

I held up the phone. I was using two hands but he yelled, "Hold it tighter, don't drop it!" I clutched the phone tightly. He laughed. "Now your hand is over the camera, see that circle at the top?"

I turned the phone tae inspect it. Chef Zach laughed. "I can see up your nose."

Master Quentin and Beaty were laughin' hard. "Verra funny, I daena want tae break it."

Chef Zach said, "I'm just kidding, you won't break it, just turn the phone around to show me the kitchen."

I turned the phone and pointed it in every direction. I heard Chef Zach say, "I told you, Emma, it's a dream kitchen, look at it."

Her voice through the phone, "It is really pretty."

I said, "Madame Emma, I ken tis a verra big decision. I want ye tae keep your family in mind. I will understand if—"

"No, we're definitely coming back, my aunt is driving me crazy. We need my parents and Zach's parents nearby. We miss the island and all of you. We'll be on the next flight."

"Och, tis good news. Ye will be here by the morrow?"

"Yeah, Quentin can send someone to get us."

Master Quentin said, "Text me once you know your flight details." The call was ended.

Beaty went tae watch her shows and Quentin and I spent the rest of the evening discussing safety and protection for the family.

He had hired a security consultant, a firm that handled big cases, and he had been thinking on it long. For a month he had been plannin' the protection of all of us, and by the end of the day I kent that it was time for us all tae come home.

*M*agnus carried Archie in his arms. I leaned against Quentin and was carried-dragged to our car. I mumbled, "We all good?"

Quentin said, "We're all good, safe, and accounted for. You, on the other hand, look like hell, like you've been on a thirty year road-trip." He lowered me into the backseat of the Mustang.

Magnus climbed into the front seat, holding Archie in his lap. Archie had been wailing but now had his arms around Magnus's neck and was looking over his shoulder at me.

I smiled. "There's your da, he's right there. I'm right here."

I looked around and woke up enough to ask, "What's happening? Where are we going?"

Quentin pulled us down a road and up to a gate, he pushed buttons and it slid open.

I said, "I have a gate? Oh my god, I have a gate?" Archie started to smile so I said, "Archie! We have a gate!" He giggled.

We drove down a long driveway, in my head I decided to call it an avenue, and pulled up to a circle of buildings. This was a freaking compound, with so many cars it was like a used car lot. "Holy shit, while I was gone did I become a drug lord?"

Because it looked like I was now a big, important person who needed gates and men to stand guard on the roof.

Magnus stood from the car and helped me out. "Come see our new house, Kaitlyn."

There was a larger house and a few smaller buildings. Quentin gestured to one. "That's the guest house, where me an Beaty live. There isn't a kitchen so we will be in your house a lot."

"No worries, I can't freaking believe there are *houses*."

He pointed, "Chef Zach and Emma's rooms are at that end of the house."

"They came back?"

Magnus said, "Aye. They are back."

Quentin opened the giant front door. "This is the main house." Across the great room was the kitchen and standing there around the kitchen bar were Zach, Emma, and Beaty.

Ben was toddling toward us.

They all yelled, "Welcome home!"

Archie called, "Bebo!" apparently a newly invented nickname for Ben and slid to the floor. They ran to the living room to see the basket of toys that was already there.

I burst into tears. Like the wailing kind. "I love you all so much. I love that you're all here. I love this new house. Thank you for getting it ready for us."

I asked Emma, "We have this much money? Wait, don't tell me, not right now, I'll worry about it later and—"

"Yes, we have this much money, you've got all that Google stock and—"

"Google stock? When did...? Have I always had Google stock?"

"It was surprisingly in your grandmother's estate."

"Oh, of course, yes."

Emma continued undaunted, "Plus the real estate, the paintings, the stock your dad bought, you have plenty. And you're actually kind of frugal considering. You drive a three-year-old Mustang, for instance. Your biggest outlays are salaries for security. But you have an offshore trust account, one that was set up in the early 20th century that your dad just located, it's full of money."

"Whoa, and I have so much to say about that when I can think it through." I took a barstool. "What are you cooking Zach?"

"Ben asked for chicken fingers and fries, if that's okay. I figured you'd probably ask for McDonald's but you'd be happy with food picked by an almost three-year-old."

I said, "Ben, you're the greatest! Chicken fingers might be the best choice after a time-jump. Is there honey mustard, no worries if there isn't, but is there?"

"There is."

I collapsed on my arms on the counter, waving my hand, my head still down, I called, "Beer!" because I just time-jumped and got to be bossy and demanding about it.

Magnus grabbed two bottles and popped their tops for us, because Zach was adding fries to a deep fryer.

"When is Hayley coming?"

"Twenty minutes."

"Good." I swigged some beer. "And where are all the vessels?"

Magnus sat down beside me. "A vault in the office."

"Awesome. I have a vault. Did I tell you guys how much I love you?"

Emma said, "Continuously since you got home."

"It's true. So totally true. And I mean it so much."

*H*ayley arrived.

She stormed into the house. "Good, you're home, we need to talk. Not now, not in front of everyone, but I've been kind of having a mental breakdown and you have to help me."

"Jeez honey, you're mental breakdowning?"

"Just in every way, but seriously, you look great." She sighed. "Like this whole motherhood thing is agreeing with you and yada yada I'm so happy for you."

"I was just at the lake house, hiding out with Barb and Jack."

She sat down, full attention. "You were? What were they doing? How long ago?"

"Before I was born. We went there to hide. They knew Magnus, so he introduced me. It was not at all as fun and wonderful and heartwarming as you might think." I took a swig of beer. "It was a lot more awkward and sad and felt like a big big mistake most of the time."

Magnus took my hand. "I am sorry for it."

I said to Magnus, "We didn't know, not really. I mean, they

were pleasant enough, but when you're around a time traveler you want to know your future, you just do. It becomes all you think about."

Hayley said, "That kind of sucks."

"Yeah, I couldn't talk about anything without worrying about what I was changing."

"You might have changed your whole life."

I shrugged. "Probably, apparently I got us even richer by talking about Google, but if I changed anything else, how would I know? I'm in it now, like it *happened*. I have no memory of it not happening. Has anything changed for you?"

"No, it's all been just..." She groaned and curled into a ball on the couch.

Ben came over and patted her on her leg. "Aywee, wha wrong?" He climbed to her lap, put his nose up to her nose, and pulled his mouth into such an epic frown that we all squealed with delight at his cuteness.

"Aunt Hayley is going through something, sweet sugar-booger, and her bestie, Katie, has been MIA for a month, so I'm feeling sorry for myself, but you're very cute."

She raised up and sniffed the air. "What is that smell, Zach?"

"Chicken fingers and fries."

Hayley said, "Is this your doings, Ben? Are you the one?" She pretended to swoon on the couch. "Why must it always be about Ben. Why can't it ever be about me?"

Zach said, "What would you have wanted, if I had asked, not that I'm asking?"

"Chicken fingers, barbecue sauce, and another beer."

Everyone laughed.

Zach said, "Done."

I asked, "Who fed you, Quentin, while Zach wasn't here? Did Beaty cook?"

He grinned. "She tried oatmeal a few times, that's pretty familiar. But she didn't know how to work much."

She giggled. She was wearing short-shorts with her legs folded up in her seat, showing off a lot of thigh. She wore a tiny crop-top. Her hair was big and flowing and bright blue, and she had on a lot of Kardashian-style makeup. I thought her smoky eyes were pretty epic. She was short and curvy and her clothes were very sexy. She looked beautiful, a gorgeous teen. And here she was, married.

Quentin looked at her adoringly.

Hayley said, "Speaking of Beaty, what's going on with Beaty? I haven't been here much."

Beaty said, "I have new clothes, dost ye like them, Madame Hayley?"

"I do, I love them, I actually want you to teach me that eye-thing you've got going on there."

I said, "I know, right?"

"I learned it on the YouTube, dost ye ken ye can learn everythin' on YouTube? I am learnin' tae play the pipes."

Quentin grinned widely.

My eyes went wide. "The pipes, as in the bagpipes? Oh — awesome."

Magnus's eyes went wistful, "Och, ye will be playin' while we look out over our lands. I will like it verra much, twill bring some of Scotland here tae our moor."

Quentin laughed. "It's a marsh, not a moor, though I can see the similarity. I warn you though, right now her playing sounds a lot like cats in heat but she practices, she'll get good at it."

She laughed merrily.

Quentin put an arm around her. "When we were tired of oatmeal, which was never quite right—"

"It dinna taste like brose, twas disgustin'. I be stirrin' it and twas awful tastin'."

He said, "After that we shopped in the frozen foods section and nuked all our meals in the microwave."

Zach groaned. "You need much better nutrition than that, I'm regretting my dinner choice tonight."

Quentin laughed. "I think chef-cooked chicken fingers are definitely more nutritious than what we have been eating..."

Beaty's brow drew down. She asked seriously, "Have ye had Scaldin' Pockets afore, Queen Kaitlyn? They will hurt yer tongue verra much if ye arna careful."

Quentin chuckled. "Mistakes were made in the cooking, definitely. The only thing we haven't figured out is oatmeal, can't get it right."

"You're going to be happy Chef Zach is home."

Zach said, "Tomorrow I'll make old fashioned oats with all your favorite toppings. Would that be good, Beaty?"

She smiled. "I would like that verra much. But let's have some chocolate chip pancakes in case I daena want the oatmeal. I mayna like anythin' from home anymore, nae much..." She sighed dramatically. "I am verra much missin' Murthy."

I asked, "Who is...?"

Quentin said, "Murthy is the pig."

"Nae just any pig, she was the verra best pig, and she was close tae havin' her spring litter. I daena ken if she is okay..."

Quentin said, "Next person who goes to the eighteenth century will check in on Murthy, I promise."

"Could they bring Murthy with them? Twould be good tae have a pig here. They keep ye warm and ye can talk tae them. Twas verra lonely here with ye all gone. I am glad tae have ye all home, I daena like tae have the house so quiet."

We ate on paper plates with rolls of paper towels because though Zach had managed to grocery shop, he hadn't fully gotten the kitchen ready. We forgave him for it since the piles of crispy chicken fingers were perfect plus he had five kinds of dipping sauce.

The table was too small so some of us ate at the kitchen counter while rest of us packed around it. During dinner we planned how to fit a larger table into the dining room and then right after dinner Quentin stood and with a big three-ring binder open went over the house rules:

Weather channel on at all times.

Monitoring the monitor at all times.

I was apparently no longer allowed a real phone, now I got a burner, like a drug dealer.

No one was allowed to be on social media.

Quentin had the safe moved into the house, but he wanted a bigger one and was discussing with the consultant about installing a panic room.

We also had a dock with a boat for quick getaways.

We also had a bigger arsenal.

Our office looked like a freaking exiled dictator lived there.

When I mentioned that, Quentin said, "Exactly, that's what our security consultant deals with. That's why I picked him. We have an exiled king. It requires the big guns."

My answer was, "Shit. That's what this is, *exile*? That kind of freaks me out."

Our meeting devolved into us complaining about not going on social media. We understood why but we weren't happy about it.

Zach said, "What about my work account: Looking for Cooking at Cooksunited.com?"

Quentin said, "Nope."

Emma joked, "What about Tumblr, Moms Who Think?"

"No, not anymore."

Zach said, "What about my online portfolio: tall cooks who dabble in cooking porn?"

Quentin feigned incredulousness. "What is cooking porn?"

"Like porn, but stuff drips off the spoon."

"Hell no."

Emma said, "So how many Facebook groups for Outlander fans are out of the question?"

"All of them."

Everyone laughed.

I asked, "How many are you in?"

"About eight."

"Jeez Louise, how many groups are you in overall?"

"About 115. Mostly parenting, Outlander, Instant Pot recipes."

Zach said, "Why on the... *why*? I so regret the chicken fingers. Tomorrow night I will make such a good meal that my wife will quit the Instant Pot recipe groups and stop cheating on me."

"And Jamie Fraser doesn't feel like she's cheating?"

"No, that just makes sense, he's totally hot."

Everyone laughed again.

We felt safe and warm and well fed. It was a reunion of togetherness.

We knew trouble was brewing, we knew this happiness wouldn't last, but still... this was good.

Archie climbed on my lap, curled on my chest, and suckled his fingers until he fell asleep and while I was pinned Chef Zach kept the beers coming.

Ben fell asleep in Emma's arms while Magnus told everyone the story of Picasso. They all marveled and said, "Holy shit," and stuff like that.

Because Magnus did a perfect impression of Picasso, touching my chin, looking into my eyes, and I was reminded how much freaking patience my husband had, how much gentleness.

The man had been trying to provoke him and there had sat my husband, on his silk chair, in the year 1904, unprovoked.

It was one of the things I loved about him, his lack of jealousy, his ability to accept, and deal and stay calm in the face of trials. I wondered at it, but thought that it was his foundation, his family, me, his loyalty — we gave him the strength to feel secure.

And I remembered back to what my Grandma said, about how he was trying to protect me, and it would be my job to be strong for the family. To let him. And grow the good memories for all of us.

We had his back. He trusted us, me, completely and not in the prove yourself way — he trusted me, that I was tying myself to his family and him in a way that was so fucking old fashioned, but also so hot — to be trusted and loved this completely, this much. He was all I ever wanted, I was all he ever needed.

And watching him mimic Picasso sprawled on Lady Mad's lap, which everyone agreed was an apt name that might need to stick, while she fed him pear slices and...

Hayley said, "Ew, really. Like sexy? Like sensual?"

She hugged an arm around Magnus. "I'm so sorry your mom has turned out to be such an icky person."

I laughed, "I'm of the opposite opinion, seeing Lady Mad with Picasso was the first sign she was a human being. I know it was hard on Magnus to deal with Picasso being such a scoundrel of a guy, but at least he wasn't evil. He wasn't trying to kill you or coerce you to kill others for sport. As a man in Lady Mad's life he actually is pretty high on the likability scale, past the drunken debauchery of course."

The conversation wound down and Magnus stood, peeled Archie off my lap, gingerly got him to his shoulder, and carried him down the hallway to our room.

Quentin asked Beaty if she wanted to go to their house across the driveway, she said yes, because there was a show she wanted to watch and followed him bounding from the room.

I watched them go and shook my head. "So let me get this

straight, soon enough this house is going to be full of the sound of bagpipes and there will be a pig, for sure, Quentin will get her one and we'll have a pig living here."

Magnus returning from the bedroom, overhearing our conversation, and completely missing the point, said, "We can put its pen near the stables."

Zach said, "I can't believe the two of them were eating microwaved food for the last month. I will have to step up my game — everyone needs vegetables, vitamins, whole grains. This is a travesty, next someone in this compound will say they are missing eighteenth century food."

Magnus said, "Tae match it ye would have tae leave away the sauce and spice and sugar and what would be left? The blood and gristle of a—"

I groaned, "Ugh, don't talk of the blood sausages, those sucked duck dong."

Hayley returned from the bathroom. "What — duck dong?"

"The food of the eighteenth century."

"Ah, yeah..." Her eyes went wistful.

I said, "Okay, we have to talk about this. Now, what is happening?"

Zach and Emma jumped up. "We're headed to bed, long day and all."

Emma said, holding Ben in her arms, "I just wanted to say how glad we are to have everyone home, new home, but under the same roof, or roofs. I had a little much to drink, but glad you're all home."

"Me too, thank you for being here to welcome me."

They left for their rooms.

*H*ayley said, "Another beer?" She brought us a round and delivered them to us on the couch and then sat down across from us on a stuffed soft-leather chair.

She sighed, deeply.

I took a swig of beer before I asked, "What's happening, out with it."

"I think I might be dying. Or — like plague or something." She stretched at the neck of her shirt.

"Honey, have you seen the doctor or—"

"No, it's not like that, I don't need a doctor."

"I think if you have the plague that's exactly what you need."

She sighed again.

"Maybe tell me, what are your symptoms?"

"I can't concentrate. I'm kind of sad. I don't want to do anything, kind of up and down and confused about what to do with all of this."

I leaned forward. I had never heard her so serious but also so vague. It was a weird combo for her. "All of what, honey?"

Her chin trembled, she bit her lip, and with the smallest voice I ever heard she said, "My feelings for Fraoch."

"Oh, *honey*."

She wailed, "I *know*."

I glanced at Magnus. He was holding a serious look on his face but I suspected he was enjoying this all immensely.

She said, "It doesn't make sense. I know it. He's awful. I mean, not at all, he's so kind and sweet and..."

I said, "Fraoch?" I looked from Hayley to Magnus. "Fraoch MacDonald?"

She continued. "I mean, he's not my type, at *all*. He's like... You know how Michael was like a puppy, I just had to train him? Keep him fed and tell him what to do? Fraoch is like a half-wolf-dog, one of those big gentle-giant dogs. The ones that sit beside you and are furry and..." She looked at me so sadly.

I said, "I honestly have no idea — can we start over? This is Fraoch you're talking about? Tell me what happened."

"I got there and he rescued me."

"From what, like a — what?"

"Like the whole century, he put me on a horse and took me to his man cave and..."

"Not to Madame Greer's house or the castle?"

"He didn't know where to take me. My existence in that time was nothing but trouble. He fed me rabbit. He hunted wild animals to feed me, and we sat around the fire and waited for you to come get me."

"Where did you sleep? Did you sleep with him, Hayley? Is that what this is?"

"No, I told him that I was married, so he just took care of me, kept wolves from feasting on me. We slept by the fire, and he guarded me all night."

"Holy shit, okay, go on, how many days was this?"

"Like three or four and then he was worried about me so he

went and got Lizbeth. She gave me a dress and took me to the castle."

"Good."

"Except, it wasn't totally. I mean, it was good for me, but then Fraoch was alone in his man cave and it—"

"Why isn't he at Madame Greer's?" I turned to Magnus.

Magnus took a swig of beer and chuckled. "She has grown tired of him. She daena like him hulkin' around inside the house, she told him tae go huntin' and leave her in peace."

"Okay, this is all so freaking juicy — so Madame Greer sent him to a man cave and then you come along, gotcha. You tell him you're married so he doesn't tend your rose garden. This is all so interesting."

I asked, "What happened in the castle, did you have trouble with the Campbell men?"

"Lizbeth sent them away to go hunting."

"This is a theme, wow, I'm learning something new. I didn't know that was a way to handle husbands."

"I am never here long enough for ye tae tire of me."

"I would never tire of you, my love."

Hayley said, "Focus on me please. I get it, you're in love, meanwhile I've just ruined my life."

"Sorry, honey, okay, you've gone to the castle, you're living there and what happens?"

"Fraoch came to see me every day. He would wear this rose scented lotion all over, because I told him that he stunk to high heaven and that he needed to wash all around his balls and ass and—"

Magnus stifled a laugh, but then began outright laughing. I had never heard him laugh so hard while trying not to. "He told me ye said this, but I still canna believe ye said it tae the man."

"I did, I couldn't bear it, he stunk, so he washed up, and covered himself in rose scent and trimmed his beard a tiny bit.

He slicked back his hair with some kind of grease, and... and... it was so freaking romantic."

I started laughing too, leaning back on the couch beside Magnus both of us dying of laughter.

Hayley looked at us with a brow raised incredulously. "Finished?"

"I am so sorry, Hayley. I have known you since you were a little girl and you have always had a much, much higher standard for what is romantic than a bath and feminine hygiene products."

"I know! This is what I'm telling you. I think it's Stockholm Syndrome or something. I've been brainwashed into thinking he's..."

She pointed at Magnus in mock anger, "Don't laugh at me, this is all your fault. You come around here in your swishy skirt and your sexy voice and—"

Magnus bit his lips. "My skirt daena swish."

"Fraoch's does, have you seen how sexy he is, Katie? In a kilt with his long beard and hair all curled and down and...?"

"God, girl, you have it bad. When he came to see you, what did you talk about? What do you have in common? I mean when Magnus was here he was seeing my world, learning about this century, we had things in common to talk about. What would you talk about that was interesting to you?"

"So much! He had a horse that I could ride, Gatorbelle. We rode every day. We hunted sometimes and we talked about my parents' divorce and he talked about his mom and dad dying and his brother, and we just talked. After a few weeks I really regretted lying to him about being married, because he was one of my closest friends. He would just listen to whatever I said. He *liked* me. He thought I was smart, and funny. We told stories and he's hilarious. And then he came to the castle and when he was with the men he was such a man. All man. It was pretty hot."

Magnus's eyes twinkled. "He is verra braw for a MacDonald."

I chuckled and then sighed, "Oh sweetie, that sounds awful and wonderful all at once. How did you leave it with him?"

"Lizbeth told me that he was wishing he could marry me, that everyone knew it, and that she had seen him praying over it, as if he was worried about sinning because I was married—"

Magnus said, "Tis a verra real worry. He is at odds with God. Twill take its toll on a man tae love another man's wife."

She clapped her hands over her mouth. "I lied to him! Who's the real problem here? Me! And I left him believing he was sinning over me. Magnus came to get me, finally, it took you two long enough, and then I left. He said some sweet things to me, and I left anyway. And now Lizbeth's going to find him a wife and..." She dropped her head to her hands and groaned loudly.

I, for lack of something better, said, "This shit sucks."

"I knew you would know just what to say to make me feel better."

"I don't. I don't even know where to begin. What are you going to do?"

"I can't stop thinking about him. His smile spreading inside his beard. His booming voice when he's insulting someone or laughing at their weakness, crowing about his strength."

My eyes went wide.

She continued, "Did you know, Katie, he's alone in the whole world? No one really takes care of him? He's like a mountain man, just needing a woman to gentle him to..."

"What the fuck are you talking about? Hayley, you're a feminist. You've been a feminist since way back. You and Michael built a relationship on absolute equality. You even had separate houses."

"Is it wrong to want to take care of someone?"

"Jeez Louise." I stared off into space. "No, it's not wrong. I mean, the stuff you're saying, some of it really worries me, but it's also true if you love him. And you sound like you love him. The truth is, I married Magnus barely having spent time with him at all." I shook my head. "Is that what you want to do, marry him?"

"Marry Fraoch? God no, never, not at all, no way.... what would that entail? I mean, that's what I can't figure out, can I marry him? Should I?"

I laughed, "I think you just gave me whiplash with that bit of logic. I don't know, did he ask you?"

"No, remember, it's a sin."

"Do you think he wanted to?"

"I don't know..."

Magnus said, "Och aye, he wanted tae. He wanted tae live with Hayley at the edge of the loch and hunt and fish with her every day and..."

"Did he tell you this?"

"Nae, but all the men kent it of him, he was plain in his intentions."

Hayley took in a deep breath. "*Katie*, what am I going to do? He's all alone there but he's scared to come here. He doesn't want to time travel again — he hates it. Could I...?"

"That is a huge question. First, the longest I have been there is a couple of weeks. Usually I carry food, equipment and supplies. You've been there longer with more deprivation, would you be able to live there?"

"I don't know. Plus, you have Magnus, he takes care of you. He protects you. When I was there, Lizbeth had to stay beside me every single moment."

Magnus said, "Fraoch is orphaned, he daena have family, tis complicated tae provide for a wife and bairns when ye daena have an extended family tae protect ye."

I nodded, "None of this sounds good, like you are not ready for this kind of life. You are a thoroughly modern woman. What about children? The first thing, the entire point of the marriage, would be to have children. What would you do?"

"I started thinking it might not be such a bad thing, I mean, I kind of like Ben. Archie is rad. Lizbeth isn't winning any mothering awards and she has babies..."

Magnus said, "Lizbeth is high born. She daena have tae raise her own bairns because she can have others do it for her. Tis her station. Marryin' Fraoch winna raise yer station. I have seen the contents of his sporran. He has only what he wears and no more. I tell ye, Madame Hayley, if he wanted tae feed ye and there wasna game about, he would have tae beg for the meal. He is cared for because I asked my clan tae care for him, and in exchange he is tae guard for the storms. He canna marry a woman such as yerself and make ye happy."

"Katie is happy. I'm not much different than her."

"Hayley," I said, "Magnus is the nephew of the Earl of Breadalbane, a cousin of the Lord of Argyll, and a king, or at least he was, and in 2020 he is fabulously wealthy."

She sighed and leaned back in her chair.

"So what do I do? It breaks my heart that I left him all alone."

There was a stack of notebooks on the coffee table. I tore out a blank piece of paper and pushed it in front of her and passed her a pen.

"Make a list, pros and cons."

She began to write:

Pros.

Underneath she wrote: I love him.

I muttered, "Jeezus Christ."

She wrote: I want to take care of him.

And then: I don't want to not have children with him.

I pointed out that double negatives didn't exactly work in the 'pros' column.

She wrote: He's smoking hot.

202 | DIANA KNIGHTLEY

I said, "Missing a tooth, add that under cons."

She scrawled it under cons then said, "He could come here and get that fixed." She drew an arrow from 'missing a tooth' over to 'pros' and over the arrow wrote: We can fix that.

Under that she wrote: Stinks when he doesn't bathe.

I groaned watching her write it.

Not great style.

Eats rabbit with his fingers.

Then she added under pros: hunted for food to feed me.

Under cons: Has never seen an episode of Friends so he misses most of my references.

I said, "Hayley, I don't think you're using this list-making tool the way it was intended."

She swigged from her beer and said, "Shhh, this is helping."

Under pros she wrote: He has no family.

I said, "Magnus already explained why that's a con."

She lifted her brow and wrote: No bitchy mother-in-law.

I said, "You got me there."

Pros: He needs me.

She leaned back on her heels. "See the pros win."

I sighed dramatically. "Hayley, you could be a grown up and say to yourself, 'I met a guy on summer vacation. He was hot. I flirted with him. He showed me a good time. We seemed like a good fit, but I couldn't leave my job, my house, my life to go to him, and he wouldn't do it for me.' Then you say 'Oh well' and then you wish him 'all the best' and let him find someone else, then you go on Tinder or Grinder or one of the other things you single ladies do, and have meaningless sex until you—"

"I don't want meaningless sex, I want Fraoch. I want a ring. I want to wake up and go hunting every single day with Fraoch."

Magnus leaned forward and waved his fingers so she would write. "Under the con one write: 'the Scottish winter will be a'comin'.'"

"Ha ha, very funny."

I said, "Seriously Hayley, write that down."

She wrote it down.

"You still think the pros win?"

"Yep."

"Does that mean you're going to move to Scotland in the year 1704? Hayley, is that what you're saying?"

"Maybe. I mean I could always come back right? Jump back and forth?"

I asked Magnus, "Would we give her a vessel?"

"You kind of owe me since this is all your fault."

"Aye, Madame Hayley and Fraoch can have a vessel tae live on the edge of a loch through the Scottish winter, nae ownin' anythin' but love, beddin' each other because tis naething else tae do, verra borin', until there are bairns all around their skirts mewlin' for milk."

Hayley wrote between both columns: Birth control is a thing.

I asked, "Do you know what you're doing?"

She shook her head. "But look at you — you love someone from the past."

"Magnus has seen the future. He knows things about the world. The first time he took me back in time I was faced with medieval rapists and barbaric murderers and the weird political maneuverings of the upper class and to make me feel better Magnus made a joke about Foo Fighters music and I laughed and we felt better. We had to have that in common... I don't know, honey, you're giving up so much."

"Yeah, and I don't know... I just think he will be worth it. When I was there it was so simple and comfortable and we had so much to talk about."

"Did you go to meetings? You're drinking..."

She shrugged. "They don't have AA meetings in the eighteenth century, but also, they... I just felt better about myself, fresh and not bored, and while I'm saying that I know it's not true. I actually was dirty, tired, and bored, and I don't know what the right answer is, except — Fraoch."

I looked at Magnus. He had his fingers resting on his lip but wasn't really laughing, just considering.

"What do you think, Magnus?"

"I believe Fraoch is a lucky man tae have Madame Hayley interested in bindin' her life tae his."

"Do you think he will be modern, and gentle, will he abuse her?"

"I ken him tae be of a mild manner when he inna beatin' me tae teach me a lesson."

I waved my hand at Magnus, "See, Hayley, he might be an abuser."

Hayley raised her brow. "How many men have you killed in the last year, Magnus?"

"If ye are speakin' on all my lives I canna count them all."

Hayley waved her hand at Magnus, mimicking me. "See? And remember that whole thing about if you're lost, stay put and...?"

I grinned. "I do. I was just telling my grandparents that of all the things they accomplish in their life, they have to make sure Grandpa Jack gets lost at the amusement park, so that I learn that lesson. I have to tell it to you so we can apply it to every single situation whether it fits or not. But Hayley, it doesn't fit in this case, who is lost?"

"Fraoch, he's orphaned, lost, and I need to go find him."

I took her pen from her hand and under her columns wrote —
Need supplies.
Need to pack.
Need to go find him.

*O*ur plan was for Hayley to leave in three days. I wish I could call our days calm and stress free but they weren't. We had, all of us, moved into a new house, and not all at once, in fits and starts. We couldn't find anything. Someone was always hollering, "Where is the...?"

Emma was muttering about the "insane people who put stuff away like idiots," sounding a lot like me when I was searching for Magnus's letter through the boxes in storage back at the beginning of all of this.

Zach was trying to toddler-proof while Ben was toddlering, and the furniture was lavish and not at all childproof. There was a pale peach velvet settee, much like Lady Mad's velvet couch, and it only took a couple of hours before there was a spilled Cheerios and milk situation on it.

Neither Ben nor Archie remembered it happening, they just found it funny.

Hayley said, "This is one hundred percent why babies aren't allowed to live in nice houses." To Ben she added, "I always know where my Cheerios are, I wouldn't leave them lying willynilly."

And Zach was irritated because he had to go so much farther to get to the grocery store, plus Quentin sent a guard with him every time and this was our life now.

The house was awesome. It was still too cold to begin using the swimming pool, and the lack of ocean-front kind of sucked, but we had an amazing yard sloping toward the marsh — a long dock stretching into the intracoastal waterway, a large boathouse with a thirty-foot get-away boat.

We were dealing with a lot of life stuff, but whenever we could we gathered family-style — breakfast out in the screened porch, a long table with chairs all around it, larger seating even than the dining room.

At sunset we gathered on the dock and sat with our feet dangling in the water, while Beaty played the bagpipes — a terribly squawking, unsettling racket that was somehow really beautiful. This was our Beaty's music, her blue hair cascading around her shoulders, barefoot and bare legged, she was learning to play by watching YouTube videos and serenading us out of a feeling of gratitude for rescuing her from her own time and bringing her here. We never ever complained about her missed notes.

A security guard stood a few feet away. Always.

We had packed Hayley's bags. She had a letter from Magnus for Lizbeth and Sean asking them to give her care and attention. Also there was a letter for the Earl of Breadalbane with a bag of gold as a gift and a request for her to be cared for.

Hayley had her own bag of gold. She was wearing an outfit from my stash, combined with some of the clothes she arrived home in so that she looked the part. She had a cooler full of food. A blade for protection.

She had long ago gone on a hormone patch for birth control and skipped her periods, so she was going to stick with that. "Something you should have done years ago," she unhelpfully pointed out.

To which I answered, "I'm trying to get pregnant."

"Ugh. Why? Your life is perfect, don't go screwing with what is already perfect. Did you learn nothing from the Katy Perry concert? We had sneaked into good seats, but no, you weren't happy, you wanted to try for front row, but that security guard found us and escorted our sorry asses all the way back to our way-in-the-back-back seats and stood watching over us. We were stuck."

"Yes, I learned my lesson, but also, I'm still trying to get pregnant. Call me a lesson-ignorer if you want, but I don't think anyone wants children because they want perfection. I kind of think you have to go into parenthood with the idea that you want to be imperfect. That's how it works. Kind of like if you wanted a perfect life you would not be heading to the eighteenth century right now. Antibiotics being something that is lacking."

She looked in my eyes. "Did you remember to pack me the antibiotics?"

"I did. Did I remember to tell you how brave you are?"

And then we were all driving in three different cars down to the south end, because we didn't want to jump from our house and draw attention to its exact location. But we all wanted to be there to say goodbye. Everyone was armed.

We parked along the road and we all helped carry a load to the sand. Ben and Archie ran chasing after a flock of seagulls though the pristine sand, pale white, not even a footstep around.

Everyone joked, teasing Hayley. She was going to stay away for two weeks, which wasn't a big deal. She was calling it a vacation, but she would stay there as long as she needed or wanted. I had taught her the night before to use the vessels. She was ready.

Zach speculated that she might come back with gray hair, and when she said, "I don't think I can stay that long," he said, "No, not gray because of age, because that Highlander is going to be such a pain in your arse."

Beaty took photos while Ben and Archie chased the birds. She raced alongside them, kicking her sandals to the side, and taking shots of the little boys against the blue skies of the clear March day.

Her internal body-temperature was all wackadoodle, like Magnus's — we were in jackets, she believed it to be warm out.

Quentin said something funny. We laughed. I rustled through one of the packs, checking it for the umpteenth time, then my eyes traveled down the beach, the distant spot where the boys were playing — Beaty was working her fingers on the back of her camera.

I asked, "What is she doing?"

Quentin called across the sand, "What are you doing, Bea?"

She didn't look up.

He cupped his fingers around his mouth and yelled it again, "What are you doing?"

She called back, some of her voice lost on the wind, "...namin' this photo, hashtag... 'the prince.'"

I stood, hands on my hips and asked Quentin, "What does she mean, 'namin' it'?"

Suddenly two big dark future-cars, raced across the road and drove careening down onto the sand.

Men in full soldier gear leapt out—

I grabbed the dirk from the bag at Hayley's feet and Quentin, Magnus, and I were in a full race toward the boys, *ohnoohnoohnononono*, Emma screamed as soldiers closed on Ben.

Zach was yelling and running toward the boys. We were all converging on the same point, the two cars, near the boys, a storm rising above them, a big terrible storm, just as one of the soldiers hit Beaty and ripped Archie from her ams. She was begging and crawling after them, grasping after the soldier's legs — he kicked her face.

Quentin was yelling. Quentin was aiming at the guards while running, commanding them to stop.

Zach was aiming his gun but a soldier was holding Ben, using him as a shield.

Magnus unsheathed his sword as he ran and was on that soldier, bellowing, "Put him down!"

I raced past Magnus, with the dirk in hand, heading straight for that asshole who was holding Archie — a struggling, screaming, terrified Archie. Like a wild banshee I brandished my blade, "Let go of him! Let go of him right now! You asshole, let go of him!"

As I gained on him I drew my hand back and plunged my dirk into his stomach, screeching. Then we were struggling over the handle of the blade, blood gushing over my hand, trying to free Archie from his grip, my hair pulled, Archie screaming, hand to hand against this monster — my arm was grabbed, yanked behind my back. Another soldier grabbed me around the waist, writhing, kicking, screaming — I was thrown onto the floorboards of a car.

Archie was screaming nearby. We were both inside the car but separated and oh god, the storm winds battered the vehicle, rocking it, a boot on my chest holding me down, my arm bent under me.

I could see through the open sunroof as the storm built more dangerously, lightning arced across the sky, and I felt it rip through my body as the time jump began.

THIRTY-NINE - MAGNUS

I gripped my sword though twas useless as the storm whipped and roared around us. I was holding Ben tight tae my chest, covering him, as sand battered us in the wind.

The cars were gone. Kaitlyn was gone. Archie.

Twas all now the sound and fury of the storm as the clouds built tae their highest position and then began tae roll back and pull away, until moments later clouds raced from the point above us.

Madame Emma reached me, taking Ben intae her arms. He was wailin' a convulsive cry, scared from his mind. He was only two years auld, a bairn, nae old enough tae be grabbed by soldiers.

I turned m'attention tae Madame Beaty, layin' on the sand her hands on her face, blood streamin' down her shirt. Master Quentin crouched beside her, pressin' a cloth tae her nose — twas slow motion around us.

Mistress Hayley beside Master Quentin, "Is her nose broken?"

He was dabbing at the blood and speakin' tae Madame Beaty tae calm her. "I don't think so, I think she's going to be okay. Can you get the monitor? I dropped it over there. We need to watch to see if more are coming."

"More could be coming?" Mistress Hayley ran tae find the monitor.

Madame Beaty was cryin', "I am sorry King Magnus, I dinna ken twas a problem. Quenny..." She clutched his shirt. "I dinna ken Insta was the problem. Ye took m'phone away, but with the camera I could post the photos. I just wanted tae put up the pretty pictures. I just..." She moaned. "If anythin' happens tae Archie twill be m'fault."

I crouched beside her and patted her hand while Master Quentin advised Mistress Hayley where tae search. "Check near your bags!"

I said, "Tis nae yer fault, Madame Beaty, ye dinna ken, tis nae... daena worry on your part in it."

Madame Emma was consolin' Ben, carryin' him tae the car.

I stood tae watch that place where Archie and Kaitlyn had last been, their struggles and screams echoin', but there was naething there—

Chef Zach stood beside me, his hand on my back. "Thank you for saving Ben, I thought — God, I thought they were going to fucking take him, to kill him — thank you."

I nodded. "I canna believe they were..."

"Do you need to go, to follow...?"

I shook my head, keeping my eyes focused on that spot. "I daena ken where they are. I have nae way of discoverin' it."

My sight had gone blurred around the edges, a pinpoint of focus in the middle, direct and straight, this — the blood on Madame Beaty, Master Quentin's voice consolin' his wife on the sand, my heart racin', my breath comin' bullish from my nose, pushed from my chest in short bursts. My sword was beside me in the sand, glintin' in the sun, heatin', I wanted tae raise it against them, tae kill them all, but when?

They were an enemy of stealth. They had waited for the right time and caught us unaware, twas strategic and brutal and final.

They had taken Archie and Kaitlyn, but nae me, because they would be usin' them tae gain power over me. I would never see them again, nae in freedom, and I would never ken peace again.

Mistress Hayley and Master Quentin fussed over Madame Beaty while she kept sayin', "My fault. Always m'fault, I daena ken the rules of this place," remindin' me of Kaitlyn, *I don't know the rules... I never know the fucking rules.*

Master Quentin pushed the hair back from Madame Beaty's face. "It's not your fault, Beaty, you just wanted to put a cool title on your photo, that's all." He helped her to sitting. She was covered in sand and blood, now drying in the cool winter sun.

I said, with my eyes on the horizon, "The blame is mine, Madame Beaty."

We loaded Hayley's bags intae the truck and returned tae the house.

We were quiet, nae one spoke. We carried Hayley's supplies tae the house and left them scattered around on the floor of the living room.

Emma came tae me with Ben in her arms and put her arms around me. She buried her head against m'chest, overcome, as we all were. "Thank you Magnus, I thought Ben was — I'm so sorry about Archie and Kaitlyn and—"

I hugged her in return. "I am glad Ben is here and is well. Your gratitude is nae necessary, Madame Emma. He is a part of m'family."

Ben looked up at me and asked, "Watee?" I kent it tae be his name for Archie.

Emma just hugged him and neither of us answered. She went over and settled onto the couch with Ben in her lap.

I stood starin' around at the gear Hayley had been takin' with her. I couldna decide what tae do, how tae proceed. My mind was a jumble of incoherent thoughts, a confused muddle of disparate images — my son and Kaitlyn, struggling, Kaitlyn stabbing a man, blood, then a storm. Kaitlyn sayin', *I don't know the rules.* The scenes from the future, the orphanage, the tent cities, Roderick standin' over me, a knife held at my throat, Bella, with her breast exposed, sayin' tae me, "I want Kaitlyn to die."

Quentin was cleanin' Beaty's face as she wept.

Without plannin' I asked, "Would someone please drive me tae church?"

Hayley said, "Of course."

Beaty dabbed at her eyes. "King Magnus, could I please come as well? I be needin' tae pray."

"Aye."

FORTY - MAGNUS

I wasna comfortable with Quentin leavin' Chef Zach and his family, they needed the protection, so twas Hayley that drove Beaty and me tae the church.

She parked and attended us in, sitting in a pew tae reflect, while Beaty and I approached the altar.

I knelt, and began tae pray.

My words rushed from me, surprisin' me with their urgency. Twas nae often I gave up action tae kneel in prayer, but there was nae action afore me... I dinna ken what tae do. I had never been so lost.

My Kaitlyn and Archie had been taken so brutally and completely. They could be anywhere, in any time.

Only Roderick would ken. But which Roderick in what time? How much time had passed since I was there? I had tae be smart and understand the game. I couldna get this wrong...

So I prayed tae God, humbled by my fear, overwhelmed by the violence and the certainty — I had lost this.

I had lost my wife and child.

I prayed more, putting tae voice how my heart was emptied

and m'mind tired. I dinna ken what tae do. I begged for help tae right myself.

And then worn and with an ache in my bones from the kneelin', the pain sharp through m'shins, risin' from my legs, through my stomach, up tae my chest, washin' the fear away with waves of pain, I continued tae pray — wantin' peace for my family, and then when I was at the end of my abilities, I asked for guidance in findin' them.

I was prayin for a verra long time.

When I raised tae my feet, my legs were unused tae bein' upright and I believed I might fall. I grasped Beaty's shoulder tae steady m'self.

I had been asking for guidance but if ye had asked me then, I would have said I dinna receive it.

I dinna believe myself tae be closer tae wisdom on it. I felt weak and small, unable tae protect my wife and child from this evil—

King Magnus, dost ye ken tae rule yer kingdom?

"Och? What did ye say Beaty?"

She was beside me as I strode down the aisle tae the doors. I had almost forgotten she was there.

We opened the doors and stepped out ontae the front stoop. The sun blinded my eyes. I winced, shieldin' them in the crook of my arm. Twas always this way, the brightness of this time, it caused me tae lose m'sight.

Madame Beaty repeated, "I was wonderin', King Magnus, if ye were given guidance tae winnin' yer kingdom?"

I shook m'head. "I daena — I wasna askin' for... what dost ye mean, Madame Beaty?"

She pulled me tae a stop with a gentle hand on m'arm and turned solemn eyes tae mine. Her face was bruised and swollen. It looked painful, and caused me tae wince tae look on her, but her shirt was clean and her bright blue hair was bright as a halo.

She was, as always, pale skinned and, as Kaitlyn called it, a sweet and silly dimple.

Now she said, "I was speakin' tae God on our current troubles and worryin' on Archie and Queen Kaitlyn, and God answered me."

My brow drew down in concentration. "What did he tell ye?"

"He said yer wisdom was in how ye would rule yer kingdom." She added, "I ken yer kingdom is lost tae ye, but I believe God was goin' tae guide ye on winnin' it again."

I considered. "I daena think it can be won again, Madame Beaty, tis too long ago lost..."

If you're lost, hold tight, someone will come and find you.

"Och," I said again.

She frowned. "Maybe, but when I was prayin' it washed over me, a feelin' of calm, that King Magnus would ken tae rule his kingdom and Queen Kaitlyn would be beside him."

Mistress Hayley approached. "Are you ready to go home? We have a lot to discuss."

"Aye."

On the way home, I was still thinkin' on what Madame Beaty said. I stared out the car window as the sand dunes and beaches of my chosen home slid by.

Twas a beautiful land.

Kaitlyn told me twas unique, a type of sand and shell that wasna seen anywhere else. While I watched the scenery I deliberated, thinking through all that would happen, all that I needed tae do, and thinkin' on what Madame Beaty had said — *God was goin' tae guide ye on winnin' it again.*

God hadna answered me, but perchance he was speaking

through Beaty. The answer dinna lie in fightin' for Kaitlyn, the solution wasna in rescuin' Kaitlyn and Archie, twas in securin' my crown and winnin' my kingdom.

The trouble was I would be loopin' ontae our lives. I would have tae give up on findin' Kaitlyn, leavin' her tae an uncertain fate, sacrificin' Archie at the age of three, tae go tae a different time.

What would happen tae them?

FORTY-ONE - MAGNUS

Kaitlyn made me promise tae never loop on my life. She said it would cause damage tae our timeline, take memories from us. How could I let go of any of our memories?

She would nae agree.

She wanted all of our memories, even the sad ones. Who was I tae make the decision for her? Tae lose what had happened between us?

She had once left me at an older age, and traveled tae me when I was younger. She had given me the chance tae live my life over without memory of the long years of war and brutal battles and... she had told me about it. I was glad tae have been spared.

Tae win m'kingdom again, I would have tae wage that war. I once begged her tae save me from that fate — now I would be choosin' it.

I wished she was here tae advise me. I dinna ken what she would say.

When she left me as Old Magnus tae come tae me as a

younger man, she did it because I asked her tae. I gave her permission tae steal those memories from me.

She wasna here tae tell me twas all right tae take memories away.

And Archie... Kaitlyn and I saved him. Kaitlyn loved him, he called her his mammy... How could I remove that from her?

She loved him.

If I played with time I might lose him.

I might. lose. him.

And wasna playin' with time the sole dominion of God?

Beaty was sure God spoke tae her, but he dinna speak tae me on it, what if she was mistaken? Might it be the work of the devil, meant tae lead me astray?

Should I dismiss it and find a way forward from here?

You aren't a god, you are only a man.

Yet I had once been also a king.

We pulled up in front of the house and walked in, still not speakin'.

We sat in a circle in the living room. Hayley leaned forward over her knees and spoke first. "I was headed to the year 1704, I had built up my nerve... but now I can't leave. I have to know what happens to Kaitlyn."

She turned a sad face tae me, "Will she be okay?"

With one hand I was massagin' the knuckles of m'other, calmin' the fingers that itched tae do somethin', anythin'. "I daena ken, I think Roderick will want tae use her tae bait me, tae do his biddin'. Bella dinna want her tae live though, she might nae..."

Hayley asked, "Why didn't you go after her?"

"I canna ken where or when she is. They were gone afore I could get tae them."

Quentin said, "It would be like looking for a hostages held in the caves in Afghanistan, except even more impossible."

Hayley nodded.

Chef Zach went tae the kitchen, drinks were poured, he returned with a tray of glasses. "Cokes for everyone."

We quieted, everyone starin' in a different direction.

I said, "I need tae speak tae everyone on what I have tae do."

They turned their attention tae me.

"I hae tae do it again."

"What part?" asked Quentin.

"The part where I lose m'kingdom. If I daena lose my kingdom none of this happens, tis the moment where it went wrong. I have it in my power tae alter the trajectory of the world. I have tae use my power."

I gave Beaty a sad smile. "God spoke tae Beaty on it. He said I was a king that needed tae rule. The more I think on it the more I ken tis the way of it."

I massaged the knuckles on m'other hand. "I canna find Kaitlyn in the future, so I must fix what has happened a'ready."

Chef Zach said, "But you can't loop back on yourself."

"I ken. Tis against the rules of the game. I also promised Kaitlyn I would never attempt anythin' like this, but I am goin' tae break my promise. I believe she will forgive me when she understands God has instructed me tae."

Emma asked, "What about Archie?"

"If I go back in time, the three-year-auld Archie we ken will be gone."

Emma said, "You could do that?"

"I canna, but I have tae. If I daena start it over he will be a captive of the soldiers. What are they doin' tae him? I canna think on..." My voice broke.

Hayley reached out and held my hand.

Beaty said, "When would ye go tae King Magnus?"

"I am thinkin' General Reyes took me away from m'purpose — tae rule m'kingdom. I should have been concentratin' on Roderick. I had the castle, I wore the crown, and I took my eyes from it tae deal with Reyes and all that has come after..."

I looked around the room. "You were in the future, when Roderick was—"

Master Quentin said, "We were all in the Safe House, but Roderick was laying siege, then we jumped away. Even Lady Mairead was there. She left too."

"Dost ye remember what day twas?"

Master Quentin said, "Not really. I was pretty worried about Beaty at the time. Your mom would know."

"I can go ask her what the date was. Then I will go tae that time and fight tae keep my kingdom."

Madame Emma said, "Archie was a baby, so yeah, you'd be able to protect him from that point."

Mistress Hayley said, "But that wouldn't change any of this, right? I'm confused."

Chef Zach said, "It would totally change all of this, all the arena, the — you couldn't come back to this point, none of this would..."

I said, "Aye, I think I would have tae loop back intae this time as well. I daena ken when..."

Master Quentin said, "So, like it's an Etch-a-sketch, you're going to shake it up and start over, Boss? How far back you going to go?"

Chef Zach said, "Whoa, nelly. No no no, you can't, you can't loop on yourself. I know Kaitlyn's not here but I am, as the resident Doctor Who/Quantum Leap expert — you can't loop onto yourself. I won't allow it."

Madame Emma said, "What are you going to do, take the keys to his car?"

"I will, I'll take all the vessels and won't let him have them."

"God told him to do it."

Chef Zach shook his head, "Oh, and I'm not allowed to argue with God? I argue with God all the damn time. You can't loop." He ran his hand through his hair. "It's too risky."

I said, "What if I loop tae a time when I am nae there? Tis nae a true loop if I wasna in the time, tis correct Chef Zach?"

"I mean, I guess, but what no one else is noticing is that Magnus means he's going to loop back on all of our lives, to start them all over from a point he decides. That means we will forget all the shit that happened between whatever to now. Are we okay with that?"

"I am nae decidin' without ye, Chef Zach. I am askin' for yer assistance in it. Can ye consider it, for a moment, that I might have tae loop tae save the lives of Kaitlyn and Archie, tae protect them? Would ye please help me determine how it might work?"

I dropped m'head tae m'hands. "I daena ken how tae do it. I daena want tae play God and risk your lives. I need yer help in the deliberating on it."

Chef Zach nodded. "Okay, yeah of course, sure..." He slumped back in his seat. "Yeah, I can help. I don't really like being the voice of reason anyway. It's exhausting and totally not my style. If you go back and fight for your kingdom — how long would that take anyway?"

"It might take years."

Chef Zach gulped. "Okay, years. You would be willing to give up years of your life?"

"Archie and Kaitlyn are captives. There is nae way tae protect them. I canna imagine what is happenin' tae them. I will be goin' tae the root of the issue and creating a new branch of time. It will take years of my life but Kaitlyn will be alive."

"I get you, you're willing to make the sacrifice." He rubbed his hands together. "If you solve all of that, in the future, why not just come back here, to now. Like last night. Won't Kaitlyn be here, it will be a different timeline right?"

"But would Archie be here? If I am protectin' him as a baby in my kingdom he winna be here... I think the loop would be unfair tae him, tae Kaitlyn. I daena understand, but I worry on him, he would be..."

"He would be looping on himself."

"Aye," I thought with my mouth propped on my fingers. "I have long been worried about him, that we have brought him here out of time, and created a certain terrible future. I wondered, with his body bruised by violence and neglect, if I have taken the easy way. Instead of protecting him from the beginning, I have neglected him and only rescued him once twas convenient. I daena like the implications. I have had grave doubts on it."

I looked around at their faces, they were all considering what I said, their faces drawn.

Mistress Hayley's mouth opened and closed, thinking of what to say, then she asked, "But then you need to come back here, right? When have you not been here?"

"I daena want tae go back too far, tis too many memories for all of us, tis too—"

Hayley said, "Because right off the bat, if you came back before Nick Reyes came here, dated me like an asshole, and took you — that would save us all a lot of trouble."

I leaned forward, my elbows on my knees. "Then I wouldna save Fraoch's life. Twould be sentencin' him tae a cruel death."

Hayley clamped her mouth shut. "Oh, right."

"It might be necessary, we need tae consider every implication, but I would like tae see if we can conjure up a better time."

Emma said, "If you need to keep all that General Reyes business, then what about after your mother met with you at the bank? She kidnapped you for Roderick, right? Katie and I returned to the beach house after, we planned your rescue, but we waited because Quentin had to take Beaty to a doctor appointment. So we were here, all of us, and you weren't. It would be perfect, you come and... I don't know, what do you do?"

"I tell Kaitlyn nae tae rescue me. I tell her I am goin' tae change time and ask her tae wait for me."

Zach said, "You'd have to do that first. Tell her to wait, and then go to the future and change the trajectory, or else none of it works."

Hayley asked, quietly, "So that means the battle of the arena isn't going to happen?"

"Nae."

"Oh. Yeah, I mean it makes sense, but then..."

"I ken."

"I mean, that's probably fine, I wouldn't meet Fraoch, would I? Right?"

I shook my head

"Okay, that's fine. It would be better actually, now that I think about it. I need to focus on the present, not throwing my life away on some guy in the past. Right?"

I nodded.

"And I won't even remember him, right? He won't remember me, so there's that."

I asked, "Ye would be willin' tae accept that?"

"For Katie? Yeah, yeah I would."

Chef Zach said, "Are we sure you won't screw up our lives? Are we sure we aren't going to end up dead or worse? When Kaitlyn was trying to save her grandmother it got worse and worse and worse."

I said, "The big things canna be changed, the small things we can alter. I daena think we will even notice they have been altered. But is there anythin' big that happened since that time? Anythin' ye might nae want tae change?"

Madame Emma said, "We want a second baby, but I haven't

gotten pregnant yet. We were putting it off a little longer, so no worries there."

Chef Zach said, "We were at your aunt's for a whole month."

"I don't mind losing that, that wasn't fun at all."

Master Quentin said, "Will we still have the monitor, all the vessels?"

"Nae. But if I am King they will be mine tae use as I wish."

Chef Zach said, "In this new life I won't have stolen the monitor from the St Auggie museum? That's too bad, that was one of my finer moments."

I said, "I will remember and we can have ye do it again."

Quentin said, "I really like this house, though I do miss the beach. I don't mind a do-over, as long as everyone is safe and just — my job is to keep security and it's been really hard to do when the future keeps surprise-attacking. They're always one step ahead of us, so I agree, if you can rule in the future we'll all be safer."

Beaty was curled up around her legs on the couch, she said quietly, "I will relive anythin' tae keep Queen Kaitlyn and Archie safe. I daena want tae have their deaths bein' m'fault."

Hayley said, "I agree."

Zach said, "This is weird though, it's a little like you're going to kill us off — the five of us in this room, to go back to our past and revive us again with different memories. I don't know... It might be too much to ask of us."

"Dost ye want tae continue livin' here with the knowledge that Roderick and his men can come upon us at any time?"

"No, I don't like that shit at all, if you can stop those guys from coming here then please do."

"Aye." I looked around at them all. "I daena ken if I will do it. I wonder if tis the right thing tae do—"

Master Quentin said, "One last thing —if you don't go back

and fix this timeline and take your kingdom, what else are you going to do, where would you go to hunt for Katie and Archie?"

"I would begin at the castle."

"A random date, arrive on a storm, knock on the front door, no army behind you?"

"Given time I might have a better plan."

Master Quentin said, "I think your path is clear then."

"I think if I do decide tae go, twould be best if we dinna speak on it anymore. Ye can wake up on the morrow, here, or ye can wake up in the beach house a month ago and nae remember this at all, but we shouldna consider it more. Twill only fill our hearts with more weight than we can bear tae hold."

Madame Emma said, "I agree. This conversation is unprecedented. It's too much power, too much control, our audacity makes me shudder, but also, if you can save their lives, you should."

Chef Zach said, "I'll make something special for dinner tonight... And I would like to say, he's really great, Magnus. You shouldn't worry about getting him at the wrong time. Archie is perfect, just the way he is, exactly your son, and he loves you and Katie, and Ben loved him a lot already. What if he's there, at the castle, right now, with Katie? What if they're waiting for you to come get them? Maybe all it will take is another arena battle. If you want to go, Quentin and I will go with you. We can talk James into it. We'll all go with you."

"Let me think on it. Mistress Hayley, would ye drive me tae the stables tae see Sunny? A ride will help me clear m'mind."

I carried a few vessels along in m'sporran. Hayley and I were quiet in the car then she pulled intae the lot in front of the stables.

I asked, "If I did go, would ye want me tae tell ye of Fraoch?"

She kept her hands on the steerin' wheel, lookin' through the front window at nothin'. "I don't know. I think so? It was an accidental meeting, I mean, we aren't meant to be together, it goes against the way time works. How can I love a man who is three hundred years older?" She sighed. "I don't know."

"I was thinkin' if ye wanted tae pass along a message, I could take ye back and introduce ye tae Fraoch."

"It might be totally different though. It's not just that we met, it's the way we met." She shook her head. "I don't think so. But I really liked him." She turned tae me with a nod. "Yes, tell me about him."

"Okay, if I go, if I decide tae, I will tell ye about Fraoch."

"Wait, don't just tell me... can you make it happen again? Like, maybe accidentally push me into the past and promise to

228 | DIANA KNIGHTLEY

pick me up the next day and... no that's stupid. Crazy. Just tell me."

"All right, I will."

"I hope this works for you. I hope you save Katie and find Archie."

"I daena ken if I am doin' it yet."

"You are, of course you are. You are doing it for Katie." She started the car again. "But what if it ends up killing her, or you, or me? What if you blow up the world?"

"I daena think tis how it..."

"I guess you have to take the chance, right? There really isn't any way to go and find her?"

"Nae, it would take too long tae find her. I daena ken where tae begin... And wastin' time is nae..."

"Want me to wait or leave?"

"Ye can go ahead and leave."

"I thought so."

She drove away and left me there alone.

I visited Sunny, grooming and speakin' tae him on the matter. Then I took him for a ride on the beach for a time, enough tae get the warm sun on my face, a breeze in my hair.

I rose above my breaths and racing heart, and gained some clarity about the issue.

Twas on the back of Sunny that it became clear —

I was a king.

Twas nae an easy position tae be in and I had been nae behavin' as one, but here twas plain — if I was a king I should be protectin' my kingdom, the prince and the queen.

Instead I was playin' at protectin' my wife and nae doin' it well enough.

Kaitlyn had once said tae me, *It's the kind of man you are. You are bound with honor... they are trying to destroy that part of you, to make you choose me or your child. I won't ever make you choose. I am safe for you...*

She was safe, trustin', and strong. She had stabbed that soldier for takin' Archie, she had been willin' tae fight for him.

She would want me tae do what it would take tae keep Archie safe, tae rescue him, even if it meant beginnin' over again.

She wasna here tae tell me, but I ken what she would say — I love you, Highlander, do what you need tae do.

Tae set out on this journey was a risk. Tae switch time. Kaitlyn did it once and there had been no repercussions. Was I clear that all was the same? Was I loopin' on anyone that would...?

I had promised Kaitlyn nae tae do it.

I dinna like doin' it tae her without speakin' tae her on it first.

What if I got us stuck in a time-loop like when she was looping for her grandmother?

And I would be takin' her tae the time before she kent this older Archie. Before Archie called her Mammy.

I think twas the happiest moment of her life and I was takin' it from her.

She wouldna remember, but... I would.

And if I intervened in the future, in my kingdom, I would be giving Bella another chance with Archie — twas nae fair tae take from Kaitlyn tae give tae Bella.

I rode along the shoreline. Sunny was light and happy tae have me home. The sky overhead grew gray and bleak, a winter storm comin', buildin' thick and oppressive. Twas dreich.

I chuckled tae m'self, Kaitlyn explainin' a cannonball, "Jump, grab your knees, tuck your whole body and plunge into the lake... Do it over and over and over again, just taking a moment to eat, then doing it again and again."

Today was a good day for a jump, and tae do it again. The air came up — cold, familiar, and calming. The air of a certainty, a feeling of trust and strength and, for once, the knowledge that I was doin' what was best.

It might take a long time, but I would be the strength m'family needed.

Then, as the rain began tae fall, I turned Sunny back toward the stables, determined tae go.

There was a weight on the edge of my bed and then Magnus whispering, his voice low and rumbling, "Good morn, mo reul-iuil."

I stretched, comfortably, luxuriously, and smiled, "Hey babe."

He was kneeling, his forearms leaned on the mattress.

"— wait... *Magnus*? Oh my god, Magnus. You were taken away from the bank by soldiers! Lady Mairead was being a total bitch. They beat you." I stroked a finger down the side of his face. "You've got no bruises, that was — I was going to go get the vessels. You said you were a distraction, right? I was going to take Quentin, James, and Hayley. What happened?"

He inhaled deeply. "Tis a great deal of talkin' ye are doing."

I clamped my mouth shut, added, "I'm just excited to see you."

Magnus folded his hands together and said, "Mo reul-iuil, I beg of ye tae forgive me..."

"Why? Oh no, *Magnus* — what did you do?"

He clasped my hands in his and kept his eyes cast down while he spoke in the dim light of our bedroom. "I have done what I promised nae tae do, I looped intae our lives and I am verra sorry on it."

"Why?" I searched his face, "Did I ask you to?"

"Nae, I had tae decide on m'own. Tis why I am here askin' ye for forgiveness."

"What happened?"

He seemed to be thinking.

Then he said, "You were taken by Roderick's soldiers. I daena ken where ye had gone. I couldna begin tae find ye. I would need tae wait for Roderick tae give me demands but what torture might he put ye through?"

I gripped her hands tighter. "I came here tae end that time-line, tae begin a new one."

"Oh, well... That sounds okay. You weren't here, you weren't and now you are, voila new timeline, and no one died, so there won't be any weirdness. This seems like a stable thing to do. But your expression is worried." I smoothed the hair from his fore-head. "You look like someone who is ashamed of what they've done — I need to know what you did that now I'm missing. What am I missing?"

"'Tis hard tae tell ye about."

"Oh. That sounds bad." I sat up, slid a leg on each side of him, settling his head into my lap.

"Tell me my love." I ran my fingers through his hair, twisting a finger through one of his locks.

His face was nestled in the crook of my thigh, his voice muffled because of it. "You and I went and rescued Archie. We found him in an orphanage when he was about three years auld."

My fingers paused their work of twisting through his hair. "You're speaking of him like he's past tense."

"He has been taken as well."

"Ah," I massaged my palms down the back of his neck and smoothed the white cotton shirt across his broad shoulders, the ridges of his scars meeting my fingertips through the cloth, familiar, yet reminding me he was human and vulnerable and —

"That's why your heart is heavy. Tell me more."

"He dinna live with us long, Kaitlyn, but he had begun tae call ye Mammy."

"He did, really?"

Magnus's head nodded against my thigh. He took a deep breath. "Och aye, he loved ye verra much. I wish I could have rescued him, but I dinna ken how and I was afraid what they might be doin' tae him. The pain and fear he might be sufferin'. When we found him, Kaitlyn he had been beaten. He was afraid of us, I... want tae protect him, but I haena, so I..." He clutched tightly around my hips.

"It sounds like you're doing the right thing."

"There is more, mo reul-iuil. I took ye tae see your grandparents." I paused my hands mid caress.

"You know I never wanted to do that. Why would you?"

"We were bein' chased, I took ye without askin' yer permission on it. You dinna like bein' there, but we all swam in the lake and did cannonballs off the dock."

"Archie met Barb?"

"Aye."

"That explains a lot, but it also raises so many questions."

"Tis our life tae be in the middle of explanations that bring more questions."

I chuckled and my stomach jiggled his head while I laughed. Then I grew serious again, "Visiting my grandparents didn't screw up my life?"

"Nae."

"Is there anything else?"

"The rest are stories I can tell ye later."

"So we had Archie but now we've lost him again? We just need to fix it and—"

He raised up, sat back on his heels, hands on his hips. He watched me, his expression one of sadness, then he shook his head. "I am goin' tae fix it. I have decided it. We arna fixin' it, we are living it through differently."

"I don't understand, not really."

"I will be goin' tae the kingdom and protecting it from Roderick the usurper. I winna allow him tae take m'crown. You told me, ye ken, long ago, that I was tae make the kingdom safe for Archie. I dinna accomplish it. I canna protect ye or m'son after Roderick becomes the king. I have tae fight him afore he takes power."

"Oh. But—"

"I am here only tae tell ye what I plan tae do. So ye will ken. So ye winna worry."

"I can come with you, I can help."

"Nae," He ran a hand through his hair. "Ye canna. I need tae be strategic. If the war is nae turnin' in my favor I will try tae fight it over. I will have tae be able tae jump if necessary. I have tae focus on the war and protect Archie and deal with Hammond—"

"And Bella."

"Aye." He looked me in the eyes. "I ken it is much tae ask, for ye tae stay here, in safety, with our family around ye. I need tae be able tae fight and win and I might have tae do things that will be difficult tae do if ye are present."

I screwed up my face to consider what he was saying. "So you are going to go away to be a king and a warrior, and you're wanting me to do as I'm told, and stay here, like a good queen, so you can do kingly things without worrying about me and without being a total pain in your arse?"

"Aye. Except ye arna a pain in my arse, nae always." He chuckled.

"But we do need tae spend some time away from each other

so you can fight a war? Didn't I promise old Magnus you wouldn't have to battle alone anymore?"

"Aye, ye did, but twas nae a promise for ye tae give. Ye tried tae protect me, but I have tae fight now. There is a war and—"

"Can't we have peace?"

"Nae, I have seen the future, mo reul-iuil, tis a bleak and violent place. You and I walked through it lookin' for Archie. There were tent cities spreadin' through the valleys and so much despair. Bella had aligned herself with Roderick and deserted Archie. But worse — King Roderick has decided tae renew the charges against ye, he is callin' ye a murderer. Bella has taken his side and she is helping him tae locate ye—"

"She is such a bitch, I hate her so much."

"Ye have every reason tae, she becomes so much worse. I will deal with her."

I said, "So the future wants me on murder charges?"

"Aye, they winna quit until they have ye."

"And being king is the only way?"

"I have had men beg me tae help them. I was their king and I ignored their pleas, I believed I could live a quiet life here with—"

"Our life is not quiet."

He chuckled. "Tis true. Lady Mairead has said ye are my weakness and I think—"

"I find that to be a ridiculous thing to say."

"I was going tae finish — I think she is wrong. You are my strength, but this time I need ye tae stay here. You bring out m'better nature. In these dealings I might need tae be barbaric." He gave me a sad smile.

"What will you need to do with Bella?"

He quietly said, "I daena ken."

"Okay." I nodded. "Yeah, okay, though I would like to be the one to kill her when it comes to that."

"You daena mean it, mo ghradh, yer days of killin' people are over, I hope. I ken ye can protect yerself but I daena want ye tae suffer in taking a life anymore."

"You would protect me from that?"

"Aye, I will always protect ye."

We stared into each other's eyes for a moment, then I asked, "So what you're saying is you've left me as Old Kaitlyn and have come back to rescue me as Young Kaitlyn. Was I terribly old? An old crone? Gray hair down to my butt?"

"Twas barely two months ago."

I grinned. "Was I wrinkled? Did I have a beard down to here?"

"You were gray and wizened and stooped over, verra beautiful."

"Very funny." I took a deep breath. "Archie called me 'Mammy'?"

"He made ye so happy ye cried on it and got verra strange in yer head about the whole experience."

"I imagine." I leaned back on my hands. "None of this is as bad as you made it out to be."

"I haena really begun, mo reul-iuil. This is only the beginnin' of it. Daena come after me. I will come home when I am finished."

"Okay, that's pretty bad." I frowned. "For how long?"

"Long enough tae bring m'kingdom under m'control. I will have tae do it as long as it takes. I winna come home right away—"

"Why?"

He put on a falsetto voice, "So if I am aged by the experience, ye winna be much younger than me. Twould be too unfair."

I batted his shoulder playfully. "There's a chance you might be old? Couldn't you come back before, tell me what's happening?"

"Every time I come home I set the time. And if I need tae return I will create a loop. There is a risk in it, ye ken."

"I do, but you could come next week or the next...?"

"I believe it should be longer, a few months here so I winna loop on anythin'. Nae risk. I want tae get ye tae a place where our lives arna a risk anymore. We should set a date so we daena have tae worry on each other. When would ye like me tae come home?"

"What about our anniversary? July 2nd, is that long enough?"

"Aye. I will be home on our anniversary, mo reul-iuil. I will tell ye all about it then."

One by one I put my feet around his ass and playfully pulled his hips forward. "And I will welcome you home."

"I ken ye will, because ye are a verra good wife."

"How long are you staying now?"

"I thought I would come and talk tae ye and then I would go... I haena changed the time of the future — Roderick is nae vanquished, I do need tae go..."

I pulled his hips even closer. "But if you think about it, my love, you're planning to go away for months and months, long months, and I won't see you until July 2nd, that's six months for me. We ought to spend a little time with each other, to tide us over until..."

He grinned. "Och, tis verra hard tae deny ye when ye are wearin' this wee shirt and these wee undergarmies, tis an enticement." He scooped my shirt off over my head and tossed it away. "Och, and now ye arna wearin' a shirt. How am I tae control m'desire for ye?"

"And if you kiss me right here," I pointed at the front of my throat, "I'll be without my undergarmies too."

"Like a magic." He kissed me where I asked while I wriggled from my panties. I lay back pulling him onto me.

He was fully clothed but that was so freaking hot, pressing my hips against his wool kilt, running my hands down his fabric bound shoulders. He was kissing me, hot breaths and — I changed my mind, it would be a lot hotter without the kilt.

I pushed him off me, stood on the mattress, slid his shirt up off his arms, and flung it away.

He stood beside the bed, wrapped his arms around my hips, and held me, his head pressed against my chest. My arms holding his hair.

We had been playful, fast, and funny, but now— "Suddenly it's real. You're really going away?"

His forehead nodded up and down, an urgent pressing against my skin. I dropped down to the bed and pulled him with me, a slow crawl to a full wrap around each other. He pulled my thigh to his waist and we held each other as tightly as we could, an embrace that meant — *I don't want to let you go.*

I whispered, "I will miss you."

He nodded, clutching my face in his strong hands, he kissed me so deeply.

"Please come home."

He stroked my hair back from my cheek. "Always."

Something about the way he said it, as if he was memorizing the way my eyes looked into his, caused tears to well up and spill down my cheeks.

"I can't believe we have to do this again."

"Again and again. Always. I daena think we can ever stop coming back tae each other."

"Yes, again, my love. Once more, but then that will be it, you regain your kingdom and then we are done. It's what you promised in the beginning and you'll have made good on it. After that we can be together."

"Aye. Then I will return for you and ye will serve me a bowl of ice cream because I winna have it in such a long—"

"They have ice cream in the future."

"Wheesht, I winna have it, daena confuse me, ice cream is only here."

"Oh, I understand, go on."

"And then you and I will go tae my kingdom. We will go see Lizbeth and Sean. We will go wherever and whenever we want, without worry, because I will be the king and you will be the queen."

"I like the sound of that."

He kissed my cheek. "I am sorry ye are crying."

"I do sometimes, you know."

"I do."

His hand slowly glided down my body, around my ass, and up my thigh, while my hands began doing their own traveling on the planes and curves of his form, memorizing the geography of him, the bound shoulders, the tight arms. My tongue explored the soft interior of his mouth.

I tasted and licked while my gliding palms brought forth heat. His motions made me writhe and press along with his palm and to wriggle in anticipation as his fingers felt along my folds and curves and my interior places of heat and wet.

There was a sexy loving-ness in our moves — not of play and flirt, but of caress and love, of deep and familiar and desire with solace and melancholy in the aching spots and small whispers, not of words but of the moans, that meant, you and I my love, and *yes* and *aye* —

and as he entered me with a sigh, and we pushed and pulled, together and apart, again and again, whispers and caresses, slow and tantalizing with the friction, we stayed wrapped, tight, not a space between us, but still I pressed more, deeper, wanting, closer — I arched to meet him and felt waves rising through me, *oh god oh god oh god*, his breath caught as he felt my rhythms and joined me. His mouth pressed against my temple, his hips thrust against me, and I held on as he pushed and pushed and pushed again, my nose pressed to his skin, breathing him in, exhaling him away, and with a rush he was finished.

I was feeling that glorious press, as the weight of him pushed me down, settled me, held me within his gravity.

"I love you."

"I ken ye do mo reul-iuil, ye bear me with a strength and patience that I strive tae deserve."

"You do deserve, you deserve so much more than—"

"Than ye? Than Archie? Than a kingdom? Nae, my love, but I will strive for it. I will gain ye back, this is the first step." He rolled off me and stared up at our ceiling fan, slowly twisting.

"You will need tae go tae your appointment for your grandmother's last will and testament. I am sorry I winna be here for ye."

"That's okay, I can do this."

"Good." He turned his head toward mine, his taut neck stretching to his collarbone, strength and power at his weakest point, his throat. I sat up to lean over and kiss him there.

He said, "If I daena leave now I might never and then we winna have any hope tae rescue Archie, tae set a new course—"

"I know." I nodded.

I remembered, "Hey guess what? When Lady Mairead took you, you didn't have this..." I pulled his sporran from the bedside drawer. "It has the shark tooth I gave you yesterday morning, for protection, and there's a photo and yeah, I'm glad you came back for it."

"Thank ye, twill be verra protective." He began dressing in his kilt.

"No shower first?"

"Nae," he joked, "I winna shower the whole time I am gone, so I will carry yer scent with me."

I rolled my eyes with a laugh. "That is disgusting and romantic and also, no one will be able to stand getting close to you, so it might be another protective shield, perfect, do that. But if someone says, a month from now, 'Ew, what's that smell?' do not say, 'My wife' or I'll... I don't know what I will do, but don't test me."

He grinned. "I winna want tae be on your bad side, I only want tae be on yer inside."

I grinned. "I like what you did there." I crawled off the bed and went to my drawer for some clothes.

FORTY-FOUR - MAGNUS

We emerged from the bedroom just in time for breakfast. Quentin had alerted the rest of the house tae the fact that I was home and nae longer a diversion in the future. They asked what happened and I said, "I am loopin'. It has only been a few weeks of time, but..."

Emma was givin' Ben a strawberry. "I thought you weren't to loop? Why would you?"

"King Roderick sent soldiers and grabbed Ben, I fought them off and got him back, twas a moment there..." I shook my head and patted Ben on the back, rememberin' his cries in m'arms. He had been so scared. "...they took Archie and Kaitlyn."

Chef Zach and Emma exchanged a look.

Chef Zach said, "Okay then, good. Sounds like a do-over is a good idea. What are we going to do differently?"

I reached intae the bowl of strawberries and dipped one through whipped cream "You are goin' tae carry on with yer days, keepin' each other safe. I am leavin' tae go tae the future and fight for my kingdom, so I can keep us all protected."

I joked, "I hae already told ye this three times."

Chef Zach laughed. "Well, I can be a bit of a stoner, I don't remember what you told me a month from now. So this is our last meal together for a while?"

"Och, aye." I sat on a barstool and Kaitlyn put her arm around my shoulders.

A few minutes later Hayley and James came intae the kitchen. James said, "Morning Magnus, we were on an errand for you this morning. Aren't you supposed to be in the future distracting someone while we steal some stuff?"

"Och, you were goin' as well, Master James?"

"Hell yeah, of course I'm going. I can't freaking wait, this time travel thing sounds epic — now we don't get to go?"

Kaitlyn said, "Not this time, but I promise Magnus and I will take you somewhere soon."

Mistress Hayley said, "But I got in all my gear! I got a couple of days off work. You were creating a diversion and I was going to go steal a bunch of vessels. I'm freaking wearing cargo pants, Mags, I don't wear those for just anyone. This was going to be a big heroic moment." She sighed.

I went tae the pantry and pulled a bottle of water from the shelf and said, "Master Quentin, could ye take me for a drive?"

Then I said, "Could ye accompany us, Mistress Hayley? I need tae speak tae ye in private."

We parked the Mustang on the south end and Mistress Hayley followed me out ontae the beach.

"What's happening, Mags? You don't usually need to talk to me privately."

I hesitated, watchin' her. "I have been in conversation with ye, a month in the future, and ye have asked me tae do somethin' for ye." I passed her the bottle of water. "Could ye put this in a pocket?"

"This is so mysterious. What, is it a surprise?"

"Aye."

I took out a vessel.

"Wait, am I going on a... what are you doing?"

"You went with Kaitlyn tae steal the vessels. You were verra heroic actually and I thank ye for it, but on yer way home ye had an accident—"

She squinted her eyes. "What are you up to?"

"I am tellin' ye." I grinned. "You went tae the year 1704. Now I have messed up the timeline and you have asked me tae help ye redo it."

"So I accidentally go to the past and... wait, how long?"

"Nae long. A day. Probably. I canna tell ye. Twill mess it up."

Her eyes went wide.

I twisted the ends of the vessel and checked tae make sure the numbers were right.

"Magnus Campbell, are you kidnapping me, am I being people trafficked? You're coming for me? What could this be? You didn't put me in a dress, where am I going? Should I be pissed off? I feel like I should be pissed."

"Nae, daena be angry, I am doin' this under orders from yerself."

I handed her the buzzing vessel. The wind rose around us, the storm clouds rising and roiling.

She clutched the vessel to her chest. Her hair whipping all around.

I said, "You are the one that is lost, stay put I will come get ye."

She yelled, "Promise this is going to be good?"

"I promise. Twas verra brave of ye tae do, but ye told me ye would do it again. Oh, and if any Campbell men ask, ye are married, daena forget."

"Okay!" She clamped her eyes shut.

I shielded my eyes from the whipping sand and backed away from the point in the storm that was a fury of wind and lightning. I made it tae the car, climbed inside and turned tae look through the glass.

The storm was wild and dark and I couldna see anyone within it anymore, but where Hayley had been was a shadow, a darkness, an echo of herself, fadin' and then gone.

They were all waitin' when Quentin and I returned.

"What did you do?" asked Kaitlyn, as I opened the door.

"Mistress Hayley asked me tae help her repeat somethin' that happened tae her. It involves Fraoch."

"Wait — what? Fraoch?"

"Aye. I will go and retrieve her after a month has passed, and she will be here tomorrow. You will need tae listen tae her on her feelings for Fraoch, they are verra strong feelings."

"What the — *what?*"

"Tis all I can tell ye. She likes him." I grinned.

Kaitlyn said, "This is not, I don't know — what? He is missing a tooth, he's all cocky and such a fricking guy."

I shrugged. "Mistress Hayley will see him in a verra different way."

· · ·

The rest of us gathered around the table for a final mornin' meal, full of laughter. I teased them on the story of Hayley and Fraoch, not givin' away too much, only tellin' bits of it.

I dinna want tae tell them anythin' about the future in case I changed the present. Twas complicated tae know what had happened, to have knowledge that others dinna have, Lady Mairead had warned me.

Our conversation turned to that last moment in Savannah when General Reyes ambushed us. I said, "I need tae ken all that happened when ye escaped to my Safe House in the year 2382."

Kaitlyn asked, "When we got there, or right before we left? You don't want to be there at the same time, right?"

"Nae, I want tae ken the final moments afore ye left."

She explained, "Hammond was commanding your army. Roderick was attacking. Lady Mairead was there..."

Kaitlyn looked like she was attemptin' tae remember. "It was a while ago, so much has happened since. It was scary, Roderick's forces were at the walls. I sent Quentin and Beaty home because Beaty was sick—"

Madame Emma said, "Ben and I came home then, too."

Kaitlyn said, "Right. Then Hayley, Zach, Lady Mairead, and I went to the guest wing looking for Bella and..." Her brow furrowed. "We went to get Archie, to get him to safety, Magnus, but someone had already gotten Bella and Archie out of the house."

She clapped her hand to her mouth. "We're there, but you might also be there, this all might be one big loop. You need to be so so so careful that I don't see you, that none of us sees you."

She added, "But also, check for Archie, if he's there... maybe you're..." Her eyes went distant. "Just be careful. This is treading really close to being a dangerous time loop."

"I will be careful, but I should go."

. . .

248 | DIANA KNIGHTLEY

I took a few of the guns, a helmet, and bulletproof vest, from the supplies they gathered for their trip to get the vessels. I put on my favorite pair of boots.

I asked Kaitlyn, "What weather was it?"

"Cold in the morning, rainy."

Quentin drove us tae the public access at the south end again, Kaitlyn accompanied me to the beach. "I'm not crying as much as I might have expected."

"Aye ye are being verra strong for me, I appreciate it."

Her chin trembled, tears filled her eyes. "Now I feel like an ass for crying."

I shook m'head. "I appreciated ye are strong for me, I also appreciate that ye weep for me goin' away. Both are needed and I thank ye for them."

She leaned on the rail of the boardwalk. "When I think of all the times I have tried to keep you here, with me, together, and now you're telling me you have to go and I'm just..." She sighed.

"You are acceptin' of it, because ye are tired of battlin'. I see it in your eyes." I brushed my thumb down her cheek, dryin' a tear that was slidin' down her soft skin. "Tis okay tae be tired of the struggle. I prayed tae God for an answer and I found strength through his answer. I ken what has tae be done, and I will take it upon my own shoulders. Twill be okay, ye daena need tae be strong tae protect me. I will do this."

"I am, I'm so tired. I just want you to be safe and all of us to..."

"I ken, ye want peace and quiet. You deserve it, mo reul-iuil. I will make it happen for ye..."

I pulled her forward to my chest and held her tight. I kissed her hair. "I winna be gone for long."

"Our anniversary?"

"Aye. I will be home then."

"I'm going to watch you go..."

I backed down the deck.

She remained, smilin' on me, leaned against the railin', a bit of sun on the tips of her hair, whipping across her face in the breeze.

She pulled a long strand loose from her lips. "I will see you soon, Highlander, be safe, stay alive."

I backed down the steps. "I love ye, mo reul-iuil. I will stay alive, this is nae the end of our story."

My feet on the sand, I strode over the dunes to the beach, and looked down on my vessel.

I set it tae take me tae the year 2382. The wind rose above me.

I looked back on her for one last time. She waved. I nodded. And then I jumped.

FORTY-SIX - MAGNUS

I landed in a spot about four miles beyond the Safe House. The spot had been chosen as the get away point and I had wondered if Colonel Hammond would have his eyes on it, but there was nae one tae meet me.

I lumbered tae my feet as soon as I was able, strapped my small bag tae my shoulder, set my helmet on, and began the long walk tae the Safe House.

When I neared the house, there were soldiers surroundin' it, helicopters on the lawn, tanks and armored vehicles ridin' the edges, and drones filled the air. Farther in the distance I could see the front line of my army fightin' Roderick's men — too close tae the safe house. A missile landed just tae the north, distant, but there were people inside the house. They were in danger.

I picked up my pace and as I came tae the Safe House held my hands in the air — lights blared on, blindin' me.

"Don't shoot!" With an elbow over my face, I shielded m'eyes.

I dropped my bag tae the ground. "I am nae armed, I need tae speak tae Colonel Hammond!"

I was rushed and surrounded by soldiers and once they understood I was the king, ushered tae a barricaded shelter where Colonel Hammond had the central command of the troops.

"King Magnus!" His smile was wide and warm.

I tried tae return it but m'opinion of him was strained by what I kent. I couldnae trust him, but I needed his help, so I had tae use him for m'aims, but I would always need tae watch him for signs of deceit.

Colonel Hammond asked, "Have you seen Queen Kaitlyn? She requested ATVs yesterday. She and Colonel Quentin Peters and two other civilians were on an errand to the past, I have seen storms behind the house and—"

"Colonel Hammond, tis imperative that ye daena tell Kaitlyn that I am here. I have looped ontae her actions, she must complete them, but I ken the Safe House is about tae fall tae Roderick. He is tryin' tae draw me out tae fight. I am here, but I canna change Kaitlyn's actions or we will lose this war."

"What do I need to do?"

"Just give her what she needs."

Hammond and I looked over the maps and discussed our battle plan — Roderick had most of his forces here, since the royal family was here, but I would remove Archie.

Then Hammond would remain tae fight on this front, while I would lead forces against Roderick's troops to the west.

I dinna ken if this would work. I wished I had known Colonel Hammond's strategy afore he lost this war. I wanted tae win it this time, but I had nae way tae ken if these were new plans or the same — the difference though was that I was here now. I had tae hope my authority would be enough tae change it.

Hammond spoke intae the radio, then reported what was

said. "Colonel Quentin Peters has left for Florida with his wife, she is ill... they expect Queen Kaitlyn any moment."

"Where is Archie?" Hammond pointed at the guest wing of the Safe House. I said, "I will need more helicopters for a diversion. If Kaitlyn discusses any of this with you, about Archie, or my presence, or anythin'—"

"My orders are to lie to the Queen?"

"Aye."

*W*ith four soldiers behind me I rushed tae the house, and banged on the door.

"Bella, let me in!"

The door opened and I entered tae find Bella, held in the arms of the man, John Mitchell, and Archie in his carrier on the floor.

Bella threw herself against m'chest. "My Magnus, I knew you—"

"There is a waitin' helicopter, grab your things."

I picked up Archie by the handle on the carrier. Soldiers yelled, "Go, go, go, go," as we raced from the house tae the waiting helicopter, rotors turnin', wind roarin' — Archie was terrified, screamin' and wailing.

Bella buckled intae the seat. I buckled a strap across Archie's carrier, strappin' it down, then commanded the pilot tae deliver them tae a bunker where I would meet them.

Three helicopters and close tae thirty drones rose intae the air at once and spread through the skies,

Explosions blasted the ground around us, gunshots through the sky, cannons and missiles and ground shaking blasts.

The helicopter carryin' Archie was hidden within their number. I watched, holdin' m'breath, willin' it tae stay safe as it flew.

I looked over m'shoulder at the Safe House as it lost power.

Hammond said, "Queen Kaitlyn is inside, she wants tae speak tae me."

"I remind ye, if she kens I am here we will lose the war, Hammond, guard this news carefully."

He left for the house.

I spoke tae the air around us. "Keep going, Kaitlyn, stay safe. Daena worry on Archie. I have him now, twill be okay."

Hammond returned a while later, "Queen Kaitlyn is going to the castle ruins, should I attend her?"

"Nae, send a soldier. I need ye here."

Then while commandin' the troops on the grounds around the Safe House, I watched as storms rose above us, and one group after another left the grounds, until I kent m'family was out and safe.

The bunker was within a cliff. There was a spare apartment meant for a commander, but I gave it over tae Bella, though she was furious on the matter. She had only Mrs Johnstone tae look after her and seemed tae think she required more help.

I lived in the bunkhouse with the soldiers, tae give Bella room tae be as irritated and fussy as she wanted tae be without bringin' me intae it.

John Mitchell looked exhausted and harried but I dinna

speak tae him on the matter. I visited with Archie and passed m'days livin' and breathin' the decisions of war.

Hammond and I were in constant contact on decisions and I came tae rely on him again, always remindin' myself that he had turned against me, takin' Roderick's side, the utmost of treasonous actions, and I needed tae keep up m'guard around him.

On the third week Hammond crossed me.

I gave him an order and he changed it on the ground. At the end of the day he had been correct tae do it, but I had a fury in m'chest over it. I kent that he was a step away from the disloyalty that had marked his career and so I demanded he come tae the bunker by mornin' and when he was led intae the command room I sent the men from the room.

We stood across from each other while I sized him up. On the walls surroundin' us were the shiftin' videos of carnage and battles and war. I had grown used tae them through the years, had learned tae rely on them.

"Colonel Hammond, I am havin' an issue with ye, tis perhaps unfair — I have seen yer future. There ye had a career that is now clothin' ye in disloyalty, of which ye are unaware. Since tis only fair tae question ye on deeds of which ye are sensible — ye were Donnan's man, were nae ye? My father?"

"Yes, Your Highness."

"You had a relationship with my mother, if I am tae believe what I hear from her, but ye were first and foremost a protector of Donnan the Second."

"Yes, I..."

"Then, when twas convenient tae ye, you became Samuel's man."

"I had no—"

"Twould be enough tae hold against ye, but then ye came tae the aid of Queen Kaitlyn. You were an advisor tae me, and a commander in my army. I have every reason tae trust ye, without question, yet I have been tae the future, twas a future that had me lose tae Roderick and I have seen ye uniformed as his commander."

I watched how that set heavy on his shoulders.

"Tis a burden on ye, tae be judged by a future action, I ken. I am tryin' tae be fair, tae nae judge ye, based on the actions of a future I am strivin' tae change. But with this knowledge, how am I expected tae trust ye will have my—"

"I have done nothing but command your troops to the best of my—"

"The exception, of course, a day ago, ye disregarded m'order and now I am left with two recourses, one, tae let ye go, or two, tae have ye strung up for treason."

"Don't," he added, "Your Highness."

"Why nae?"

"Because I am loyal and will fight on your side."

"Why, ever, would I believe ye tae be loyal?" There was a knock on the door and I called, "Come in!"

A soldier entered. His eyes shifted back and forth between his king and his colonel and to the video on the wall of an explosion on a local road. He said, "Your Highness, you're wanted on an urgent call..."

"Have them hold, I am almost done."

He bowed from the room.

As soon as the door closed, I lunged, grabbing Colonel Hammond by his shirt, shovin' him against the wall, growlin', "I daena have time tae discuss or test — you have asked me tae trust ye beyond what I have seen with m'own eyes. I canna have a traitor in my command. I am goin' tae have tae relieve ye of duty."

I was furious and breathin' heavy, glarin' intae his eyes.

"You have to trust me. I don't have anywhere else to go."

My brow furrowed. "Why nae? Ye could live your life, nae fight anymore. In yer place I would take the chance in a second."

"I can't tell you because you will kill me for it."

"I daena understand. What have ye done tae deserve tae die? Ye have been my commander."

"I haven't done anything but be born."

"Ye have tae explain yer meanin'. All of us die, but I believe it takes more than bein' born tae deserve tae go." I let go of his shirt and shoved him for good measure.

He collected himself, straightening his uniform over his barrel chest.

"Explain, I am runnin' out of time and might need tae kill ye just tae bring this conversation tae an end."

He exhaled a deep breath. "You and I share a grandfather. I am your cousin. I have a claim, that I don't want, to your throne."

"What dost ye mean?"

"My father was Lidan. He was killed by Tanrick many years ago in the arena. Donnan, my uncle, retrieved me from my home. I was eighteen. He told me I could serve him or die in the arena. I chose serving him. In exchange he hid my parentage so I would not be challenged. Since Donnan was killed, I have had to pledge my allegiance to my uncle Samuel, and now my cousin."

"Why daena ye just quit and leave?"

"I know that wherever I am, whenever I go, I will not be safe. There will always be a brother or a cousin to find me. Living in hiding and fear is no way to live. I just want to live without worry. If I serve my king I will have foreknowledge of what is coming."

I leaned against the desk. "I understand that wish, but what of your family?"

"I don't have one. I have not been free to have one."

"Oh."

We stared at each other across the command room.

I asked, "Ye daena want the throne?"

"No. Never. I can not imagine a worse fate."

I nodded. "I agree." I let out a deep breath of air.

The large projection loomed on the walls, enclosin' us — two men with a war tae wage, we dinna want tae fight but we had tae win.

"I have interrupted the work for too long, I need tae give this room over tae the soldiers again."

"I understand."

"My apologies, Colonel Hammond, for threatenin' ye. As my commander, as long as I am king, ye will have safety within my service. I canna hold yer bloodline against ye." I added, "How can I? Tis the same as mine."

"You can call me Hammie, the other is too formal. And I'd like to get back to work, Your Highness, this war won't win itself and now I really need you to remain the king."

FORTY-EIGHT - KAITLYN

The day after Magnus left, Hayley returned by storm.

I mostly thought Magnus would accompany her, so I raced to meet them, with Quentin driving, but there in the sand — just Hayley.

I tried very hard not to be disappointed.

I dropped into the sand beside her and stroked her arm. "Hey babe, ready to get up? Where'd you go?"

Her eyes fluttered open and she looked up into mine. She frowned the kind of frown that bordered on comical, the kind that you have to really work on to get it to frown so much, and said, "Oh no, I think I made a mistake."

Once she was ready, Quentin helped me pull her to standing. We helped her teeter to the car and climb into the back seat. As we drove her home, she had a dazed look on her face, her brow drawn down, her expression confused and bordering on hopeless as she watched the houses slide by. I kept looking at her over my shoulder. Quentin checked her with the rear view.

"How's it going, Hayley?"

"Not good, I think..." Her voice trailed off.

I met eyes with Quentin. "Want to talk about it? Where'd you go? How long?"

She sighed. "I'll tell you about it when we get to the house."

∽

At the house she ate a meal that was enough for ten men, so much meat and cheese I warned her she was going to get sick.

She said, "Bring it on! Better sick than starving."

She dipped rolled up roast beef into a rich cheese sauce, moaning rapturously, swigging a dark ale to wash it down, until she groaned collapsing on her arms on the counter.

"I was so freaking hungry." Then she vomited all over her lap.

I held her skirt up so it wouldn't drip on the floor, and directed her to the bathroom to strip down. And then I sat on the bathroom counter while she showered. "So where were you? Eighteenth century by the looks of it, but maybe you should give me the details."

"I was with Fraoch and Lizbeth. She's wonderful by the way, she sends you her warmest regards."

I said, "I miss her so much, she's awesome isn't she? How long were you there?"

She was lathering suds in her hair. "A month, a whole fucking month, because your husband promised to come back for me after one day, but guess what? He lied."

I clamped my smile down in my teeth. "I'm sure he had a very good reason?"

She waved that off, "Whatever," finished rinsing her hair and stepped out of the shower, wrapping in a towel for her body and another one for her hair.

She asked for my big fluffy robe to complete the comfort level she required after, as she put it, "Your husband kidnapped me and stranded me in the eighteenth century."

I said, "I can see you're in a mood, how about you come to the living room and tell me all about it."

She sat down on the couch in a big huff. "I'm hungry again."

"No wonder, and how long were you in the eighteenth century?"

"Long enough to eat blood sausage."

Chef Zach grimaced. "I'm getting you cookies and a glass of ginger ale, stat."

She wouldn't talk until the plate of cookies and glass of ginger ale were in front of her and she had started eating. Then she leaned back on the comfortable couch wrapped in all the luxurious white fluffy terry and settled her eyes on me. "I saw Magnus, he said to tell you that he loves you very, very much."

"Aw, that's really awesome." I sighed. "He's been gone for a full day and it feels like forever."

She squinted her eyes and looked at me long.

Finally I said, "Wait, how long has he been gone?"

"He said it had been nine months."

"Oh. Whoa."

"Yeah. He said to tell you that he thinks the war against Roderick is turning, and there will be an end to it in time. He looks really tired though, Katie, and sad. He was glad to see Lizbeth and Sean and Fraoch."

I sighed, "Remind me again, why he can't come home?"

"I think he wants to get this done. He's worried that if he comes home before he's beaten Roderick's army that he'll give Roderick the chance to take over again. He sent this letter and this present. He might explain it better." She dug through the leather pouch she had carried with her and brought out a package wrapped in a square of cloth, a deep vivid royal blue wool. It was Magnus's favorite color.

Inside was a leather bound book, a journal, beside it what looked like a long jewelry box. I pried the box open to find a gorgeous gold fountain pen. I clutched it to my chest while I opened the book, blank, except for, on the first page, in my husbands scrawling hand:

> And I will come again, my Luve,
> Tho' it were ten thousand mile.

And under it, he wrote:

The book is for ye tae list what we will do next... I will see ye on July 2, 2020

Love,

Magnus

"Oh." Tears welled up. I clutched the book to my chest too.

Hayley nodded.

Then she sighed.

Then she said, "We get it, we know, he's the most amazing romantic man in the world, but can we please talk about Fraoch? I think I... I don't know... Like, he wore rose-scented lotion for me."

I placed my present on the side table, wiped my eyes, and attempted to focus for my friend. "He did what?"

And then she told me the whole story.

And after she told me the whole story we wrote a list of pros and cons using my luxurious new gold pen.

She added many more pros than cons but they were ridiculous pros, like she could 'bring him here to get his tooth fixed.'

I explained that she wasn't doing the list right.

We finally agreed to 'agree in principle' that she might need to go see what comes next with Fraoch.

We also agreed that, because she could go back to any time of her choosing, she would wait until after Magnus was home. And that if we could Magnus and I could accompany her to the past. All of us together.

To protect her. And support her.

"That would be good," she said, "it sucked not having you guys there, when Magnus arrived everyone treated me so differently, so much better."

"Good, when he is home we'll all go together. You can tell Fraoch you're sorry you lied to him and then, you can spend some time with him, with us there, too."

"Like a double date."

"Exactly. A double date. And you will be able to decide what comes next."

"Maybe I stay."

"God, would you, Hayley? Really?"

"I might. I might if he needed me to."

"You are a terrible arse."

"I have to be to keep up with you."

FORTY NINE - KAITLYN

The next few days I spent hanging out, resting, relaxing. I couldn't remember the last time this happened. It was melancholy, but also, not.

I felt strong. I knew in the marrow of my bones that my husband would be home in a few months time, exactly as he said he would be. I also knew from the tip of my head to the ends of my toes that I was for perhaps the first time in my married life, safe.

He was creating the future for me — one in which no one would be hunting for my murderous ass. One I would be the queen of.

And if he accomplished all of that I would make damn sure the future didn't have that bitch Bella in it.

I hoped it would include sweet Archie.

Magnus said Archie had been almost three years old and that he called me Mammy.

I wrote in my journal a lot.

I walked on the beach looking for shark teeth, enjoying some solitude. And then I had an appointment with the lawyers about

AGAIN MY LOVE | 265

my grandparents' estate, much larger than I ever imagined. Grandpa Jack had done very well for them in tech stock.

I had some of the paintings appraised. My father's investments of Magnus's money made for a nice pile, but then also, one day I was looking through the finances and found an old British bank account in my name with tons of money inside. It had been receiving investments and deposits for over a hundred years, a lot of European real estate and never before seen art — I was the main beneficiary.

It all added up to an amazing amount far beyond what I imagined ever needing.

And then one night about three weeks in, Hayley showed up with a six pack. "Beer!"

Zach teased her, "I shop, I have beer stocked in the fridge."

"Sure, but you get all judgy about your beer. This is my beer. It's light and delicious. And I can have as many as I want."

She put it down on the counter and started popping tops. "Beaty, you about killed me when you changed your status from 'single' to 'in a relationship'. I was thinking, 'How crazy is that? An eighteenth century married lady just figured out Facebook.'" She handed her a beer, then took it away. "I forgot, your married ass is underage."

Beaty giggled. "I like Facebook verra much, did ye see the picture I posted tae day? Tis of Ben?"

"I did, did you take the quiz I sent you: How to Know What Character of the Office You Are?"

"Aye, I was Michael Scott. I daena think I understood the questions."

We all laughed.

Quentin popped the lid off a Coke bottle and brought one to Beaty too. He was enjoying his job these days. He took a shift as a guard and then got to relax, because most of our danger was over. "I'm thinking you're a lot more like Pam."

Beaty giggled. "I think I am like Dwight. I do love beets."

We all cracked up about that one.

Hayley said, "I was thinking, since you're all gathered here — what if you bought a house?"

I looked around at the interior of the beach house. "This one is pretty good, plus this is the one Magnus knows and..."

Hayley leaned forward. "But does it fit you?"

"Not really, the style is pretty weird, too much glass, and there are not enough bedrooms, for sure."

"Exactly, I have to sleep on the couch when I want to come have a beer with my bestie. Plus, I'm bored and have too much to think about so I spent the last couple of days looking at real estate. I found you a house. And I would like to mention, there is an island real estate agent, your mother, that I'm kind of in competition with. I would love to sell you this house."

"What kind of a house?"

"It's a mother-flipping mansion, and it's on the beach, on the south end. It has wings, and a circular drive, seven bedrooms, eight bathrooms, you're welcome." She swigged from her bottle, then added, "It's a half mile from Amelia Stables. An easy walk."

"Near Sunny?"

"Aye," she joked.

"Oh my god, I don't even have to look. Can I afford it?"

"The question is, can you afford not to? Also, Zach, Emma, Quenny, what do you all think about it?"

Emma said, "Sounds great, we really need a bigger place."

I looked around at all their faces. Magnus's family, packed into this beach rental, and he would be home on our anniversary and— "I could buy it for him for his anniversary?"

"That's way too fucking extravagant," said Zach. "I mean, are you trying to kill him? You can't buy a man a house for a gift. He will never live up to it. He'll never be able to top it."

"Oh, right, so you think he will mind if I move him while he's away?"

Zach said, "Nah, I'm kidding. Magnus won't care at all. You know where he wants to live? With you and me and Sunny. That's it. If we're all in a bigger house he won't care as long as the three of us are there."

"Truer words were never spoken."

We all raised our drinks.

I said, "To Magnus, King of the future, and a Man of Simple Tastes living here in Florida. Give him a private chef, a warm bed, and a horse, and he's completely happy."

We drank.

Hayley grinned. "So I can sell you the house?"

"I'd like to see it tomorrow, but yeah, let's buy a house."

FIFTY - MAGNUS

I landed in Paris in the year 1904, nae long after Kaitlyn and I had left. I was almost three years older though, and had the weight of the years on me. But I had won the war. Roderick's forces were down tae an insignificant threat in the eastern region and he had gone intae hidin'. I had soldiers huntin' for him, but I had given up carin'. Twould take too many years for him tae regain his forces, and I was enlargin' my own army, strengthenin' my armaments, and building loyalty in the ranks.

I remembered how my troops had turned on me in the past. I was keen on growing respect amongst m'men and it was working.

The kingdom was mine and I had solidified m'power. Now I needed tae ask for Lady Mairead's help in the matter.

I aimed m'landin' for a place farther from Paris and then I hiked intae the city. M'clothes were patterned on the uniform of the time, wool pants and coat, a vest and a linen shirt. I wore a hat and looked the part of a gentleman.

At Lady Mairead's house I rang the bell.

She called down, "Who is it?"

"Tis Magnus Campbell."

Her footsteps descended the stairs. She opened the door, but left me standin' on the stoop. "Why are ye here?" Her eyes squinted. "Ye have aged. Where is Kaitlyn?"

"I will explain when I am nae on the stoop of yer house."

"Fine," she huffed as she led me up tae the sitting room.

"You have been gone a week, yet ye have the look of someone who has been gone a verra long time. Out with it, what has happened?"

I sat in the same chair I had sat in with Kaitlyn perched on the arm, while Picasso had lounged with m'mother. "Where is the baby-man?"

"Pablo Picasso?" She laughed. "He is nae a baby-man, he is a genius. I have told ye this, but he is nae here. This morn he was in a fury about something and has stormed—"

I said, "Much as a baby-man would behave. I am surprised ye want tae care for a bairn, ye dinna want tae care on yer own."

"Verra funny, Magnus. I have sent Pablo home until he can return with an apology."

She smoothed her skirt. "Answer my question."

"I wasna able tae keep Kaitlyn and Archie safe, I—"

"I told ye this, I told ye that ye—"

"I ken what ye told me."

"But ye ignored me, though I have proven myself tae have abilities and wisdoms that are necessary in this game. Ye ignored me much as a baby-man might do."

I scoffed.

She shrugged, leveling her eyes on me while I continued, "Ye have also proven yerself tae have evil machinations and terrible judgments on character, so I canna trust ye on principle. Though in this instance, tis true, ye were right on this."

She raised her chin haughtily. "Good. So tell me what has happened."

"King Roderick's soldiers captured Kaitlyn and Archie. I couldna think where they had gone."

She winced. "I daena like the idea of that man having the upper hand on ye, Magnus. He daena deserve tae be a threat tae ye, he is—"

"Allow me tae finish, Lady Mairead. When I realized I couldna win against him, I restarted the game."

She leaned forward, her eyes wide. "What dost ye mean?"

"I went tae a time verra near the beginning of the war and intervened. I fought the war against Roderick and I have won, after almost three years, I have won."

Lady Mairead clapped her hands together. "Finally! Are ye then the king, Magnus?"

"Aye, I am King Magnus, construction is happening on m'castle, now called Caisteal Morag."

Her eyes gleamed in a way that looked as if she might cry.

I continued, "I have brought ye a present." I pulled a small box from my coat pocket and passed it tae her.

She pried open the lid and a tear did spill over and roll down her cheek.

I explained, "Tis a matchin' set — the Campbell crest on a brooch for ye, along with a sgian dubh."

She fingered the pieces delicately. "Tis beautiful."

"The brooch is inscribed for ye, after Mary Stuart, 'In My End is my Beginning.'"

"Och, this is verra beautiful, Magnus, I thank ye."

"I kent ye liked her words."

"I do, she was desperately ill-used. I have often wondered on going back tae advise her on her path, I suppose..." Her eyes grew wistful.

"Tae change her course might mean tae alter too much of your own."

"This is true." She folded her hands over the brooch and dagger. "Where is Kaitlyn?"

"I left her in Florida for the time so I could handle the war, the kingdom, and Archie, but now I would like tae return for her."

She closed the lid on the box. "So why are you here?"

"I would ask ye tae attend me tae the future. I have finished fighting, I need ye tae guard and guide the kingdom in m'absence. Also, you should see yer grandson."

"Aye, ye are lookin' haggard. I can see the war on yer face." She added, "As tae the other reason, grandsons of a young age are nae tae my interest. I will meet him when he is of an age tae be useful. And I daena ken if I want tae attend ye tae the kingdom. I have a life here, I—"

"Lady Mairead, I have done what ye asked, taken m'throne. I have a kingdom, and tis firmly mine. Ye have always wanted me tae ascend tae power, tis done. Tis time for ye tae come and assist me in m'duties."

She sighed. "I have always wanted tae be the Queen Mother, think of the intrigues!"

"Och aye, I ken ye have a great deal of fun here, but imagine the trouble ye can get intae in the year 2386?"

Her smile widened and her eyes twinkled. "But Pablo was goin' tae paint me again. He has a grand idea for the pose."

I grinned. "I remind ye I brought ye that bonny jewelry."

She sighed. "I could come back to see Pablo of course... and twill keep him guessin' if I leave him. He does thrive on melancholy and unease. Okay, I will come tae the future with ye, Magnus. Will I have tae deal with Kaitlyn?"

"Nae, our deal is that ye winna deal with her at all, ye will treat her with the respect she deserves or I will finish ye with the dagger I just gave ye, out of a sense of poetry."

"Ah, my son has threatened tae put a dagger through my heart, he sounds like a king. What else am I tae do, besides suffer yer wife? Must I also suffer your long beard?"

"Aye, Kaitlyn likes it, so I have grown it for her."

"Fine, what else?"

"You will also need tae respect Colonel Hammond, he has—"

She threw her hands up. "Why is he still there...?"

"Because I have decided it. I ken the reason he has done what he does and I trust him."

"Enlighten me."

"He shares m'bloodline. He is a cousin. He daena want the throne, but Donnan threatened tae kill him. His mischief with ye was because he lived under Donnan's threats. If I am king he is safe from challenge or intrigue. We have come tae a mutual agreement."

She huffed. "Well, fine, but he doesn't have a mutual agreement with me."

"As the king, I demand ye treat him with respect as an officer under m'command."

She rolled her eyes. "Fine, I have tae treat everyone with respect," she huffed, "And have ye given Bella a new chance tae redeem herself, tae prove she would make a good wife?"

"In the other future, the one I am writin' over, she has used ye terribly—"

"Me? How can that be?" Her brow furrowed as if she was searchin' her memory. "Bella kens I am her superior. I can break her in a second, she kens this, I daena believe she would..."

"She and Roderick had ye imprisoned, and they sentenced me tae death in the arena. Kaitlyn rescued us both—"

"Imprisoned! For what offense?"

"For nae bein' useful tae their aims, for bein' an impediment — do with the information what ye will."

I took a deep breath. "I ken that Bella has always been reactin' tae her circumstances. In this timeline I have tried tae be patient. I have given her a home, safety, the chance tae follow a different path, but I believe she haena been a good mother tae Archie and she has embarrassed me by seemin' out of my control—"

"I have heard enough, Magnus. Give me the date that I am expected." She reopened the box lid on the brooch and the dagger.

FIFTY-ONE - KAITLYN

e had spent the day touring our new home. It was perfect. But actually that wasn't the right word: perfect would have fit us. This was too big, too majestic, too gorgeous. A Kardashian would use this house to get away from the paparazzi, or some old duchess with a healthy dose of agoraphobia would hide here, or maybe if Batman needed a beach estate...

It wasn't the biggest house. I had seen big houses in Malibu, but this was Florida big, lavish and more than enough.

It was a hacienda style with large sprawling archways along outer hallways, a delicate cream color with an orange tile roof. There were large windows looking over decks, a pool, and a long walk to the beach. The beach was almost private because the house took up so much beachfront land.

The house was furnished with tile, wood, wrought iron, leather. It seemed perfect for Magnus — oversized, comfortable, built of sturdy materials. My husband would be comfortable here.

The house had wings, and enough bedrooms for Zach and

Emma to have a whole section of the main house with two bedrooms and an office.

Magnus and I had two bedrooms, an office, and a guest room, as Hayley pointed out, "For me!" with easy access to the main living room.

There was a separate guesthouse that Quentin and Beaty wanted. It had its own kitchen, living room, and bedroom, all that they needed. I had offered the guesthouse to Zach first, but he had pretended to hyperventilate at the idea of waking up every day to a teeny tiny kitchen. "It would be devastating to my psyche, Katie. I need to wake up and go down the hall to the main kitchen. I have to, it's important."

I said, "All right, it's a deal."

While we walked around touring and planning and picking our bedrooms, Beaty spent the whole time on her phone, scrolling. Finally, she said, while we were all standing in the kitchen, "How dost one get a hair color such as this?"

She turned her phone to show us a teenager with bright, peacock blue hair.

I grinned. "It's a hair dye."

"Can someone such as me dye m'hair?"

"You want to do it?"

She asked, "Quenny, mighten I dye m'hair the color of the sky?"

He took her phone and held it up to her hair. "Looks pretty, I don't see why not."

Emma said, "All right then, on the way back I'll stop at the drug store. When can we move in here, by the way?"

Hayley said, "It will take at least a couple of weeks or so. And while you're at the drug store can you get a few extra pairs of the gloves? I want to help Beaty turn blue."

∾

Emma placed a box of peacock blue hair dye in front of Beaty, "For you."

She tossed a package of latex gloves in front of Hayley, "For you."

And she placed a brown paper bag in front of me.

"What's this for?"

"You'll see."

Inside the bag was a pink box, a pregnancy test kit. I squinted my eyes and leveled them on Emma. "Why did you get me a pregnancy test?"

Emma shrugged. "I don't really know. I just have a feeling. You should pee on the stick."

I stared at it dumbfounded. "Why would you have a feeling and I not have a feeling? And now I have to pee on a stick? That's not usually the way these things work. When would I even have gotten pregnant? Magnus is away."

"Magnus jumped back into your life a little over four weeks ago, did you have sex?"

"Uh, yeah, of course."

"Well, I don't think you've been paying attention. Pee on the stick."

I glanced at Hayley. "Do you hear this, Hayley?"

"Yep. You should pee on the stick."

My eyes went wide. "This kind of feels like a mutiny."

We were all in my master bathroom. Beaty had a towel wrapped around her shoulders and parts of her hair piled on her head.

Emma was sitting on the counter reading the hair dye instructions. Hayley had on the gloves and was, "Preparing to turn this eighteenth century girl peacock blue."

I was sitting on the toilet, not preparing to urinate, trying to build up my courage *to* urinate. I didn't know why I needed courage, not really — until thirty minutes ago peeing on a stick hadn't even been a thing.

Now the box was sitting on my lap and I was freaking out.

What if I was pregnant?

What if I wasn't pregnant?

God, I couldn't pee on the stick. I should just wait until — Magnus's cocky smile, *when ye are squat as a broody hen we will ken.*

There was no way I was peeing on this stick.

FIFTY-TWO - MAGNUS

*L*ady Mairead had been in all the meetings of my cabinet, she understood m'wishes on the runnin' of the government. I dinna trust her, but I had enough threats over her tae keep her willfulness under control. Hammie was again m'closest advisor and kent my thoughts on issues.

I planned tae leave for Florida, and after some time there I would return with Kaitlyn. I wouldna be gone long, but there was nae way tae communicate with m'kingdom. Creatin' a government that would proceed in m'absence had been my aim.

The only issue I hadna solved was Bella's obstinance. She had her own estate and we had long ago decided nae tae speak tae each other. It had been easy because I was oft away at the battlefront.

She seemed tae believe that if I would just acquiesce, she could be the queen.

I refused her so we were at an impasse.

I hadna gotten to see Archie much with the pressing needs of the war. I had lived away from court and he was verra young.

Twas difficult tae see him, and I couldna bring him tae me on the front lines.

From afar I had tae watch him as he began tae walk and then talk. I wanted sole custody, but I was away fightin', and I kent a battle with Bella about Archie would cause many difficulties.

I wanted Archie tae have his mother. The trouble was, Bella wanted tae live a life of parties and wild excesses. I believed in the beginnin' that she was doin' it tae make me jealous, but as I dinna care she did it more and more. Twas nae about me at all, nor about Archie, twas only about Bella — her only thought.

When I was returned from war, m'heart was heavy with worry for him. I dinna ken if she had always been like this, or was now neglectin' him tae spite me. She was off travelin' and partyin' for weeks on end.

Security kept me informed. Bella's household staff was carin' for him. We argued about it. I told her she was nae tae leave him anymore, and she reformed for a couple of weeks. But then I was told she was away again, and there was naethin' tae be done as I was meeting with Hammond and fighting a war.

When Lady Mairead arrived over dinner one evenin' I brought up the subject of Bella. "She is neglectin' Archie."

Lady Mairead folded her napkin, finished with her meal. "Tis nae matter in it, Magnus, he will become a strong independent man, like his father. The more important matter is that her behavior is embarrassing tae the crown."

"I agree tis embarrassin'."

"I will set up a meetin' tae discuss it on the morrow. Will ye be able tae attend?"

"Aye."

Bella curtly nodded when I sat down across from her at the long conference table in Lady Mairead's office. Twas Lady Mairead's favorite way tae conduct business, pacin' around a long table, sneakin' up behind ye unawares, and threatenin' ye from behind yer chair.

The video images along the wall shewed Bella dancin' at a party the night afore with many different men. Lady Mairead asked, "What of this news? Do ye hear what they are sayin' on ye, Bella?"

Bella tossed her hair. "I do not pay attention to them."

The images on the wall shifted tae one where Bella was at another party with another man. "You should. You should have more wisdom about your conduct. You haena helped Magnus in ruling his kingdom—"

"Why should I? I am not the queen."

Lady Mairead turned tae me, "Has it caused ye trouble and worry tae have a mistress that is so poorly behaved? She is traipsing around the city without care while ye have been at war, barely attending tae her son — has it caused ye trouble, Magnus?"

"Aye."

"And how does it look tae the people of the kingdom tae have ye behaving like a harlot while we are at war? Has Magnus spoken tae ye on the matter, Bella?"

"Yes, he has, but..." She shook her head and changed her expression tae one of indignation. "I should have taken Roderick's side when I had the chance."

I worried Lady Mairead would have a fallin' down fit there on the table.

She stood, leaned over the desk top, her voice menacing. "I want ye tae understand this. King Magnus has complaints on your conduct. I have argued with him in your favor, but I hae seen the headlines, I ken ye have nae performed your duties as the heir's mother. I am shocked. I believed ye tae be clever. Is your son the heir tae the throne?"

"Yes."

"You are enjoying the king's generosity, his wealth and power. Have ye been performing your duties?"

Bella batted her eyes. "I offered to take him to bed, but he is content with his prostitutes I suppose."

"King Magnus daena keep prostitutes. You ken this is true. If ye attempt tae ruin his good name I will have your allowance removed and your household dissolved. Do ye understand me?"

"Yes, fine."

"Magnus is going away for a time. I will be in charge. What is on your schedule for the next week?"

"The Westlands Film Festival begins in two days, I have plans to attend."

"Nae, I hae events tae organize. I need ye tae help me host and plan a party tae announce I am the Queen Mother and will be ruling on Magnus's behalf while he is away. You will have tae clear your calendar. The castle has been rebuilt and Archie must have his photo taken. He will need tae be outfitted for the festivities."

"But I have plans tae be at the Channing After Party at the Nebula."

Lady Mairead looked furious. "You will have tae cancel your plans! As the mother of the prince ye hae responsibilities. You have duties tae perform that repay King Magnus for his care and attention tae your safekeeping."

"Magnus could make me the queen. He does not do anything for me—"

Lady Mairead threw her hands in the air. "King Magnus has been living here, fighting a war, ruling his kingdom for years without bringing his wife tae support him. If ye had been smart, ye would have been a help tae him politically — yet ye have chosen instead tae be a beggar, a waste of his time, and an extra burden on his shoulders. I expected better of ye, but there ye have it. You arna necessary except for the duties that come tae ye from being Archie's mother. In exchange ye will continue tae have the estate, the security staff, the cars, and you may continue with your parties if ye accomplish your duties first. I recommend ye perform them without complaint. Magnus has a patience that I daena and I am in charge while he is away."

Bella stood. "Can I be excused?"

"Of course, I will see ye in the morn for our plannin' meeting."

Bella swept from the room and Lady Mairead sat stiffly in a chair. She inhaled deeply with a scowl. "She is a verra irritating woman."

I said, "I find it interesting that your biggest problem with her haena been the threats against me, but that she haena fulfilled her duties tae the crown."

She said, "I take m'duties verra seriously, Magnus, and ye do as well. You have lived here for how long, alone, fighting a war?"

"A couple of years or more, I forget on it."

"Roderick is still out there."

"Aye, and there are other men as well, some I haena even heard of yet. I daena think ye should talk tae her so threateningly. I am worried what she might do, who she might align herself with."

Lady Mairead humphed. "She should try and cross me, just try. Where is Archie now?"

"He has been stayin' with her this week."

She said, "You could have her arrested."

"I remember too well what twas like tae have him hidden from me, taken from me. I want tae try tae cooperate with her. How would it be tae have his mother arrested and jailed? What if he dinna forgive me on it?"

"Ye are being too fair tae her."

"I am in a difficult position."

Lady Mairead came tae m'apartment bangin' on the door. "Magnus, awaken, something has happened."

When she entered she looked overly excited. "Bella is downstairs, asking for refuge, there has been some mischief."

I rushed to the elevators and down the main foyer. "What happened?"

Bella was wearin' a silk robe, with a wool blanket wrapped around her shoulders, her hair stickin' up as if she had been in bed. Archie was wailin' desperately in Mrs Johnstone's arms.

Bella said, "Magnus!" and fell against m'chest. "He was after me! He barged in! He tried to..." She began tae sob.

"Who did?" I looked around at the security for answers. "Who was there?"

Sergeant Melber, head of Bella's security, said, "Your Highness, we didn't see anyone. They're searching the estate now. She wanted to be brought here, to you, directly."

I reached for Archie tae comfort him. As Mrs Johnstone passed him tae me she whispered, "He has a bruise here."

I brushed his hair away from his forehead tae see a purple bruise. He flinched in fear.

"Och," I held him close. His wee arms went around m'neck. I stepped away from Bella. "Who was it? Was it Roderick? His men?"

"Yes!" She sobbed more and was unable tae continue speakin'.

I said tae Sergeant Melber, "I'll take her up tae m'apartments."

FIFTY-THREE - MAGNUS

*M*rs Johnstone turned on the lights.

I led Bella tae the couch and sat beside her and requested food and drink tae be brought for her. I tried tae console Archie.

Lady Mairead stood on the edge of the living room, her eyes narrowed at Bella. "What happened tae ye? Security needs be tightened, who are we looking for?"

Bella looked from Lady Mairead tae me, then she dove at me, shrieking, and thrust a blade intae my abdomen, a sharp pain, a stab, furious, deep and shocking.

In m'pain I hurled Archie off the couch, accidentally bangin' him against the table.

His cries crescendoed as I looked down at m'front, a dagger hilt juttin' from m'body, blood rushing from the wound — "Och!"

Lady Mairead pulled Bella off me, holdin' a dagger at her throat.

Security guards rushed in through the doors.

Bella screeched, "I hate you! Roderick is the true king! Long live Roderick!"

Soldiers surrounded her, subduin' her and bindin' her arms, arrestin' her in front of our frightened, screaming son. "Mrs Johnstone! Take him from the room!"

Blood poured down my front, Archie was wailing in fear and pain.

Soldiers lifted me tae rush me tae the infirmary.

I woke in a stark room with Lady Mairead near m'bed.

She said, "Tis about time for ye tae awaken. There is a mess ye need tae be dealin' with."

I looked up at the plain ceiling. "I have been here verra many times."

"What, the infirmary?"

"Nae, with a mess tae deal with." I felt the bandages on my stomach. "What of m'wound?"

"It could have been worse, you should be able tae leave the infirmary by tomorrow morning."

"I wanted tae return tae Florida today."

She shrugged. "You might have tae wait a few more days afore ye can travel, but ye will need tae decide on Archie first."

"Och."

"Bella was in contact with Roderick. If I had been here earlier, I would have been listening tae all her conversations. You were too kind. She has given Roderick many details on ye."

"Tis nothing new. My adversaries are always with more information than I have."

She primly folded her hands in her lap.

"What am I tae do with Bella, I am sure ye have thoughts?"

"I do. I daena think ye want a trial. She is the mother of Archie. Twill nae be in the best interests of the prince tae have a mother who is a criminal, it looks verra bad. His step-mother is already a murderer—"

"Careful."

"Fine."

"What do ye suggest?"

"She was taken, ye ken, from a village when she was young. By Donnan who as ye ken had a horrid penchant for cruelty. I will return her tae the village, she can return tae her humble beginnings—"

"Nae, this is also too cruel. She has grown used tae comfort. You should take her tae someplace that has modern medicine, basic luxuries."

"Och, ye want tae be magnanimous? Ye daena have sense in ye, Magnus. You should feed her tae the dragons. Fine, I like New York, I have friends there."

"The time daena overlap with Kaitlyn?"

"Nae, they winna cross paths."

"Good, thank ye."

"I will do it first thing. Then when ye are released, ye can return tae Florida for a time."

*H*ayley was massaging the blue dye all over Beaty's head, dividing her hair into thick sections and working the blue down the lengths.

Emma watched and teased Beaty about the instructions on the dye kit. "It says here that it could turn orange if we leave it on too long."

Beaty said, "Och, tis a terrible color, Quenny winna like that."

Hayley rolled a thick strand between her palms coating it generously. "She's just kidding you, Beaty, this is only going to be blue, but if it does turn out orange we can shave it all off."

Beaty said, "Och, I better take a photo with m'long hair for m'Insta in case tis gone later." She held her phone up and took a sweet and silly dimple-accentuating selfie with a glob of blue dye on her cheek.

I was still on the toilet, pretending to be engaged, while also pretending not to be freaking out. They all knew I was freaking out. You could hear it the way they were talking, pretending not to be aware that I was freaking out.

Finally, I stood, shoved down my pants and panties, and sat back down, ripped open the box, ripped the bag enclosure with my teeth, yanked out a stick, and jabbed it in the space between my legs. "Fine. Happy now? I'm whizzing on the stick, thank you very much. You'll see, I'm going to prove you wrong and then..."

I forgot to keep talking as urine streamed onto the stick and then I managed to wipe, stand, pull up my pants and holding the stick behind my back went and stood by the rest of them.

"Beaty it looks great so far, really great," I said absent-mindedly.

Hayley said, "Well, so far it's the color of a peacock which is, I guess, what she is going for."

She said, "It will match m'pipes."

I asked, "Your what?"

"M'pipes, they are goin' tae be blue and green, and Quenny bought them for me. He said they would be delivered in the new house."

Hayley said, "Just so we're clear, by pipes you mean, bagpipes?"

"Och aye, I miss the sound of them echoin' through the castle, tis a beautiful music inna it Mistress Hayley?"

"Um, yes, I suppose so. I did like it a lot echoing around the castle in Scotland, though I'm wondering what it will sound like in Florida?"

Beaty said, "Twill be beautiful."

I said, "I didn't know you played the bagpipes, Beaty."

"I daena but I be goin' tae learn tae on the YouTube."

Emma chuckled, "Thank heavens we're getting a bigger house." She dropped the dye instructions to the side. "Okay, Katie, let's see it."

I shook my head. "Nope. I changed my mind on the whole thing."

Hayley, her hands in Beaty's hair, said, "The thing about

Katie, Emma, is she is one big chickenshit. Like she never wants to know anything that could be good or bad. She'd rather suffer not knowing than—"

She dove at me with blue, dye-covered hands. I was shriek-laughing. She messed up my skin, my shirt, my pants and my hair, and wrestled me to the ground. Finally, against my squealing protests, she yanked the stick away, and sitting astride my body, held it up high in the air.

My hair was wild from the wrestling and there was a streak of blue down my arm and a blue handprint on my shirt. "Nice, I've been assaulted, great." Then I said, "Don't get it blue, we won't be able to tell what it says, and I'm not peeing on a stick ever ever ever again."

She turned it over, looked at it, then shoved it in my face. "See babe, you're pregnant."

She dropped the stick onto my chest, climbed off me, and started working on Beaty's hair again. I lay on the floor of the bathroom holding the stick up, trying to make sense of its meaning.

Emma was watching me with her lips clamped between her teeth.

"I'm pregnant?"

Emma nodded.

I clutched the stick to my chest and burst into tears.

FIFTY-FIVE - KAITLYN

*E*mma helped me sit up and then I sat there on the bathroom floor, just like that last time when I was pregnant and — except Magnus wasn't here.

"I'm pregnant."

Emma watched me for a moment and then said, "This is literally all your dreams come true."

"Except Magnus isn't here."

"This is true, but he will be here, he'll be here in a little over four months."

"Oh."

Emma worked on her phone. "And by my calculation you're due October 20th."

"Oh." I said again.

Hayley said, "Are you sure you should be talking about due dates and stuff, maybe just take it easy, not think about it, wait and see."

"Right," I said, "we don't know if this means anything at all. I don't even know I'm pregnant, this could just be..."

"What?"

"Like an anomaly."

Emma said, "No, not, I mean, just because you've lost a baby before doesn't mean you will again."

"Really? Because suddenly this seems really real and scary."

"It's not, this pregnancy is going to go great. You've got all of us to take care of you and your husband is off doing big manly things to keep you safe."

Hayley snapped the plastic cap onto Beaty's head, peeled off the latex gloves, and dropped down onto the tile floor beside me. "Emma is right, this is going to go great. Do you need to go get Magnus, tell him to come home early?"

I dropped my head back against the wall. "I don't really have a way to tell him."

Emma said, "And maybe no jumping for now."

"Yeah, and he'll be home on our anniversary. I can tell him then."

Hayley rested her head against mine, "Remember that whole thing I said about you earlier?"

"Where you called me a chickenshit?"

"Yeah, that was an unfortunate display. On further consideration I regret saying it. You're pretty brave."

"Thanks nut job."

"We should go celebrate with some margaritas."

"I don't think I'm supposed to drink."

"Holy shit, now explain to me why this is something you want to do?"

"You know why I want to do it."

"Yeah, I do babe, and congratulations."

"Thanks." I looked back down at the stick, the little blue plus sign staring up at me.

～

The super sucky part about being pregnant?

Morning sickness kicked my ass again.

And really brought out my complain-y side. Hayley was very exasperated and called me a big wallowing wuss.

In answer I threatened to throw up on her shoes.

She said, "Like you've been doing ever since I've known you?"

The cool part about being pregnant? I didn't have to help us move. I was in my bedroom, shades drawn, moaning from nausea while everyone moved my house. Then they moved me to Campbell Castle with a tray of Rice Krispies treats on my lap like I was an invalid queen.

I loved my new house so much. It was luxurious and vintage, but state of the art and modern. Zach hummed the whole time he was in the kitchen, dancing and cooking, playing his favorite music epically loud.

There were no neighbors nearby.

Which meant Beaty could practice her bagpipes on the back deck. And as she got better at playing she serenaded us when we walked on the beach.

I walked every afternoon, once the full-day nausea turned into just-in-the-morning nausea, and then finally subsided. As the weeks went by, the nausea ended, and it was becoming summer, the days growing hot.

I was busy with projects: working on the books, having the art appraised. Emma and I began the work of building a charitable foundation, and worked together through piles of paperwork.

It was nice being busy.

It was important to keep my mind occupied because simmering just under my skin was a bubbling pool of self-doubt — was I capable of this?

The fear — that this was just another moment where 'Kaitlyn got her hopes up' — stayed.

Until day after day slid by on the warm spring breezes and then my hopes settled in with the heat of the summer.

I was capable.

FIFTY-SIX - KAITLYN

hen, like magic it was July 1. I had suffered the spin of the earth for 156 days, as my friends noted, hardly crying at all. They mentioned I was being rather stoic actually, brave and strong, and surprisingly grown up. Emma teased me that maybe big hormones were actually good for me, making me, for once, kind of reasonable.

July 1. It was the day before Magnus would come home.

Zach and Emma shopped for food.

Quentin and I discussed the plan: he would meet Magnus's storm. I would stay here and greet him when he arrived at his new house.

Surprise factor.

It was going to be so cool.

I barely ate.

I hardly slept.

I went to a yoga class and then, when I needed something to do, watched two movies back to back with Hayley. Afterwards I joked, "What did we just watch?" Because I could barely concentrate over my brain — Magnus was coming home.

FIFTY-SEVEN - KAITLYN

*A*nd then it was July 2.

The kind of waiting through moments that crawled by... Had I just spent eight minutes brushing my teeth? Or... I looked down at the toothbrush in my hand. Had I forgotten to brush my teeth?

I brushed my teeth again.

I dressed in tiny panties.

I wore Magnus's favorite color, a blue dress, flowy and flirty, maternity-style, it fit over my rounded tummy and showed off my tan legs.

My Highlander was going to go weak in the knees.

I ate some breakfast because Zach made me.

And then I sat on the back porch and watched the sky.

Quentin was on the upper deck and yelled down, "See it?"

"I do. Oh my god, oh my god, oh my god. It's him, right? That's a storm, right?"

Zach rushed out the door, "Katie, the monitor is blowing up."

"Oh my god, it's a freaking storm. Quentin! It's a storm!"

Quentin rushed down the stairs, keys in his hand, he bolted to the door.

My voice following him, "Should I come? I shouldn't, right? Yes, I should, no, not—"

But it was too late, he was gone.

I ran up the stairs to stand on the top deck and watch as the storm furiously billowed farther to the south. The spot where we jumped in and out of the island wasn't that far away, a mile perhaps, but there were trees covering the area, nothing to see, just—

I sighed.

I should have gone with Quentin.

The storm was gone. I decided to go out and wait on the driveway.

FIFTY-EIGHT - KAITLYN

I stood on the driveway for what felt like forever until finally the car was coming.

It pulled up and into the garage and then—

"Quentin!!!!! Where's Magnus?"

He rolled down the window. "Don't panic, he's here, he walked up the beach, because... reasons, he's probably at the back deck by now."

"Really? Shit, you gave me a heart attack."

I raced up through the front door and then to everyone in the house, "Oh my god! He's walking up the beach. I have to pee! I'm so freaking excited I almost peed myself!"

I rushed into the tiny bath beside the kitchen and peed as fast as I could and rushed out, "Oh my god, I'm totally freaking out. Is he here?"

Emma smiled her 'calming' smile. "No, not yet, deep breath, you look beautiful. Now go on out."

I rushed out the door, trying to be calm, and not freaking out. I walked down the length of the boardwalk, long, out over the dunes to where the stair at the end dropped down to the sand.

I stood at the top, in the light breeze of a hot summer day, and watched, as there down the beach —

Magnus.

I waved.

My breath quickened, but I waited.

Magnus led a horse, a big beautiful horse, and held a little boy in his arms, Archie —

His son's wee arms were around Magnus's neck, a neck obscured by a long full beard, accentuating the crinkle under his eyes, that meant — *I have been gone long, mo reul-iuil, yet now I am home.*

He drew near. "Och," he said, "look at ye."

A tear rolled down my cheek.

His eyes traveled down my body to my stomach "Kaitlyn... are ye with bairn?"

"Yes."

His hand gripped the rail, warily. "Och, tis a marvel, are ye...? Is the bairn...?"

"I'm farther along than before, the doctor says we're both perfect."

His eyes got misty. He said, "When I decided tae bring ye the gelding, I forgot tae consider how tae get him home." He tied the horse's reins to the rail.

"You brought him for me?"

"Aye, his name is Osna. I am glad ye brought our home closer so I dinna have tae walk as far."

"Do you like the house?"

He squinted in the bright sun. "Aye, tis a braw house."

He climbed up the stair and rubbed my stomach, the expression on his face one of marveling. "We are havin' a bairn?"

"Yes, we are."

"Och." His hand rubbed along my form again, massaging my stomach, feeling it's roundness.

I rubbed the back of Archie's hair. "Hey sweetie, you must be Archie." He hid his face in his da's shoulder, still sniffling from the jump. I said, "I'm Kaitlyn, I'm very glad you're here."

Magnus gripped the rail and gingerly lowered himself to his knees, tears glistening on his cheeks. He hugged around my hips with his free arm, holding me close. His forehead pressed against my stomach, he said, "Hello wee bairn, I am Magnus, yer da. I have only just come home, tis why ye haena heard me afore, but I am here now. I promise I am here now and I canna wait tae meet ye."

I held my arms around their heads, clutching them closer.

The three of us.

Make that four.

"You're home."

"Aye."

"Archie, I barely recognized your da." He clutched tighter to Magnus's neck.

Magnus said, "I am older, not so much in years but the weight of them."

I lifted his chin, his forehead gleaming in the hot air, eyes squinting at the brightness. "How long have you been gone?"

"Almost three years, mo reul-iuil."

"Did you finish what you needed to do?"

"Aye. I have fought a war, vanquished m'enemy, subdued m'mother, and rescued m'son."

"You did all of that?"

"I also brought ye the horse, Osna, he is for an anniversary present."

"I love him. He's perfect."

He grinned. "Aye, I think I deserve a special amount of welcomin'. If ye think on it I might deserve the most amount."

I smiled down on him and sighed. "God yes, definitely. I can't wait to welcome you home properly. And, Archie, I'm so glad you're here. I'm so sorry about how you got here, that feels awful, I know, but through the doors of this house we have cookies waiting for you, and we're going to make it all better."

Archie sniffled and nestled more into his father's shoulder.

"You will make it all better, mo ghradh."

Magnus rubbed his face on my stomach with a low growl. "Och, ye are broody." He grinned up at me, clutching my ass in his hand. "Your arse is wide and heavy."

"Magnus Campbell, I have barely put on any weight, just enough. My doctor says it's a perfect amount. I'll have you know."

"Och, tis perfect." He lumbered up to his feet and hugged me, walking forward, walking me backward, kissing me, loving me, "Tis perfectly braw yer arse, just right for a broodin' hen."

I threw my arms around his neck. "I missed you so much."

"I missed ye too." He picked me up around my waist. "We should be inside m'braw castle." He carried me and Archie into the house saying, "Tis hot as the underside of a dung heap out here," and calling up to Quentin, guarding on the upper deck, "Master Quentin, could ye see tae Kaitlyn's horse?"

FIFTY-NINE - MAGNUS

*M*y new house was big, far bigger than the one afore. Twas interesting tae have the full memory of a lifetime that Kaitlyn could nae remember, but she had one of me from long ago, Old Magnus, and here I was again, if nae old, at least older and wiser as well.

I greeted m'family. They hadna seen me for months, for me it had been years.

I wasna famished, but I had been hungry without Chef Zach's food and Madame Emma's attention, Master Quentin's security and Madame Beaty's reminiscences of home, and Kaitlyn — her smile, her laugh, and though my arms ached from holding wee Archie, his weight was welcome as well. M'family was growin' and it was a comfort tae be in the middle of it.

Kaitlyn hovered around Archie and me. She gave us a tour, she offered him a cookie and sweetly smoothed his hair from his forehead and spoke tae him and opened her heart tae him again and after I had been home for an hour, I asked tae pass him over so I could step from the room, and Archie held his arms out and took tae her lap.

As I placed him there, I asked, "He is too heavy for ye?"

"Never, he's a wee spider monkey, I like the weight of him," and this was a loop of us, the good kind, the kind that repeats the story and fills in with the details.

Chef Zach had told me a story once, that the footpaths of auld had worn intae the earth, gone deeper and deeper until they had become a groove, and those grooves had continued on, becomin' roads and highways, historic paths. I liked tae think we were doin' that, walkin' a path taegether, creating a groove in the earth, through time, in our hearts.

Archie wrapped a hand in Kaitlyn's hair and put his two middle fingers intae his mouth tae suckle on while he slept and by the time I returned from the bathroom he was nappin' on her front.

Her eyes were misty, her smile wide.

Hayley was there, tae greet me. "Last I saw of you, Mags, was at Balloch," she said.

"Aye, and how are ye feelin' now on Fraoch?"

"I miss him so much."

"Are ye keen tae go?"

Kaitlyn said, "She made a list of the reasons to do it, and seems pretty set."

"Still?"

Hayley said, "Still. I'm going to take a vacation from work next week. I'll go for a while, just to see. Katie promised me you wouldn't mind if I borrow a vessel."

"I daena mind." I put my hand out on Kaitlyn's rounded form. "I believe I am grounded for a time. I am happy tae be. I am glad ye are capable of going on yer own. Fraoch will be happy tae see ye."

"Will he? You're sure?"

"Aye, he was yer man, through and through. You just need tae claim him."

I raised m'beer. "Tae Mistress Hayley and her future in the eighteenth century with the man, Fraoch, an orphan from the clan MacDonald, formerly scurvy-ridden, with the manners of a pirate, and the scent of roses — the kind of man I call a true friend."

Hayley laughed. "Thank you Mags, I'm glad you're home."

"Aye, me as well."

Just then there was a movement under my palm.

Kaitlyn said, "Put your hand here." She adjusted Archie tae the side so I had more area tae feel. A form within her rolled from one side tae the other. "Och, our bairn."

I concentrated on that spot, then folded across her, wrappin' her in m'arms, Archie and Kaitlyn and the bairn that was comin', and held her close, forgettin' we were in the midst of our family.

I nestled intae the edge of her neck and whispered, "I love ye, mo reul-iuil," and then I cried, against her skin, in front of my family.

I dinna ken why. Twas because of the long time away, and the relief tae be home, but also twas like I had been carryin' the burden of our lives for a long time alone and it had been verra heavy.

I was nae complainin', twas necessary, but I had placed the burden now at Kaitlyn's feet, askin' her tae help, and she was takin' it up. She had waited for me with strength, and had embraced Archie, my past, and would help me raise him, without question or judgment, she would open her heart, and now she was bringin' forth a bairn. She would be the mother she had wanted tae be, and I kent that from now on, as the queen, she would be able tae help me rule, with all that came next.

I wouldna have tae do it alone. She was here, waiting, and we were ready for what came next.

. . .

304 | DIANA KNIGHTLEY

Chef Zach grilled steak and potatoes upon an outdoor grill on the back deck of the house.

Beaty emerged from her guest house with bagpipes. I said, "Madame Beaty, I do verra much admire yer hair."

"Ye do?"

"Aye, it reminds me of home."

She grinned, "Balloch?"

"Nae, Florida."

She played us a few songs. The pipes lilting, only sometimes squeakin' and squawkin', out over the sand dunes.

When she finished we cheered and clapped. Archie sat on my lap, watchin' Ben, ready tae play but bein' shy on it, not sure he wanted tae be away from me tae do it.

I said, "Tis alright wee'un, ye will have the morrow," and it was true.

Archie fell asleep and I carried him intae the bedroom and put him intae the middle of our bed. Then I returned tae the decks tae talk more with our friends.

Kaitlyn said, "I want to hear all of it, all of the whole three years, but first, how did you get Archie?"

"It has been verra complicated. Bella was a great vexation. I dinna ken how tae deal with her, but then she solved the dilemma by attemptin' tae kill me and—"

They all said, "What?"

"Aye," I raised m'shirt tae show them the cut, still fresh but healing. I joked, "Attempted murder of the king was the final straw."

Chef Zach said, "I guess so — what the hell? That lady was nothing but trouble."

Kaitlyn frowned. "Does that mean she's in jail forever or worse?"

"She was, but I dinna want a drawn out trial. I worried on Archie tae have his mother charged with treason. The punishment of the crime is death, I dinna—"

Kaitlyn said, "I would be worried about that too, my love, that would be tragic."

I clasped her hand. "Aye, so Lady Mairead removed her tae another time. She has been left without a vessel."

Emma said, "That's diabolical!"

"Aye, Lady Mairead is often diabolical. She was also helpful which she rarely is." I took a swig of a beer. "Bella winna be botherin' us again. Roderick, though, is still unaccounted for. He has been beaten, but is in hidin', and daena have any vessels. I daena think he can cause trouble."

Quentin said, "Good, perfect."

Kaitlyn asked, "So Bella isn't coming back for Archie?"

"Nae, mo reul-iuil. She dinna like him much anyway."

"That's awful. She's so freaking mean, I hate her mean bitchface so much. We really never have to deal with her again?"

"Without a vessel she inna much more than a terrible memory."

"There is so much good news, I mean, except for the whole three years worth of war."

I said, "We are rebuildin' the Caisteal Morag now, and Hammie is helpin' tae run the government. I am tryin' tae improve the kingdom."

"And Lady Mairead is helping you?"

"Aye, she is in her element, runnin' meetings, negotiatin' treaties, lordin' over all the men. I gave her a dagger. She wears it every day and takes it out sometimes just tae hold while she makes commands. She is verra contented."

Kaitlyn laughed. "I never thought I'd say this, but that's great. I'm glad she has something to do to keep her busy. Here we were struggling against the idea of you becoming a king and against trusting Lady Mairead and somehow by just embracing the two things, becoming king, and bringing her into your court, you got so much safer. It's kind of a miracle. And just so we're clear, Archie lives with us now, here, wherever we are?"

"Och, aye, he daena have another home except for ours."

Kaitlyn said, "That is..." Her voice trailed off and she held my hand tightly. Then she stood and raised her juice glass. We all held up our beers. She said, "To Magnus, for making our future safer, for making our family larger, and for coming home."

Everyone said, "Hear hear."

SIXTY - MAGNUS

*A*s the night grew long, Beaty and Quentin retired tae their own house.

Zach instructed me tae work the intercom system. "You push this button, see? And say, 'Chef Zach, I need ice cream,' and I'll rush out and meet you here in the kitchen. The house is too large to hear you, so don't forget."

"I winna forget. I daena want tae deal with yer fury if I made m'own snack at night."

"Good, as long as we're clear. It's been fucking boring here for months and months. No one ever lets me get them stuff, so you know, maybe tonight ask for something because I bought all this ice cream and..."

Emma grabbed his arm, with a laugh. "We get it, you missed him. You want to feel needed. He'll call you on your little bro phone."

Zach pretend sniffled. "I just want him to understand how important it is to me."

She dragged him from the room.

Hayley said, "I get the guest room tonight?"

Kaitlyn said, "Of course, just go there soon. I need to welcome my husband home and we have a young child in our bed."

"Ugh, that is too much information. Especially since I've been months with no, you know, in months, literal months."

Kaitlyn chuckled. "Can't believe you're about to go three hundred years for a booty-call."

I asked, "What is a booty-call?"

"Sex."

I joked, "Och, three hundred years? I have been almost three years without a booty-call, and have just traveled almost four hundred years tae get one from m'wife."

Kaitlyn laughed. "I love that my Highlander is joking about a booty-call, and he is exactly right, nighty-night, Hayley."

Mistress Hayley said, "All right, I'm going to my room. If you get up for a snack though, call me by intercom. I want some too, and Zach won't wake up for my late-night snacking needs."

She kissed us both and retired tae her room.

Kaitlyn cuddled under m'arm and looked up in m'eyes. "I am so glad you're home."

"Thank ye for makin' a home tae come tae. Tis a braw house. I can see we will be verra comfortable here."

"I want to take you to bed. You are just home from battle, Master Magnus, and you need to get onto your back so I can welcome you home. Also you need to get onto your back because my stomach makes lying on my back uncomfortable."

"I have just put a wee'un intae our bed."

"We have a deck, Master Magnus. It's a private deck looking out over the ocean, and there is a cushioned deck chaise out there — it's not wide, we can't get acrobatic, but we can definitely get busy."

"I like the sound of it."

She stood and led me tae the stairs.

*W*e snuck past Archie through the doors to the deck.

"Och, we should put a bed out here."

"I agree, one hundred percent. See, there's no way anyone can see us. And check out the stars." We both looked up at the sky, encrusted with tiny stars strewn from one end to the other.

While Magnus gaped at the stars, I slipped my dress off, unfastened my bra and slid off my sandals. Then I looked up at the stars again like I hadn't done anything unusual.

Magnus chuckled, "The Madame Campbell has lost her clothes. I believe she might be overly wantin' her husband." He looked down on me and shook his head, saying, his voice low and deep, "Tis a bonny sight yer wee stomach all round and hopeful."

He sat down on the side of the chaise and I stood in front of him so he was eye level with my stomach.

Then he looked up at me with a mischievous grin,

"What?"

"Yer breasts, usually the size of a hen's egg are now—"

"I know, closer to the size of an apple."

"Nae," his eyes twinkled, "now they are closer in size tae a cow's udder. You will need tae have much bigger undergarmies."

I groaned. "Magnus Campbell, I am naked before you and you're going to compare my breasts to cow udders?"

He ginned. "I am only havin' some fun, ye are beautiful, mo reul-iuil."

"Get to your back, Highlander." He lay back on the chaise and I worked the button on his pants. "Wow," I teased, "you've grown bigger too, or are you just happy to see me?"

"Och, I have a present for ye in m'pocket." I stood up while he fished it out and passed me a small jewelry box.

"You didn't need to, Magnus, you brought me a horse. You came home."

He leaned up on one arm, still fully clothed.

I was completely naked, pregnant, round in lots of ways, and on display.

"Open it, mo reul-iuil, tis nae much, just..."

I pried open the lid. "Oh." Inside was a beautiful gold locket on a delicate chain. *Oh*.

The locket was an oval shape, and on the outside was a beautiful pattern, a Scottish knot, around a heart. Inside on the left was a photo of Magnus, one where he was laughing, the crinkle in the corner of his eyes, prominent.

He said, "I thought ye might put another photo, maybe of Archie if ye wanted tae."

I had tears streaming, naked and crying. "I do want to, I'll put a photo of both our bairns there. We'll photograph Archie holding the baby and..." I wiped my tears, closed the box, and clutched it to my chest. "I didn't get you anything."

"Och, ye are sayin' this tae me, while ye are growin' a bairn? In a house ye bought for me and are callin' Castle Campbell? I think tis enough."

I blew out a breath of air. "God, I want you so bad."

His eyes twinkled and he scrambled to hurriedly unbutton his pants.

I joked, "Faster faster."

He said, "I am out of practice on undressin'." I helped him pull his pants down and we tossed them aside.

"Tis okay, we winna hurt the bairn?"

"No, you aren't that big." I pulled his shirt off over his head.

"Och, hae ye seen me? I'm massive."

I giggled, "Oh yes, I'm seeing you. But still, it's perfectly safe."

I slowly climbed onto him, and even slower settled onto him. I was mindful of his healing wound, but not minding the lack of all the playing, this was a 'welcome home', and an, 'it's been a long time,' and an especially necessary, 'I needed you' kind of sex — we got to the business of it before we even kissed, which was kind of hot, to be astride and looking down on him, taking in the hotness of him, watching his eyes appreciate me against the dark sky on the deck of our Florida home.

Then sinking down more with a low moan and breathing him in, the scent I had missed, that warmth and comfort against his skin, and collapsing on him and nestling, his arms around, while we moved, in and out and the sweat of exertion between us, and the heat of a high summer night, wet and sticky and lovely, oh so fucking lovely — *god, I love you.*

Aye, I love ye too.

Afterwards, we snuck into the bedroom, put on our pajamas, and climbed into bed. Magnus on one side of his son, I on the other, curled facing each other, looking at Archie in the muted darkness of a moonlit night in our room where, again, I never liked to pull the shades, preferring the open starlit sky on a night like this.

"I don't know if I've ever been this happy."

312 | DIANA KNIGHTLEY

"Tis a joyous day, tis nae improvin' on it. But..." He smiled. "Let's see if we can make it even more."

He jumped from the bed and strode tae the intercom and pushed the button. "Chef Zach, tis me, Magnus, I am needin' an ice cream feast for all of us."

I giggled, "All of us?"

"I am wakin' everybody up. Tis m'first night home. They have had two hours tae sleep. We will eat ice cream and then go tae the beach for a walk, perhaps Madame Beaty will play the pipes for us on the sand."

"That might be too loud for one-thirty in the morning, but the rest of it sounds perfect."

He lifted Archie gently from the bed. Archie clutched his shoulder, "Da?"

"We are havin' a treat, wee'un, in the middle of the night."

Archie looked across Magnus's shoulder at me. He put his arms out and reached for me, and Magnus passed him into my arms.

SIXTY-TWO - MAGNUS

*I*n the darkened kitchen, Chef Zach was already preparin' the bowls. I used the intercom tae bring Hayley and Quentin and Beaty tae the kitchen as well, with a great deal of jokin' about how tired they were and a bit of grumblin' about havin' their sleep interrupted, but they all understood m'need — tae be surrounded by them, tae be happy and at peace.

Soon enough we were all eatin', and then the bairns had fallen asleep again, so the rest of us traipsed out tae the end of the boardwalk and down the steps tae put our feet in the sand. We walked out to the edge of the ocean and warm water lapped our toes.

I hugged Kaitlyn tae me and enjoyed the moment, warm and safe, a high sky, a beautiful beach, a full stomach, bairns tae protect, and Kaitlyn in my arms.

After a minute of quiet, Hayley said, looking up at the sky, "Ugh, all this love stuff, you guys are the worst." Then she added, "...completely unrelated. I think I'm going to leave first thing tomorrow. I mean, I've been packed for ages. I should just go, right? I should do it before it's too late."

"Aye, tis a fragile thing, life, ye need tae jump if ye are going tae, Mistress Hayley."

"Yeah, right Mags, I'm going to jump."

THE END... FOR NOW.

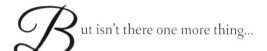 ut isn't there one more thing...

HAYLEY - SCOTLAND, 1704

I woke up lying in the dirt of the familiar Scottish clearing. My eyes opened on dirt, leaves, detritus, and then a foot beyond, boots, loose leather reins, higher — rough hands holding the reins loosely, and then bare knees crouching beside me, kilt draping over them.

I moaned, every bone, muscle, sinew was in agony.

I turned my head just enough to look up at the face that was crouched beside me.

"Fraoch?"

"Aye, Madame Hayley."

He was looking down on me, his eyes concerned. "Ye have returned?"

"Yes," I brushed hair from my face. "I came back."

"Och." His hands fiddled with the loose rein. He added, "I daena understand what ye mean with returnin' alone."

I pulled myself up to sitting, arms wrapped around my knees, surrounded by bags and boxes, gifts and packages for Magnus and Kaitlyn's family. "Funny thing, Fraoch, I'm not married."

His brow drew further down.

"And I kind of thought I might come back to rescue you."

He grinned, a cocky look spread across his face. "Madame Hayley wanted tae come back tae rescue Fraoch MacDonald, from what danger are ye goin' tae rescue me?"

"From being alone, Fraoch."

"Och," he said simply, watching my face.

"This is where you should say something amazing to mean I didn't just do something really really stupid. Because you're kind of acting like I'm being really really stupid."

"What should I say?"

I groaned. "Like that you are..."

He shook his head so I faltered. "What?"

Then he spoke. "Madame Hayley, I haena had peace in my head or m'heart since ye arrived. I wish I had spoken tae ye on it, but twas nae m'place tae tell ye, as ye were married, and — I dinna want ye tae leave."

"I'm sorry I did, but I came back as soon—"

"Lizbeth and Madame Greer have found me a wife, Madame Hayley."

"Oh, you are married?"

"Nae, but they are setting tae the plannin' on it. I have spent the afternoon discussin' with her father."

"Oh."

We both sat quietly for a moment.

"This is complicated huh?"

"Aye, tis."

"You're already rescued?"

He chuckled. "I am verra glad tae see ye, Madame Hayley, I..."

I rested my cheek on my knees, waiting for him to finish but instead he seemed unable to.

I nodded, "I'm glad to see you too."

The End

THANK YOU

There are more chapters in Magnus and Kaitlyn's story and in Fraoch and Hayley's story as well...

Review Book #9, Again my Love

As you all know, reviews are the best social proof a book can have, and I would greatly appreciate your review on this book.

If you need help getting through the pauses before the next books, there is a FB group here: Kaitlyn and the Highlander Group

Thank you for taking the time to read this book. The world is full of entertainment and I appreciate that you chose to spend some time with Magnus and Kaitlyn. I fell in love with Magnus when I was writing him, and I hope you fell in love a little bit too.

Kaitlyn and the Highlander (Book 1)

Time and Space Between Us (Book 2)
Warrior of My Own (Book 3)
Begin Where We Are (Book 4)
A Missing Entanglement (now a prologue within book 5)
Entangled with You (Book 5)
Magnus and a Love Beyond Words (Book 6)
Under the Same Sky (book 7)
Nothing But Dust (book 8)
Again My Love (book 9)
Our Shared Horizon (book 10)

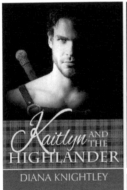  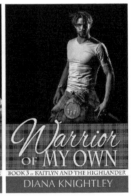

SERIES ORDER

Kaitlyn and the Highlander (book 1)
Time and Space Between Us (book 2)
A Warrior of My Own (book 3)
Begin Where We Are (book 4)
A Missing Entanglement (short, optional, between 4&5)
Entangled With You (book 5)
Magnus and a Love Beyond Words (book 6)
Under the Same Sky (book 7)
Nothing but Dust (book 8)
Again My Love (book 9)
Our Shared Horizon (book 10)

SOME THOUGHTS AND RESEARCH...

Characters:

    Kaitlyn Maude Sheffield - born 1994

    Magnus Archibald Caelhin Campbell - born 1681

    Lady Mairead (Campbell) Delapointe she is the sister of the Earl of Breadalbane

    Hayley Sherman - Kaitlyn's best friend

    Quentin Peters - Magnus's security guard/colonel in his future army

    Beaty Peters - Quentin's wife. Born in the late 1680s

    Zach Greene - The chef

    Emma Garcia - Household manager

    Baby Ben Greene - born May 15, 2018

    Sean Campbell -Magnus's half-brother

    Lizbeth Campbell - Magnus's half-sister

    Sean and Lizbeth are the children born of Lady Mairead and her first husband.

    Baby Archie Campbell - born 2382

    Bella Florentin - mother of Archie

Colonel Hammond Donahoe

The Earl of Breadalbane - Lady Mairead's brother

Uncle Archibald (Baldie) Campbell - uncle to Sean and Lizbeth

Tyler Garrison Wilson - Archie's alter-ego

Grandma Barb

Grandpa Jack

Pablo Picasso - 1881 - 1973

Picasso's friends - Max Jacob and Guillaume Apollinaire

Fraoch MacDonald - born in 1714, is aged 26 in 1740 when he meets Magnus is pretending to be a MacLeod

Colonel Hammond - Magnus calls him Hammie, come to find out — cousin.

King Roderick - now just plain Roderick, because Magnus has kicked his arse and sent him into hiding.

~

The line of kings in the future-future

Donnan the Second - murdered by Kaitlyn Campbell in the year 2381

Samuel - Donnan's brother. Attempted takeover during the transfer of power between Donnan and Magnus, uncrowned. (Killed in the arena by Magnus.)

Magnus the First - crowned in 2382 shortly before the birth of his son, Archibald Campbell, next in line for the throne.

Roderick the Usurper - son of Samuel. Claimed a right to the throne. Raised an army and overthrew Magnus the First in 2383. Bella is with him. Wait — now that never happened...

Magnus the First

~

Some **Scottish and Gaelic words** that appear within the book series:

Chan eil an t-sìde cho math an-diugh 's a bha e an-dé - The weather's not as good today as it was yesterday.

Tha droch shìde ann - The weather is bad.

Dreich - dull and miserable weather

Turadh - a break in the clouds between showers

Solasta - luminous shining (possible nickname)

Splang - flash, spark, sparkle

Mo reul-iuil - my North Star (nickname)

Tha thu a 'fàileadh mar ghaoith - you have the scent of a breeze.

Osna - a sigh

Rionnag - star

Sollier - bright

Ghrian - the sun

Mo ghradh - my own love

Tha thu breagha - you are beautiful

Mo chridhe - my heart

Corrachag-cagail - dancing and flickering ember flames

Mo reul-iuil, is ann leatsa abhios mo chridhe gubrath - My North Star, my heart belongs to you forever

Dinna ken - didn't know

A h-uile là sona dhuibh 's gun là idir dona dhuib - May all your days be happy ones

Tae - to

Winna - won't or will not

Daena - don't

Tis - it is or there is. This is most often a contraction t'is, but it looked messy and hard to read on the page so I removed the apostrophe. For Magnus it's not a contraction, it's a word.

Och nae - Oh no.

Ken, kent, kens - know, knew, knows

iora rua - a squirrel. (Magnus compares Kaitlyn to this ;o)

scabby-boggin tarriwag - Ugly-foul smelling testicles

latha fada - long day

sùgh am gròiseid - juice in the gooseberry

Beinn Labhair - Ben Lawers, the highest mountain in the southern part of the Scottish Highlands. It lies to the north of Loch Tay.

> *"And I will come again, my love, though it were ten thousand mile..." is from the beautiful* **Robert Burns** *poem,* O my Luve's like a red, red rose, *written in 1794 after Magnus's time.*

beannachd leibh - farewell or blessings be with you.

> *"Fra banc to banc, fra wod to wod, I rin, Ourhailit with my feeble fantasie, Lyk til a leif that fallis from a trie..." is from a Sonet by* **Mark Alexander Boyd**. 1563-1601

Locations:
Fernandina Beach on Amelia Island, Florida, 2017-2020
Magnus's home in Scotland - Balloch. Built in 1552. In early 1800s it was rebuilt as Taymouth Castle. (Maybe because of the

breach in the walls caused by our siege from the future?) Situated on the south bank of the River Tay, in the heart of the Grampian Mountains. In 2382 it is a ruin.

Kilchurn Castle - Magnus's childhood home, favorite castle of his uncle Baldie. On an island at the northeastern end of Loch Awe. In the region Argyll.

The kingdom of Magnus the First is in Scotland, his Caisteal Morag is very near Balloch Castle.

Paris, Montmartre, 1904.

~

True things that happened:

Sir Colin Campbell of Glenorchy (1521– 1583) did claim to have chosen the site of the Balloch Castle on the spot where he first heard a blackbird sing.

In 1787, Robert Burns described the beauty of Balloch Castle and its surrounding lands in verse, as follows:-
The Tay meandering sweet in infant pride,
The Palace rising on its verdant side,
The lawns, wood fringed, in Nature's native taste,
The hillocks dropped in Nature's native haste...

Madeleine was the name of a model who posed for Picasso and became his mistress in the summer of 1904, but that is all we know. Where she came from, where she went after leaving Picasso, when she died, and even her last name are lost to history.

I have posited here that this is because she was actually a time traveler. Whether that is true or not is impossible to prove. She appears in some of Picasso's late Blue Period works.

～

Coutts bank is a real bank formed in 1692 by a young Scots gold-smith-banker, John Campbell. Cynthia Tyler tells me to get in I need a minimum deposit of £500,000 pounds, or total assets of £5,000,000. Lady Mad only banks with the best family banks.

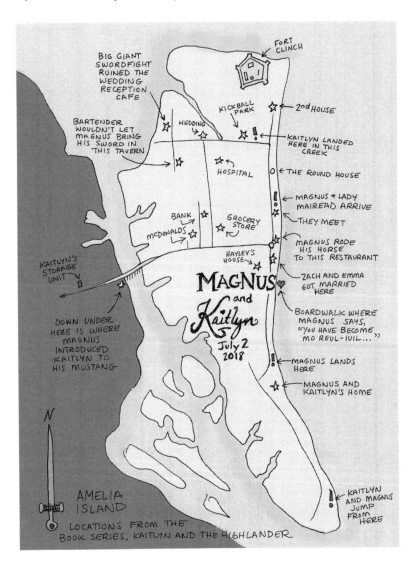

FORT CLINCH

BIG GIANT SWORDFIGHT RUINED THE WEDDING RECEPTION CAFE

KICKBALL PARK

2nd HOUSE

BARTENDER WOULDN'T LET MAGNUS BRING HIS SWORD IN THIS TAVERN

WEDDING

KAITLYN LANDED HERE IN THIS CREEK

HOSPITAL

THE ROUND HOUSE

MAGNUS + LADY MAIREAD ARRIVE

THEY MEET

BANK

GROCERY STORE

MCDONALDS

MAGNUS RODE HIS HORSE TO THIS RESTAURANT

HAYLEY'S HOUSE

KAITLYN'S STORAGE UNIT

ZACH AND EMMA GOT MARRIED HERE

MAGNUS and Kaitlyn July 2 2018

BOARDWALK WHERE MAGNUS SAYS, "YOU HAVE BECOME MO REUL-IUIL..."

DOWN UNDER HERE IS WHERE MAGNUS INTRODUCED KAITLYN TO HIS MUSTANG

MAGNUS LANDS HERE

MAGNUS AND KAITLYN'S HOME

N

KAITLYN AND MAGNUS JUMP FROM HERE

AMELIA ISLAND

LOCATIONS FROM THE BOOK SERIES, KAITLYN AND THE HIGHLANDER

ACKNOWLEDGMENTS

Thank you to Jessica Fox for being the very first reader to accomplish the full read through. You sent me a list of loves and very few issues, but reminded me that Magnus needed to grab the bag of vessels when he rescued Hayley, thank you! I really thank you for reading, your compliments reminded me to breathe again.

∿

A big thank you to David Sutton for beta-reading again. It was a tight deadline this time, but thank you for all your thoughts. From urging me not to let Magnus pack protein bars for Hayley before she went to re-meet Fraoch, to sending me a video about skinning a rabbit, urging me not to let them jump near the house, and reminding me that ginger-ale is for nausea and that absinthe is green. Thank you for all of your insights, every suggestion helps make the story better and better.

∿

A huge thank you to Heather Hawkes for beta-reading yet again. I thought this installment was without a cliffhanger until you sent me a barrage of gifs and:

"So when is book ten gonna be started?? Tomorrow? I'm coming to your house so you can fill my ass in. I'm gonna die waiting. How can you do this to me??? I thought we were friends?!"

I am very glad we are friends, that you care this much about the story and have invested your time in it, thank you.

Thank you to Kristen Schoenmann De Haan for always being available to beta-read, and getting it done during family time on this crazy tight deadline smack dab in holiday hoopla. I really appreciated your thoughts and your kind words. There was a section there, the bit where Hayley says "It was odd how much the world kept being the same." I had taken it out, you told me you loved it so I added it back. Thank you.

And a special, gigantic thank you to Cynthia Tyler for pointing out that bears were extinct in Scotland, to noting there were many cars in Paris in 1904, to making sure that my its and it's were right and loving Hayley and Kaitlyn's pros and cons scene, and the million other things you found and noticed. I'm filled with gratitude about your wonderful editing, for going faster than seems humanly possible, and helping me get this super polished to a high sheen just in time for release. You are so darn good at this, thank you.

And a very big thank you to Keira Stevens for becoming the narrator of my audiobooks and bringing Kaitlyn and Magnus to life. Now, when I'm writing, I hear your voices in my head and they have become even more living breathing friends to me. I adore the way you do this, all of this, from beginning to the very finished end. And thank you for finding the perfect voice to read POV Magnus beginning in book 4 and becoming a collaborator and manager and all the new things you have to do to make that happen.

~

And thank you to Shane East for joining the team and voicing Magnus. He is perfect.

~

Thank you to *Jackie Malecki* and *Angelique Mahfood* for signing on to help admin the big and growing FB group. I'm so glad you're there!

And thank you to *Anna Spain* for starting the weekly book club, it means so much to me that you started it for the group, I know it takes time and I don't know what to say, but thank you.

Which brings me to a huge thank you to every single member of the FB group, Kaitlyn and the Highlander. Every day, in every way, sharing your thoughts, joys, and loves with me is so amazing, thank you. You inspire me to try harder.

Thank you to *Sandy Hambrick, Linda Rose Lynch, Dianna Schmidt, Jenny Thomas, Molly Lyions, Tracey Rountree-Bristow, Nadeen Lough, Jessica Blasek, Lillian Llewellyn, Ginger Duke, Donna Hughes, Christine Cornelison, Gail Bissett, Kathy Ann Harper, Christine Todd Champeaux, Lisa Greer McKinnon, Jenny Thomas, Ishka Arnold, Lesli Muir Lytle, Nancy Josey*

Massengill, Nadeen Lough, Georgene K Jacobs, Sharon-Nick Palmer, Tara Smith Blake, Yvette Brown, Melinda Flanagan, Sammie Moore, Karen Ingersoll, Noelle Pratt Blosser, Sheri Nolte-Ochoa, Stacey Eddings, Jenni Branchaw, Mary Pahs, Debbie Olson, Joanne Watkins, Faith Ransom, Sarah J Thomas, Roseanne Russell, Neshama Fried Mousseau, Alix Cothran, Emily Smith-Haskins, Nicky Scott, Julie Schmitz Stephens, Nakia Brown, Sara Bacher, Peggy Locke, Carol Leslie, Esther Lee, Lissette Capote, Diana Rhodes, Janet Zidoff Lukach, Michelle Lynn Cochran for all your posts and comments in the group.

And when I ask 'research questions' you give such great answers...

I asked: Time and money is no object, Magnus gets something for Kaitlyn for an anniversary present. (Three years!) What does he get her?

There were 87 wonderful replies. Our Magnus ended up giving Kaitlyn more than one.

Teri Gutermuth, Liza Gee, Sammie Moore, Sly Greenberg, and Sara Bacher came up with leather journal.

Sandy Hambrick, Lisa Zimmerman Moon, Linda Downing Carlson, Tara Smith Blake, Christine Cornelison, Lisa Hostetler, Barbara McPherson, Jackie Malecki, and Leondra Workman all said a horse.

Susan Nilsson, Tori Brouhard, Cathy Cannizzaro, Nadeem Lough, Cheryl Strother hoped for a locket

----

Marlene Villardi and Deborah Garver, Donna Hughes, Beverly Leonard, Dee Spencer Hentz, were answering the question about anniversary gifts, but gave me the idea of giving the traditional brooch and sgian dubh to Lady Mairead.

I also asked if you could add to Kaitlyn's backpack, what she might take to the past? The list was long and thorough, but sadly, Kaitlyn never got to pack this go around, hopefully I can use it next time!

And I asked for your help picking the new house for the gang. I didn't know at the time that the gang would be moving twice in this book. Hundreds of you weighed in and helped me pick real estate, thank you so much for the help.

I also asked: Kaitlyn finds herself wearing a Tshirt to sleep in. Just some random, funny, weird or ironic Tshirt. Magnus is away for the night so it doesn't have to be cute. Trouble is, the shirt ends up being something she has to wear for longer and in public. She might regret it, or at least it's not really what she would want to wear. What does the Tshirt say?

There were so many great comments, I hated having to choose just one, so I picked Liza Gee's choice: I'm only here for the men in kilts, but then at the last moment I picked Kathryn Denton's choice: Team Edward. Because ultimately it needed to be something that Quentin could see on video and recognize immediately.

For book 8 I asked the group to name a meal that Barb would make for Kaitlyn. Since I used it again, here are my thanks again. Thank you for Chicken and Dumplings *Phyllis Phucas, Michiko Martin,* and *Sara Bacher.*

If I have somehow forgotten to add your name, or didn't remember your contribution, please forgive me. I am living in the world of Magnus and Kaitlyn and it is hard some days to come up for air.

I mean to always say truthfully thank you. Thank you.

~

Thank you to *Kevin Dowdee* for being there for me in the real world as I submerge into this world to write these stories of Magnus and Kaitlyn. I appreciate you so much.

Thank you to my kids, *Ean, Gwynnie, Fiona,* and *Isobel,* for listening to me go on and on about these characters, advising me whenever you can, and accepting them as real parts of our lives. I love you.

Can he see to the depths of her mystery before it's too late?

The oceans cover everything, the apocalypse is behind them. Before them is just water, leveling. And in the middle — they find each other.

On a desolate, military-run Outpost, Beckett is waiting.

Then Luna bumps her paddleboard up to the glass windows and disrupts his everything.

And soon Beckett has something and someone to live for. Finally. But their survival depends on discovering what she's hiding, what she won't tell him.

Because some things are too painful to speak out loud.

With the clock ticking, the water rising, and the storms growing, hang on while Beckett and Luna desperately try to rescue each other in Leveling, the epic, steamy, and suspenseful first book of the trilogy, Luna's Story:

Leveling: Book One of Luna's Story

Under: Book Two of Luna's Story

Deep: Book Three of Luna's Story

ABOUT ME, DIANA KNIGHTLEY

I live in Los Angeles where we have a lot of apocalyptic tendencies that we overcome by wishful thinking. Also great beaches. I maintain a lot of people in a small house, too many pets, and a to-do list that is longer than it should be, because my main rule is: Art, play, fun, before housework. My kids say I am a cool mom because I try to be kind. I'm married to a guy who is like a water god: he surfs, he paddle boards, he built a boat. I'm a huge fan.

I write about heroes and tragedies and magical whisperings and always forever happily ever afters. I love that scene where the two are desperate to be together but can't because of war or apocalyptic-stuff or (scientifically sound!) time-jumping and he is begging the universe with a plead in his heart and she is distraught (yet still strong) and somehow, through kisses and steamy more and hope and heaps and piles of true love, they manage to come out on the other side.

I like a man in a kilt, especially if he looks like a Hemsworth, doesn't matter, Liam or Chris.

My couples so far include Beckett and Luna (from the trilogy, Luna's Story) who battle their fear to find each other during an apocalypse of rising waters. And Magnus and Kaitlyn (from the series Kaitlyn and the Highlander). Who find themselves traveling through time to be together.

I write under two pen names, this one here, Diana Knightley, and another one, H. D. Knightley, where I write books for Young

Adults (They are still romantic and fun and sometimes steamy though, because love is grand at any age.)

DianaKnightley.com
Diana@dianaknightley.com

ALSO BY H. D. KNIGHTLEY (MY YA PEN NAME)

Bright (Book One of The Estelle Series)

Beyond (Book Two of The Estelle Series)

Belief (Book Three of The Estelle Series)

Fly; The Light Princess Retold

Violet's Mountain

Sid and Teddy

Printed in Great Britain
by Amazon

15733800R00198